TERROR

The first gunshot brought Mase instantly out of his bedroll. By the time he got his boots on, he was wide-awake and reaching for his rifle.

He could hear Pug shouting orders and the pounding hooves of running cattle. He ran to his horse. As fast as he could, Mase slung a saddle on, buckled it, stuck the rifle in its rig holster, and jumped aboard, kicking the stallion into action.

He could see the starlight glistening off the horns of his cattle as the herd milled and bawled, many on the south end stampeding away. A muzzle flash showed from down that way. Was that one of his men trying to drive the cattle back into the herd? Or someone trying to split up the herd? An unfamiliar voice warbled a Rebel yell. Rustlers!

RALPH COMPTON

RED TRAIL

A RALPH COMPTON WESTERN BY

JOHN SHIRLEY

BERKLEY
New York

BERKLEY
An imprint of Penguin Random House LLC
penguinrandomhouse.com

ISBN: 9780593102343

First Edition: December 2020

Printed in the United States of America
1 3 5 7 9 10 8 6 4 2

Cover art by Steve Atkinson
Cover design by Steve Meditz
Book design by George Towne

THE IMMORTAL COWBOY

This is respectfully dedicated to the "American Cowboy." His was the saga sparked by the turmoil that followed the Civil War, and the passing of more than a century has by no means diminished the flame.

True, the old days and the old ways are but treasured memories, and the old trails have grown dim with the ravages of time, but the spirit of the cowboy lives on.

In my travels—to Texas, Oklahoma, Kansas, Nebraska, Colorado, Wyoming, New Mexico, and Arizona—I always find something that reminds me of the Old West. While I am walking these plains and mountains for the first time, there is this feeling that a part of me is eternal, that I have known these old trails before. I believe it is the undying spirit of the frontier calling me, through the mind's eye, to step back into time. What is the appeal of the Old West of the American frontier?

It has been epitomized by some as the dark and bloody period in American history. Its heroes—Crockett, Bowie, Hickok, Earp—have been reviled and criticized. Yet the Old West lives on, larger than life.

It has become a symbol of freedom, when there was always another mountain to climb and another river to cross; when a dispute between two men was settled not with expensive lawyers, but with fists, knives, or guns. Barbaric? Maybe. But some things never change. When the cowboy rode into the pages of American history, he left behind a legacy that lives within the hearts of us all.

—Ralph Compton

CHAPTER ONE

Central Texas, April 1874

THE RANCH STRETCHED out near far as the eye could see, flat and sun warmed below them, green with springtime, in places dappled light brown by the herd of longhorn cattle. Mase and Katie Durst sat astride their horses, poised on the bluff overlooking their ranch. The bluff was set amongst the San Vincente hills, just about the only elevation hereabouts, and Mason "Mase" Durst could see most of the 2,340 longhorns. He gazed upon them with considerable satisfaction, for they'd been hard-won. Years back he had hired Crane Williams, young Lorenzo Vasquez, and Pug Liberty to help him "scrape" the start of the herd from the underbrush around the Brazos River. There were said to be a hundred thousand such cattle, descendants of strays, free and legal for the taking in that wild region of Texas. Most of the cattle on Durst Ranch were the offspring from those captured by the Durst hands. It was dangerous work, driving the wild longhorns from the brush-choked oak mottes around the river into the ramshackle pens they'd set up to contain them. Herding the feral cattle back to Durst Ranch carried its risks, too. Mase had gotten badly gored in his right leg from one of the longhorns—but once the cattle were contained on his medium-small ranch, he'd bred them and built up his herd. For some years he'd sold off part of his herd every spring, but for the last four, he'd simply built it up.

They'd lived lean these last years, but Katie never complained. Not even when he'd signed on for other ranchers' trail drives, to be gone for months at a time for a hundred dollars and a chance to learn the trails. He glanced at her affectionately now. His wife was a sturdily attractive woman, the kind people called handsome due to the strong planes of her face, her piercing dark blue eyes, her strong chin. Her shoulders were wider than most women's, her hands a little bigger. He was six feet one himself, and she was five eight. An armful and a sweet one—but tough as leather when she needed to be. She wore buckskin riding breeches today, cut for a lady, and a tan top, the sleeves rolled to her elbows. She had smooth, flawless skin, a contrast to his own craggy, weather-beaten features.

"There's Jim and Curly," Mase said, pointing to the south.

They could see their son, Jim, riding his small cow pony on the flatlands below and doing a good job of it for a nine-year-old boy. Riding alongside him on a quarter horse was the only full-time hand the Durst Ranch had, Carlos "Curly" Chavez. He was a kind of unofficial uncle for the boy, as well as a ranch hand. Curly lived with his family in a sizable cabin in the hills beside the ravine through which ran San Vincente Creek.

Katie grinned. “Look at Jimmy waving that lasso!”

“He’s driving a cow back into the herd. Not that she needs it. She’s just looking for sweeter grass.”

“We’re lucky we got those early rains,” Katie remarked. “Gave us the good grass, the extra grazing.”

“Lucky in some ways, darlin’,” Mase said. “But it’s flooded a good deal of the trails north. And that’s not all we’ll be facing. . . .”

“You’re still fixed on driving the herd up north this month, Mase? There’s that trouble with the Comanches. Railroad north of Dallas is cut by the Indians—won’t be running for another month or so . . .”

He nodded. “The Chisolm Trail’s so overrun with Apaches and Comanches and Comancheros, the Army’s shut it down for a good while. Same with the Shawnee Trail. Anything west of that’s a long distance out of our way. Was I to wait for those trails to open up, we’d be competing with the big herds for grazing, for trail headway, and they’d get the jump on me with the buyers.”

“You already have that buyer. Mr. Osgood seems a decent sort. He said he’d buy every steer you’ve got if you could get ’em to the railhead—and I believed him. Why not just take his word for it?”

“I do believe he’s reliable. But he’s practical, too. He’s got only so much money to spend, and if the other herds get there first with good beef, he’ll buy from them. He’s offered me top dollar—I want to get that herd to him.”

"We've got no choice but to wait, Mase, unless you want to herd them east to Louisiana."

"Wouldn't get as good a price there. No, I'm for Wichita. You know, Crane Williams found another trail a couple years back. I'm going to talk to him about it. . . ."

YOU MAKE THIS work for me, Fuller, and I'll cut you in," said Tom Harning. "Hell, that ranch should have been mine all along. Mase Durst horned in and moved in with the help of his Yankee friends!"

Ralph Fuller squirmed in his chair. He was sitting behind a small desk in an office that was barely larger than the desk, in the back of the Clinton Bank, the only bank in the county. He was a man whose pallid, round-cheeked face was softened even more by indoor living, whose small mustache twitched from side to side as he considered his reply.

"I don't know about that, Tom. The government men did say the land was his, but the way I heard it, Durst got there first and legally staked his claim."

"That's what they tell you—but they're lying!" Harning said, standing up and leaning vulturelike over the desk. He was a wide-bodied man of forty-five, with a square-cut beard to hide his jowls and bristling eyebrows that seemed to bristle even more when he was angry. His small gray eyes got smaller as he narrowed them at Fuller and went loudly on. "I'll not have you naysaying me on that or anything else, Fuller! I know what you did, and *you* know what you did!"

Fuller winced. "Now, these allegations—they come

from a man who drinks too much, and we had to let him go—"

"You let Barney Kaper go because he saw you pay that gambling debt off with the bank's money!"

Fuller licked his lips. "That's . . . I have sat over the books with the accountant and—"

"Oh, you juggled things around and made it work, and I hear that you put that accountant in for a raise! But your boss, Mr. Gaffell, will be interested to have a closer look—if I give him the clue!"

"He'll just misunderstand it all, Tom, if you go putting a bee in his bonnet—"

"You will do as I say, or that bee will be buzzing right in his ear!" With that, Harning slapped his right hand flat and hard on the desk, making the bank manager recoil in his chair.

Fuller gulped and spread his hands. "I can't just call in the loan on that ranch when it's hardly in arrears! Why, we give all these folks a good while to sell their beef so's they can pay us, Tom! That's how it's understood! It pays off, too."

"Doesn't have to be that way! You call it in—and you see the bank sells that place to me!"

Fuller looked desperately at his blotter, as if it might offer some way out. "It's not that easy to get people out of a place they've been rightfully established in—"

"I'll deal with that, Fuller! Now"—Harning stood up straight and crossed his arms over his chest—"are you going to do it, or am I going to get in touch with Mr. Gaffell?"

Fuller closed his eyes and let out a long breath. "I . . . Yes, all right. Very well. I seem to have no choice."

* * *

Mase Durst and Crane Williams sat out on the broad farmhouse porch, drinking hard cider and watching the moon rise over the flowering Texas plains. A biting breeze was sweeping down from the north, making Mase shiver. The Williams farm was eighteen miles south of the Durst Ranch. Mase had come here hoping to recruit Crane as a partner and work out the substitute trail with him.

Crane was fifteen years older than Mase. Once a cowboy, he was now settled on his own quiet farm, which mixed sheep, a few hundred steers, twenty dairy cows, and a great many chickens; and he was doing well enough with it. He was a major supplier of dairy, eggs, chicken, and steaks to two nearby towns. He had a gray-streaked brown beard, long graying hair because he didn't bother to cut it, and a crooked nose because when it was broken, he hadn't bothered to set it. Four years ago he'd gone on what he swore was his last drive. He and his wife, Azalea, had two kids left of the three—little Judd had died of the galloping ague—and Crane was reluctant to be far from his homestead.

"And that's why I'm telling you, no, I cain't come with you, Mase," Crane was saying. "Hell, I lost four men on that trail—and two hundred twenty head of cattle. It's dangerous! There are outlaws aplenty up there, and you may run into hostile Cherokees. The route takes you through canyons twisty as an angry rattler. And it's a fair narrow way, too. That land is as rugged as anything you can squeeze a cow through. Why, we had to dodge a landslide—lost poor Henry Domingo to them rocks!" He took a pull on his can of cider and went on. "Also, you're probably going to have to stop in Leadton for supplies. Never met such a pack of scoundrels."

"You make it sound like it ain't passable at all, Crane."

"I proved a drive can pass that way and come out the other side. Anyhow, maybe you'll have better luck than we did. I do think your Katie's right—it's better to wait and choose one of the marked trails. But if you're of a mind to go right quick, it sure looks like Red Trail is your only way to get where you're goin'. And it does seem the other trails are closed for now."

"It was another drive that forced you on the Red Trail, wasn't it?"

"That SOB Charles Goodnight. Got it into his head we were stealing his stock. Wasn't ready to take his drive north and didn't want us to go either—said we'd use up all the graze. Made a deal with the Choctaw to close the trail to us. Being as we couldn't get through on the Chisolm, we struck west, lookin' for a way around. . . . A band of Chickasaw told us about a trail through the canyons north. Chief name of Cloudy Moon. Not a bad sort. You run across him, give him my regards. We paid him fair, and he let us through and pointed the way."

Mase grunted. "Not sure I can even find this Indian."

"If you listen close and look at the map I made, you'll find your way to the trail all right. It ain't so hard to get to." Crane gave Mase a gap-toothed grin. "It's just hard to get through with all your fingers and toes!" He puffed his pipe alight, then passed a hand-drawn map over to Mase.

Mase unfolded the paper and held it out to catch the lamplight. "Looks like the route starts where the Shawnee Trail crosses the Red River."

"Sure enough. Y'all can take the Shawnee up to Denison and across the river into the Indian Nations. Ten miles north and you'll come to an old buffalo trail heading northeast"—he leaned over and tapped the map with his pipestem—"there. Now, you'll be crossing two rivers, and then you follow this one northwest, and you'll find the entrance to the canyons—and Red Trail. See it? Right there. That's where you got to start watching your back. . . ."

KATIE DURST WAS sitting by the fire, reading to her son, but her mind kept wandering to places north. She wanted to go on the drive with Mase, just to help him get through it. They had been partners in everything, and she wanted to be a partner in that, too. She knew herself to be capable of it. But he was worried about the ranch, the stock—though Curly would stay here and look after all that. There was Jim to think of. He didn't want the boy to be left without his mother, though he'd be fine with the Chavez family; he'd stayed with them before. True, it'd be an awful long time without his ma.

But she knew there was something else. Though Mase placed a lot of trust in his wife, he was scared for her to go. The Red Trail was especially dangerous. Of course, every trail to the railhead was tough. She had heard the stories: men swept away by floods, trampled by stampedes, caught in unseasonal blizzards and frozen to death, attacked by Indians and rustlers, blasted by lightning—the cause of a surprising number of cowboy deaths. Endless long, very long days in the saddle. And if you took sick in those harsh conditions, you were very far from a doctor.

She'd be willing, anyway. But she admitted to herself that if she went along, she'd start in worrying about Jimmy after a day or two.

"Ma?"

"Yes, Jimmy?"

"You stopped reading about Robin Hood and all."

"Oh—I'm sorry. But you know what? I was just coming to the part about Maid Marian. I thought you said you didn't care about that part!"

"Well—I'd like to hear that'n, too."

"I thought so! Thinking about maidens at your age!"

He snorted and shook his head. Katie closed the book on her lap and looked at him, a tanned boy with his father's sandy hair and the eyes he'd inherited from her, so dark blue they were almost black. That endearing spray of freckles across his nose was all his. "Maid Marian can wait. It's time for you to hit the bunk."

Jim yawned. "Where's Pa?"

"He's gone to Crane Williams's place to talk some business."

"How long's he gonna be gone on that drive?"

"Oh, upward of two months."

"We could go with him. Or anyhow I could. I could help! I'm pretty good on a horse, Ma. I can catch the fence post every time with a loop."

"That's true. You're more than half a cowboy already, Jim. The time will come when you'll go with him. But Pa says this time you got to stay here and take care of me and the ranch."

"Oh, Ma, you could take care of the ranch your own self. I've seen you do everything he does! You'd be fine and dandy!"

Katie laughed. "Well—I'm touched by that tender concern for your mama. Come on, off to bed. I've got sewing to do."

He shrugged and picked up a wood chip by the fire and tossed it at the tabby cat. It was a game they played. The cat tensed—and smacked it back at him.

"Varmint, come on with me," he said. He picked up the cat and carried it toward his room.

Katie watched him go and thought again of trying to convince Mase to wait for the other trails to open. Anything would be better than the Red Trail.

Katie sighed. Mase was a stubborn man once he'd made up his mind. Luckily, what he made up his mind to do was pretty much always worth doing. But this time—she wasn't so sure.

This time, Mason Durst might not come back alive.

CHAPTER TWO

SOME OF THE men who'd come to the hire that drizzly morning scarcely needed to be hired. Mase was always ready to ride with Perry "Pug" Liberty, Ray Jost—an old friend who'd sided Mase on two drives with other outfits—and Lorenzo Vasquez. Soon as they expressed themselves satisfied with the proposed pay, they would be hired.

The other four men standing in front of the barn at the Durst Ranch were unknown to Mase till this morning. A compact little waddy with a door-knocker mustache, compensating for shortness with a ten-gallon hat, identified himself as one Andy Pike. He had worked for the Circle H, he said, and had left because "he didn't like Mr. Harning's ways." He claimed to be a good horse wrangler and an experienced drover. Mase had indeed seen him riding along the property line with Harning's men, and figured he was likely experienced enough. From Alabama, and the son of a

Confederate colonel, Pike proudly announced he had ridden behind General Lee himself. "So you know I can hold my own in a fight."

Mase's father had died in the War Between the States, fighting for the Confederacy, and Mase had chosen to stay behind and run the farm for his mother and sister, his older brother having ridden off with his father to join the Rebels. Despite his father's allegiances, the whole idea of splitting up the United States had gone against Mase's grain. Then the elder Durst had been killed, and Mase's brother, Hiram, had come back from the war a haunted, bitter man, caring only for cheap whiskey, loose women, and easy money. Mase hadn't seen Hiram in five years.

Anyhow, Mase just wasn't impressed with Civil War stories. But he needed men—four others he'd approached had said no, not wanting to ride the Red Trail—and he was going to be short on hands as it was.

"All right, you're hired," he told Pike.

Jacob Marsh was a black man, about forty, who'd been recommended by Crane Williams as "tough as old leather and quick to get things done." He stood there, a little apart from the others, hat in hand, and just listened. They'd met the day before, and Mase noted Jacob to be a man of few words but a steady gaze. He had never been on a long drive before, but he was a good all-around hand, according to Crane. Jacob was to assist the cook and the horse wrangler and, when he wasn't doing that, to ride drag or swing.

Harry Duff was twenty-one and just plain skinny; a rancher's son, from the Triangle D off to the south a fair piece, he wore ram's fur chaps, a new Stetson, and a Colt Army on his hip. "Everybody just calls me Duff, except my ma and pa."

Duff was shivering without his jacket, and that made Mase doubt him. "You feeling chilly, Duff? It might get mighty cold up north. Spring ain't summer, and in them hills, about two in the morning when you're on night guard a long way from the campfire, you'll feel cold and then some."

"Why, I can handle it, boss!" Duff declared, tilting his head proudly back.

Pug snorted. "Boy, you'd better be able to—I've seen it so cold in April out on the prairie, with that north wind sheering in, a man's eyelids freeze shut!"

"That ain't nothin'," said Ray Jost. "I saw it so cold on night guard, a fellow froze to his horse, the horse froze solid, and they both died so stuck together, they had to be buried in one grave, the horse standing up. That was a deep hole to dig, too."

The other hands stared for a moment and then burst into laughter at this windy.

Mase only chuckled—he was used to Ray's ludicrous stories—and turned to young Duff. "Tell me something, Duff—why do you want to go on this trip?"

"Mr. Durst, my whole life I've only been but eighty-five miles from my pa's ranch! I want to see the elephant! And—well, my old man didn't think I'm man enough for it either. So I had to do it!"

Mase nodded. Having to prove something to your father was something he understood. It was a powerful motivation. "How're you for horse wrangling?"

"Why, that's most of what I done on our place! My pa breeds horses as well as cows, Mr. Durst."

"I'm shorthanded, so I reckon you're hired. You'll handle the remuda, and sometimes you'll trade out with Ray Jost so you can ride drag. Not the best jobs but you're green, and that's what you're offered."

The young man grinned, a very wide and bright grin, and stuck out his hand. "Happy to do anything you need, Mr. Durst."

They shook hands, and Mase turned to the man who was likely to be his trail cook.

Mase had met Mick Dollager on a recent trip to town, finding him fruitlessly searching for work "as a chef," as he put it. Mase had already as much as hired him. He had invited him to the ranch to demonstrate his cooking, and the results had more than impressed both Mase and Katie. She had even asked him for the recipe for what he called officers' stew.

Dollager was a big, heavy-bellied man with a curling brown beard and curled-up mustaches. He wore a bowler hat, a threadbare dusty blue suit, and a frock coat. Standing there holding his lapels and emanating self-importance, he had the air of a politician about to give a speech, or so it seemed to Mase. He seemed to know his job—he told convincing stories of having been a cook for the British Army in India—and Mase found the man entertaining, even likable, despite his pomposity. But would he be able to abide the long trail north?

"Boys," said Mase, "this is Mick Dollager. He's from far-off Britain. If we come to an agreement today, he'll be our cook."

"Who's he loyal to?" asked Pike, looking at the Brit askance.

"Here now, what's all this, young man!" Dollager

said, frowning at Pike. His British accent made the men chuckle.

"Is you loyal to the king of that England or to this here US of A?"

"Why, are you planning to make war on the United Kingdom, young man?"

Pike seemed taken aback. "Me?"

"In point of fact, sir, I am . . . I am *soon to be* an American citizen. I want nothing else. My loyalty is to good men, sir. Are you a good man?"

"Why, in course I am!"

"Then I'll be loyal to you. 'Nothing is more noble, nothing more venerable, than loyalty,' so Cicero tells us."

"Is Cicero workin' with this outfit?" Pike asked, scratching his head.

"Is Cicero—?" Dollager looked at him in amazement.

"Never mind about Cicero," Ray said. "The question, Dollager, is, are you a biscuit shooter—or a belly cheater?"

The other cowboys nodded approvingly at that.

Dollager cleared his throat. "I am not entirely familiar with your nomenclature, sir, but I assure you that as a cook, I will cheat no one's belly! You shall have all I am allowed to give you, and you shall have it cooked to that degree of perfection that is permitted by conditions."

"Fair enough," Ray said with his trademark crooked smile. He thrust out his hand and the two men shook, Dollager adding in a small bow.

"I know you can cook, Dollager," said Mase. "But can you drive a team of oxen?"

"Can I drive—!" Dollager raised his eyebrows. "Sir, I drove a cook wagon for Her Majesty's Army in India. Oxen were my constant companions! I am richly experienced in the matter!"

"Now, suppose we're attacked out there. What will you do?"

"As to that, I am no man to glorify violence. Our camp was overrun in the India Rebellion, there was a terrible loss in our ranks, and I was forced to shoot two of the invaders. It saddened me. But I will do it again if necessary! I will exhibit caution but not cowardice."

Mase nodded in approval. He suspected there was much more to Dollager's life story. The man was a fish out of water here in Texas. How had he come to be here? Why was he so eager to be an American citizen? He could be running from something. But trail-worthy cooks were hard to come by. "You're hired, if you agree to the wages."

Mase stepped back and looked them all over, then said, "Boys—the same goes for you all. You're all hired if you agree to the wages. I will need you to meet me at the north gate of the ranch, Monday morning—Curly will show you where it is. The chuck wagon and oxen will be there, too, loaded and ready. I want you there at one hour before dawn! That's *before* dawn now! You can bring your own horse, or you can use only the remuda. But you're responsible for any mount you fork."

"Who's trail boss?" Lorenzo Vasquez asked. The vaquero was a cheerful, medium-sized man with big brown eyes and curling mustachios; he wore a modest sombrero, a short deer-hide jacket sewn with intricate patterns, black trousers with a white strip of embroidery on the sides, and deer-hide chaps.

"I'll be my own trail boss," Mase replied, "but I'll be drovin', too. Pug is your foreman. We'll look into hiring some more help up near the Red River, but till then, there's a heap of cattle and not enough of us."

Mase had a tough exterior, but he quietly arranged to pay each man—at the end of the drive—a mite more than the average drive boss. A hundred thirty dollars and found. Pug would get a hundred sixty-five dollars and found because he was to be foreman.

"Just one thing, Mr. Durst," Pike said after they'd gone into the barn, where a table was set up, to sign the hire contract. "Some bosses will pay an advance if a man's hard up. Harning fired me after I done spent my pay, and well, I got a debt of twenty dollars. I don't want to go on the trail owing folks."

"How am I to know you won't just take it and spend it all on whiskey?" Mase asked.

Pike scowled. "That how you see me?"

"I don't know you. Well?"

"No such a thing. I want it for a debt."

"All right, though it's not something I like doing. I'd better not see everybody else line up for it either." He fished a double eagle from his pocket and handed it over. "Now—this'll be taken out of your pay. And if you don't show up Monday, when I come back, I'll take it out of your hide!"

Pug chuckled at that. "He will, too."

Pike nodded. "You can trust me, Mr. Durst."

ANDY PIKE STOOD in front of Tom Harning's desk, hat in hand, and said, "After we signed the contract, boss, he gave us the lowdown on the drive.

They're heading up the Shawnee Trail, then over west to somethin' he calls Red Trail, north on that through the Leadton hill country."

"You don't say. When do they leave?"

"Monday morning at dawn."

"Was you not my top hand, I'd send you along to do a job for me. I don't want Durst finishing that drive."

Pike was a little startled at that. He didn't mind pretending to sign on with Durst—and getting twenty dollars out of it, too—but what Harning was hinting at stuck in his craw. A man could hang for that. And he had no intention of riding north on the Red Trail.

"That's not my kind of work, boss." He licked his lips. "But I know a man . . ."

MASE AND KATIE were sitting up in bed, having perhaps gotten a start on a second child; he was studying Crane's map for perhaps the tenth time, and she was scratching Varmint behind the ears, the cat now curled up on her lap. Katie glanced thoughtfully over Mase's shoulder at the map. In the yellow light of the oil lamp, it looked to her like not much more than chicken scratchings.

Katie sighed. "That sure don't look like much to go on. Can't I talk you out of it, Mase? Later in the season the Chisolm will open up. . . ."

He dropped an arm around her shoulders and pulled her closer. "I'm afraid not, darlin'. I'm going to get those cows up north before everybody else. And this is the only way to do it."

"You know, I heard from Elsie Sorenson that Tom Harning's lawyer has got something in the court docket, and it might just be our ranch, Mase. You know what Harning thinks."

"I know what he pretends to think. It's all puffery. Don't mean a thing."

"Without you here . . ."

Mase frowned. "Without me here—what?"

"I just don't know what he's capable of. I've heard some stories. And he shot the Sorensons' sheep."

"He shot a few of them that came onto his land. Or anyhow he said he did. He had to pay them for 'em, too. He pushes, he gets pushed back."

"His ranch is on three sides of us. Seems like it bothers his mind not to have it all."

"Hell, he's not making money like he used to. You know, I sell these cattle, I just might buy some of his ranch from him. Who knows? Maybe he'd sell out to me!"

Katie snorted. "Not likely. I feel sorry for his wife. He only married Gertrude for her pa's money."

"He's managed to sire a couple of children with her."

"Managed to!"

Mase blinked. "I say something wrong? I never know—"

"Well—just because she's not a pretty woman . . ."

"Oh, she's fine, just fine," Mase said hastily. "She seems a decent sort when I see them in town. Never seems happy with that sourpuss, and I don't blame her. Anyway, you don't worry about him. He's all hat and no cattle. Can't back up anything he says. And I know something else for sure—Tom Harning's no match for Katie Durst!"

She smiled. "You think so?"

He kissed her. "I know so."

"Mase—did you think on what I asked about—for Monday morning? It'd make Jim feel good, and you can use the help getting those beeves on the trail."

"Well, you keep a close eye on him, and you two can help us drive 'em up to the crossing at Butner Creek. But no farther!"

"He'll be thrilled!"

"We'll see how thrilled he feels when you get him up about two hours before dawn. . . ."

EVERYONE WAS THERE well before dawn, Monday morning, including Katie and a sleepy young Jim Durst. Katie had set up a campfire near the wagon, just to make the "Arbuckle," and Jim was yawning as he poured water from a bucket into the enormous coffeepot.

Working under a lantern, Mase and Dollager went over the goods packing the chuck wagon, the cook noting everything down with a pencil and paper, including all the dry goods and hardware.

They would be hiring more men on the way, and Mase had stocked up for them, too. The victuals list included two hundred fifty pounds of salt pork, four hundred pounds of flour, forty pounds of salt, ten pounds of pepper, ninety pounds of coffee, one hundred fifty pounds of ground onions, four hundred pounds of beans, fifty pounds of sourdough starter, four hundred pounds of potatoes, sixty pounds of dried chilis, thirty-five pounds of dried garlic, fifty pounds of lard, and two hundred pounds of dried fruit. In addition, Dollager had brought along two chests of his own, including one for "various spices," and twenty pounds of butter. The butter was a treat that they would soon have to do without; it would be used up in the first week and not replenished, for it would not keep as long as lard. There were a hundred pounds of salted beef, from an older steer Mase didn't think would make it to Wichita, and half a dozen smoked hams.

Besides food supplies and water barrels, the chuck wagon carried pots and pans; tin plates and forks, which the cowboys liked to call "eatin' irons"; two spare wheels strapped to the sides; lanterns and five gallons of kerosene; and kegs for holding sourdough, a small barrel of horseshoes, spare oxen shoes, small barrels of nails, two boxes of tools, and a small anvil. There were a big box of rifle ammunition, a long box for shotguns, and two big coils of rope. The possible various drawers and cubbies in this Charles Goodnight–style wagon contained bandages, needles and thread, vinegar, and a few patent medicaments. A Dutch oven stood just inside the rear gate of the wagon, and alongside it was a three-gallon coffeepot. Lucifers and extra blankets rounded out the storage.

As they went over these goods, Dollager, so it seemed to Mase, had the grave and reverential air of a priest preparing for a mass.

"Well, coosie," said Mase, "I'll tell you true—"

"Pardon me, sir?" Dollager asked, brows knitted in puzzlement. "What did you call me?"

"'Coosie'—it's what we call the cook on the drive. Now, I've been scrimping for this drive for a long time. Selling what I could sell—even sold ten acres. These supplies cost me close to three thousand dollars. And that's not including the cost of this wagon. Just see you guard the whole shootin' match with your life!"

A twinkle in his eyes, Dollager saluted him in the snappy fashion of the British Army. "Very good, Captain!"

Mase grinned. "Come on, let's look at the oxen."

The sturdy oxen were fully grown but relatively young, and they seemed to champ at the bits, stamping their hooves as if in a restless hurry of their own.

The two men inspected the animals' hooves—carefully, not wanting to be kicked by the enormous bovines—and peered at the oxen's eyes and mouths.

"They seem well enough," Dollager declared. "Have they names?"

"Well, they're brother and sister. You can name them if you care to."

"I shall call them Albert and Victoria."

"Suit yourself. Now, we won't tussle with the stove this morning, but we'll have a short breakfast of coffee, biscuits, and dried ham before setting out. Katie's made the biscuits and coffee, but you can hand it all out and pour the coffee. After this, you're on your own, except maybe if you get some help from Jacob!"

Mase went to inspect the remuda. There were twenty spare horses hobbled there, within a circle of roped stakes. The horses were another daunting investment for Mase, for these were all trained cow ponies, stock horses used to being haltered, herded, and corralled; they were responsive to cowboys, ready to turn to face the wrangler once roped from behind, and experienced at driving cattle. Such horses did not come cheaply.

Harry Duff had come over to the ranch the day before to inspect the remuda horses and to make their acquaintance. Now he was among them, checking their legs and backs one last time, patting them and clucking to them and removing their hobbles so he could prepare them to be driven alongside the herd. He had done so for short drives of seventy-five miles on two occasions, and Mase worried he wasn't going to be experienced enough to handle these horses on a long drive. But there was no time now to find a better horse wrangler.

"You think you can move all this horseflesh up with the herd, Duff?" Mase asked.

"Yes, sir! Just you watch me!"

Mase looked around, seeing the cowboys sitting on their saddles near the milling herd of longhorns; the cattle were a bit stirred up, having been driven close together beside the gate, closer than they were used to; they milled and bawled and clacked their horns. Curly Chavez was there on his mule, keeping watch. He was a stocky man with a round face, a mass of curly black hair speckled with gray, and a small mustache. He had cut out Ol' Buck from the herd and kept the enormous steer up at the gate. Ol' Buck had led two other herds for short distances, had indeed led many of the cattle here from the Brazos—for every herd had a leader. Hence, he was not fated to be a meat animal. Mase was hoping Buck would be able to lead the herd all the way to Wichita with the help of the drovers.

The cattle looked good. "Fat and sassy" from two months of rich grazing, as his father would have said. They'd been brought here by himself, Jim, Katie, and Curly the day before, to give them grazing in the general direction of the drive, and now they seemed eager to move on.

Katie called out, "Biscuits 'n' coffee!" And shortly

the men were gathered around the fire. Jim was given a cup of coffee heavy on the milk his mother had brought along for the purpose, and like the men, he ate the bacon Katie had cooked the night before, between two biscuits.

Dollager filled their cups and stoked the fire under the portable grate. Mase looked around and noticed that Pike had not shown up. Somehow, he wasn't surprised. Was he reporting back to Harning now? Well, he'd see that Pike gave him that double eagle back one day.

The dawn was breaking when Mase called out, "All right, men, listen up!"

He cleared his throat and boomed out, "Boys, we can't fly like the crow so we can't get to Wichita in a straight line! It'll be around six hundred miles of crooked trail from here. We'll try to go fifteen miles every damn day, but many days it'll be somewhere between eight and twelve. We'll have to stop sometimes for grazing and watering and a half dozen other causes, and maybe the terrain just won't let us go as fast as we want to. This is going to be a pretty long drive. It's going to take time, but I'm hoping we'll all be getting paid in Wichita come early June! We're shorthanded, but we'll take on more hands up the trail. I've got a friend on the lookout for me at Red River station. Even with more help, we've got two thousand three hundred and forty cattle to move—not as big as a lot of outfits but big enough. So that's more than enough work for every man. We're going to run into some rough weather, like as not! But being as it's a wet spring, we might eat less dust than we'd have to later in the year. On the other side of it—we'll hit mud! We'll have cattle getting stuck, and horses have got to be watched for seedy toe from all that damp. We're going to have to swim the herd across a couple of rivers. We could run into Comanches and Comancheros! We're going to have some long hours and not enough sleep! Well, complaining does not go here—but if you've broken a bone or you get a high fever, sing out! Apart from that, stick to the job no matter what! And listen here—Pug there is your foreman! You do what he tells you! Now, a few other things—there's *no liquor in the camp*. Nor in the saddle. If you've got some, leave it here. You can have a gun in the saddle in case you run into trouble, but in camp you leave your weapons with the coosie. And gambling of an evening—you can use twigs, you can use matches, anything but money. We'll have no fights on this drive! If you've got a problem with a man, tell Pug or me, as long as it ain't minor. Now—is everybody agreed?"

They all shouted assent, some with a *Yes, sir!* and some with a *Yo!* Jim gave a loud shrill *Yahoo!* and the men laughed, but there was fondness in their voices.

"Now, Jim and Katie are giving us a hand this morning, so you boys are going to have it easy as far as Butner Creek—let's saddle up!"

The first leg was indeed fairly smooth. Ol' Buck was trotting along in fine form, leading the herd. Dollager drove the chuck wagon to the left and a little ahead of the herd, and he seemed to have a steady hand with the oxen. Ray Jost and Pug Liberty rode both point and swing on the left, shifting from position to position as needed.

Not needing to ride ahead as yet, since he knew this patch so well, Mase rode point and swing on the right, aided by Katie and Jim, who—Mase noted with approval—was holding his own. Jacob rode drag, staying on top of the job, and sometimes Duff dropped back from herding the remuda to help with drag when dilatory cattle, trying to stop and graze, offered too much resistance for one man. The boy had good cow sense.

Lorenzo rode right point, and Curly rode right flank and wherever he was needed to keep the herd reasonably close together and moving ahead.

They stopped at half past noon for a quick meal of salt beef and corn cakes—the corn cakes provided by Katie—taking fifteen minutes to eat, as Duff and Jacob rode slowly around the herd, keeping it contained. The well-trained remuda horses took their ease cropping grass nearby, none of them offering to run off.

The men who'd eaten saddled up without being told, as Duff and Jacob returned for a quick meal. They, too, were soon saddled, and the herd was on its way again.

Mase smiled, hearing Jim mutter that his rump was getting sore, but apart from that, the lad did not complain, even when he was sagging in the saddle toward evening.

When they approached the ford at Butner Creek, Mase sent Katie and Jim up ahead with the chuck wagon to cross the creek in advance and make camp on the far side. This first workday was a fairly short one, because of the presence of Katie and Jim, and because the cattle were still getting used to the routine of the drive.

Jim and Katie slept beside Mase that night. After breakfast, he walked them to their mounts, which were saddled and ready, held by the smiling Pug Liberty. Curly was already mounted on his mule.

Katie put her hand on her husband's face and looked him in the eye. "You'd better come back to me, Mason Durst."

"I will, darlin'."

"You watch where you go all the way there and back!"

"I surely will!"

She turned to Pug and jabbed a forefinger at him. "And you watch his back trail, Pug!"

Pug took off his hat and nodded somberly. "My solemn word on it, ma'am."

Mase took his wife in his arms and kissed her. Then he turned to Jim, looked into the boy's eyes, and spoke gravely. "I'm going to tell you something, Jim, and I ain't foolin'. I expect you to watch over your ma and the ranch! You and Curly are the men of Durst Ranch till I get back! I mean that, Jim! That means you do every one of your chores and anything else that needs to be done, and you give her no trouble!"

Jim's eyes widened. He swallowed. "Yes, sir."

"And listen here—Curly is not your damn babysitter! You help him with whatever he needs help with!"

"I . . . I'll do it, Pa."

Mase nodded one time and stuck out his hand. They shook like two men agreeing on a deal. Jim's hand felt so small in his. And he'd be leaving the boy for perhaps two months. Could be more.

Mase cleared his throat, which seemed strangely obstructed. He reached out, picked up his son, and set him in the saddle of the pony.

Then he turned to Curly. "Can I count on you, Curly? All the way down the line?"

Curly simply nodded. "Of course, Senor Durst. Always."

Mase reached up and shook Curly's hand. *"Gracias."*

Katie opened her saddlebags and took out a cylindrical brown package. She handed it to Mase.

"This for me?"

"Well, open it up."

He unwrapped it—and found a brass telescope. "Why, look at that!"

"They say it's the kind the ships' captains use."

"That what the drummer tell you, did he?" Mase extended it, put it to his eye, and looked out over the plains. "By jingo, it works good!" He grinned at Katie. "Thank you, darlin'!"

"You just see you use it. Keep an eye for what's coming at you out there."

Mase bent over and kissed her on the cheek—tasting salty tears. Katie pushed him gently away and turned to Bonnie, her mare.

"June, then, Mase?" she asked, climbing on her horse.

He smiled and nodded to her. "June, darlin'."

"You'll drop us a line when you can?"

"I will, Katie. In Denison and wherever else I can find the post."

She bit her lip, nodded, and turned away. "Come on, Jim."

With that, Katie and Jim trotted their mounts off. Curly touched his hat and called, "*Vaya con dios*, Senor Durst!" Then he cantered off after Katie and Jim.

Mase watched them ride off, proud of Jim and already missing him and Katie. He used the telescope to watch them more closely for a time, till they became hard to see clearly.

Then Mase Durst turned to the camp and shouted, "Saddle up! We're ho for Wichita!"

CHAPTER THREE

ANOTHER MORNING WAKING without Mase.

Katie sat up, sighing. He'd been gone only a week, but she ached for him in the mornings. It was hard going to sleep without him there—the bed seemed far too big with just her in it—and maybe harder on her feelings when she woke up without him. They'd often dallied in bed a little while—moments of tenderness, even lovemaking, early in the morning when the boy was deeply asleep. Just waking to find Mase there had been deeply reassuring to her. He'd gone off on long trips before, hiring out on drives to learn the trails and make some extra cash, but this time the Red Trail cast a shadow over their separation. The risks seemed foolhardy to her. Sometimes she seethed in quiet anger at him for refusing to wait.

But now the rooster was crowing, and those morose thoughts fled, driven away by duty. Katie was soon up, dressed, and heading to the barn to milk the cow and feed the chickens. This done, she lit the stove and prepared porridge and bacon for her and Jim, and coffee for herself. She schooled him at home, for there was no schoolhouse close enough, and they would have an hour of reading and figures before they undertook the day's chores. It was lonely for him here without his father. But she made sure that when they went into town, Jim had time to mix with the other children, and she sometimes took him to a church picnic. He was friends with Curly's son, too, though Hector Chavez was almost three years older than Jim. Hector, already something of a vaquero, was patient with Jim and treated him like an equal.

"Jim! Get your lazy bones out of bed!" she called, ladling out the porridge.

They had just finished eating when there came a distinct light knock on the door she knew to be Curly.

"Morning, Curly," she said, opening the door. "Bless me—" She peered past him at the road to the ranch house. "Are those riders coming here?"

"Yes, senora, that's why I come to the door. It looks to be Tom Harning. And one of his men—Andy Pike, that one."

Frowning, Katie went out on the porch to wait for the rancher. Harning and his hand trotted their horses up. "Morning, Katie," Harning said though she did not think of them as being on first-name terms.

"Mr. Harning." Because it was the way of the frontier, she said, "Will you men come and have some coffee?" She hoped he'd refuse.

"I believe I will," Harning said. "Pike, you wait here. Keep an eye out."

"Yes, sir."

She noted that Pike had a six-gun on his hip. Ranch hands didn't often wear them when just visiting another spread. Well, Curly would keep an eye on him.

Harning dismounted and stalked past her into the house.

"Jim!" she called. "Go and grain the mule!"

Jim stood up from the kitchen table, but hesitated, staring at Harning. "Maybe I should stay in here with you, Ma."

"That will not be necessary, young man," she said, hastily clearing the dishes. "Run along now. Maybe you and Hector can check on the horses. Go on."

"Yes, ma'am," he said reluctantly, leaving the room.

Harning ignored him and sat down, awaiting his coffee.

Katie went to the china cabinet. "Will you take some cream with that, Mr. Harning? Fresh this morning."

"I believe I will."

She set a china cup before Harning, poured his coffee from the tin pot and cream from the pitcher, then sat down across from him.

"How is Gertrude?" she asked.

"Gertrude?" He blinked as if the question surprised him. "She's well enough."

Katie waited for him to elaborate, as most husbands would have, but he merely sipped his coffee.

"What brings you out this way?" she asked as equably as she could. "On your way into town?"

"I am at that. But I wanted to see you, too." He smiled at her. It was like a smile carved on a wooden statue.

"About what, Mr. Harning?"

"How about you call me Tom?"

She wanted to demur. But she thought it best to avoid friction. "If you like. Tom."

Another wooden smile, and then he put down his cup and leaned a little toward her. "Katie, it's my understanding Mase is going to be gone for a good long while."

"He's taking a herd to Wichita," she said. "It takes time."

"How many head?"

"About twenty-four hundred."

"Neither big nor small, that herd. But still a sore trial for any man—and now, with the Indian troubles, and trails washed out, and the Army holding up the Chisolm and the Western Trail . . ." He shook his head sadly. "And the spring rains, too! Up in the Oklahoma hills, he could hit snow." He regarded her with cold, narrowed eyes. "How's he going to get through Oklahoma Territory so early in the year?"

Instinctively, Katie decided not to give Harning any more information than she had to. "Oh, he's got a good route. I expect he'll take the Shawnee Trail far as he can. Apart from that"—she shrugged—"I leave it to Mase. He'll figure something."

"Suppose something should happen to him? Here you'd be, all alone!"

"Not alone. I trust Mr. Chavez and his son. And I can take care of myself."

"No doubt." He sipped a little more coffee. "But, Katie, you should know that if anything happens to Mase—and may God forbid it!—you can come to me. I will give you a good price for this ranch. It's like to fall to me anyhow, if the court sees it my way. In fact, was you to—"

Trying to contain her anger, she quickly stood up. "Mr. Harning—*Tom*—I would not sell you this ranch if it burned down and was overrun by locusts. Nor will my husband fail to return. He's as strong and wise a man as any in Texas!"

"I did not mean to suggest—"

"Now—if you will excuse me, we still have chores to attend to." Her tongue felt thick, and she had to work at keeping the tremble from her voice. "My son is still young enough he needs me to hand when he sees to the stock. Do take your time and enjoy your coffee."

She turned and strode from the room—just catching a glimpse of the amazement on his face.

SEVEN DAYS INTO the drive.

The herd was following the Brazos north, and Mase, acting as trail boss, was upriver from the drive, on a windy but sunny morning, scouting for the ford to see how much the rains had swollen the river there. Upstream they'd come to a wide, shallow reach, a ford when the water was low. Shouldn't be too deep even now. Once across, they'd be well and truly on the Shawnee Trail.

He reached the ford and saw that the Brazos was swollen, but the herd wouldn't need much swimming to get across. The chuck wagon would take the ferry if it was running. Otherwise, he might have to add some horsepower to the oxen to get it across the high river without incident. If the current was too deep and fast to ford, they could continue northwest till they passed the headwaters of the river, but that would take them at least two days out of their way.

No. They would cross here.

Mase turned his horse and rode at a canter back toward the herd. Three and a half miles and he reached the chuck wagon. He raised a sign for Dollager to pull up, and the cook shouted at the oxen to halt, tugged on the reins, and pulled the brake lever.

"How looks the trail, Mr. Durst?" Dollager asked. He was dressed now in tweeds and tall boots, which he had said were used by British men on "walking tours," and he had a deerstalker cap shading his eyes.

"The water's high for the Brazos, which runs kind of shallow, but it's not bad at the ford." With a straight face he added, "With a little luck the wagon won't overturn and drown you."

"How you Southern Yanks love to practice your sense of humor on me!" Dollager said, shaking his head. "And it's a comic turn that's dark as a moonless night!"

Mase grinned. "I'll take that as a compliment." He had been joshing—but he also had wanted to see if Dollager scared easily. "If the ferry's running, you'll cross on her. It's big enough for the wagon and the team."

"A ferry! That sounds lovely. I've been dreading a water crossing. But will the herd get across all right?"

"Most of the ford'll be a wade. It'll be some deep in the middle, but cattle will swim if the water's not too fierce."

"May I ask, sir, if the men find my fare to be palatable?"

"Your cooking, you mean? Haven't you seen how they clean their plates?"

"They're hungry enough, they'd probably eat sautéed

rawhide, sir. But all I get are queer looks and raised eyebrows for my efforts."

Mase chuckled. "Some of that is your talk, which puzzles them some. They'll get used to it. Now, the food's some different, too—though your fried steak is more or less Texan chuck. That yellow stuff you put in the stew . . ."

"The curry?"

"It's not usual, but I like it. I find it puts a spring in my step. And I distinctly heard Ray say, 'Good chuck!' last night."

"Is 'good chuck' an accolade?"

"A what? Well, anyhow, it's a compliment, and for a cowpuncher it's nigh to enthusiasm." Mase turned to look at the herd. It was straggled out more than he liked. Of course, once at the ford they'd need it a mite bottlenecked to keep order.

"How are we for"—Dollager looked around nervously—"Indian trouble?"

"Indians? Here?" Mase looked at him in surprise. "Why, the few Indians hereabouts are peaceable as lambs at the suck. But once we cross the Red River, we'll have to go careful. Don't be quick to shoot at a redskin, Mick. That's asking for trouble, and it could be a powerful injustice."

"Quite, Mr. Durst. Where do we camp, come nightfall?"

"There's a tributary of the Brazos out northeast—we'll cross it and make camp. It's still a day's drive from here. Keep the king and queen there moving. We'll have a rest once we're across the river, and then we move on. . . ."

Dollager touched his hat, and Mase rode back to

check on the remuda. They'd been moving since dawn, and he wanted to change out his mount. . . .

He thought of Katie and Jim—they were never far from his thoughts—and he wondered if indeed there'd be trouble with Tom Harning.

Let the man howl in the courtroom if he wanted. He would accomplish nothing. Mase had the deeds and all the proofs he needed. The bank was solidly behind Durst Ranch.

What could that fool Harning do against him?

GERTRUDE HARNING LOOKED at the grandfather clock across the dining room and sighed. It was nine. She decided to give up on waiting for her husband to eat breakfast with her.

She took the cover off the chili'd eggs and spooned herself up a couple. Despite her lack of appetite, she made herself eat them, for her mother had been quite firm that it was sinful to waste food, and when Gertie turned her nose up at a meal, it was as if her late mother were there at her elbow, shaking her head in dark disapproval.

The big clock ticked with loud deliberation as she ate eggs and bacon and sipped her tea. Tom's plate was set out, and she'd hoped to discuss the matter of the buggy repair with him, and ask, once more, if he would come to mass with her this Sunday. Tom had more and more refused to go to church, saying it was a waste of his valuable time, and he acted as if her household concerns, too, were frivolous. She wanted to ask him for a new churchgoing dress for their daughter, Mary—for at ten she was growing out of her old dresses; and Len needed a tutor. He was thirteen but read like a much younger boy. Those permissions she might still have from Tom Harning if she bearded him in his office. He did at least have some concern for his children.

She dabbed at her lips with the napkin and got up, moving the heavy chair back alone. If she'd called Francisco, their cook, he'd have happily helped her from the chair—for she was a small, rather frail woman—but she was embarrassed for him to see that her husband spurned even a meal with her.

Gertie straightened her ankle-length black skirt and went to the oval dining room mirror to make sure of herself before she should enter Tom's office. He criticized her appearance with so little provocation. Her brown hair was properly layered up in a double bun; her white blouse was smooth enough. Everything seemed in order. She remembered him snapping at her, after the last time they'd gone to church, about the expression on her face. *When you get that hang-dog expression, that big nose and small chin of yours make you look like a hound! Try to smile, woman, if you're out with me.*

She closed her eyes, dismissing the pain of the memory, and went to the door of the little smoking room he called his office. She raised her hand to knock on the paneled door—and froze, hearing an unfamiliar voice from within. A deep male voice, certainly not her husband's.

"I could do it, Mr. Harning. But that could put the law on me. And I have no wish to hang."

The remarks startled Gertie. Who was this man talking of the law coming after him—and of hanging?

The voice was somewhat muffled by the door, but she could hear it well enough. He was none of her husband's ranch hands; she was sure of that.

"You've got to do it smart," Tom was saying. "Make it look like a misadventure. An act of God. Or if there's lead flying anyway—Indians and such—if you're careful, a bullet of your own will seem to have come from those other guns."

"I could work it that way, I reckon. Pike said you'd pay me, but didn't say how much."

"Two thousand when I have confirmed to my satisfaction that Mason Durst is dead! Once he's out of the way, I believe Katie Durst will sell out to me right quick."

Gertie gasped. Her husband was asking this man to kill Mase Durst!

"How do I know you'll pay me?" the man asked.

"It'll be safer to pay you than not to, of course. But if you want five hundred dollars more, you'll scatter that herd so that they'll never recover it. I have a plan for that. . . ."

"How do I find the drive?"

"He's signing more men on, up in Denison. You ride up there and wait for the herd. I'll give you a hundred dollars' stake money. . . ."

Gertie felt dizzy. She certainly couldn't face her husband now.

She turned and walked dazedly away and took herself to the parlor. She sank mutely on the settee, wringing her hands, panting softly. What could she do? What would Tom do if she confronted him? He had slapped her for less. If she went to the county sheriff—

how would it go? Sheriff Beslow was not unfriendly with Tom. He'd be reluctant to believe such a story. He'd accuse her of having misheard. And she could imagine the lawman pointing out that even if she'd heard rightly, no murder had yet been done. There'd only been talk of one.

But suppose the sheriff did take the matter in hand? Suppose Tom was arrested for plotting a murder?

She would have to testify in court, if it was permitted for her to testify against her husband. And the children—how would they feel? It could end with him being released and taking Len and Mary away from her.

Gertie felt paralyzed with indecision. But—what of Mase Durst? He'd always seemed a good man. His wife came to mass twice monthly, when she could get there—Fuente Verde, the nearest town, was yet a fair distance away—and was always ready for a friendly chat afterward, never remarking on the enmity between their husbands. How could Gertie allow this crime to be carried out upon these good people?

She had to think. There was time surely. It was hard to know what to do. Perhaps she could not act at all. She might have to hope this strange hireling failed in his attempt at murder.

But how could she live with what she had heard?

It came to her then that she had never truly known her husband. She had thought him a cold man. His courtly chivalrousness had vanished soon after their marriage. Just as soon as he had laid hands on her money. He had slapped her on occasion and frequently demeaned her appearance. He thought of her as a kind of nanny to his children, at best.

But murder? She had not thought him capable of it.

She had never seen how black his heart was till now.

And yet, for the sake of her children, it might be that she must go on as she had always done. She must live with this man.

Covering her eyes, she wept as quietly as she could.

CHAPTER FOUR

HIRAM DURST STOOD at the rail of the balcony overlooking the only street to be found in Leadton, Oklahoma Territory. Freight wagons trundled noisily below; a drifter bellowed at the barkeep who'd ejected him from the Stew Pot, and there was out-of-key piano music jangling from the doorway behind him. The Stew Pot Saloon wasn't roaring yet, but it was waking up.

Hiram was rolling a cigarette, watching the sunset between the steep hills to the west, and thinking he should leave Leadton. The Kelso brothers hated him—he had knocked Rod Kelso out cold just two weeks before and now there was that business of Phil Kelso's hat—and when drunk, they were both reckless. In addition, Sheriff Greer didn't like him because of Queenie; she preferred Hiram's company to the sheriff's.

Anyhow, Hiram had nothing going here but playing the part of official fine and tax collector for the three merchants who called themselves the town council.

The job required him to go toe to toe with querulous drummers, cowboys with trifling little herds, surprisingly truculent sheepherders passing through, and the like, to squeeze money out of them for the city coffers. It was distasteful work—and worse, it paid badly. So why not hit the trail? He seemed to have lost touch with his gumption, was why. A peculiar tiredness was forever snapping at his heels.

He lit his cigarette and thought about Mase. He had more and more caught himself wondering about his brother lately. Was Mase making a better living than Hiram was? Mase and his wife had a ranch somewhere south of Fort Worth. Hiram had been through there just once, meeting Katie and a four-year-old boy, little Jimmy Durst, who'd called him "Unca," and he'd left as soon as he decently could. They'd treated him well but the whole interlude had made him mighty uncomfortable . . . or had it just been envy?

"Here you are," said Queenie, coming out onto the balcony as he drew in the tobacco smoke. "I thought you'd done rid out on me." She came to the rail beside him and put out her hand for the cigarette. He handed her the smoke, and she took a puff and handed it back.

"You're always thinking I'm gonna ride out on you, but I haven't done it," said Hiram.

She shrugged. "It's on your mind to go. I can feel it."

She was right about that. He glanced at her. Queenie had put on that blue dress he liked, cut low and cut high. She was a head shorter than him, but she looked taller with the dress showing so much of her legs. Her blond hair was swirling over her shoulders and her China blue eyes held a sparkle as she gazed up at him.

"Well, Queenie," he said, "don't you ever think of doing something different than running this place for Sanborne?"

"Sure I do. I think how we could go to New Orleans, start our own place. I got some money saved. Or maybe Virginia City. It's booming there." After a moment she added, "You hear that? When I said *we*?"

"I did. Hon, we've only known each other since February. I don't even know your real name."

"How do you know it's not Queenie?"

"You going to tell me, or ain't you?"

She sighed. "It's Amaryllis."

"Like the flower? Say, that's a beautiful name. Why'd you change it?"

"I don't want every man who pays to spend time with me to know my name."

He nodded. "Well, since you've worked for Murch Sanborne, you haven't had to . . . to spend that kind of time with anyone. And you don't charge me."

"Of course I don't." She put her hand on his arm, clasping his elbow the way a wife would with her man when they walked down the street. "Maybe I should."

"Nope." He turned to her and lifted her chin and kissed her. "No, you shouldn't."

"Durst!" It was Greer's voice.

Hiram turned to see Sheriff Greer glaring at him from the balcony door. Mike Greer was a barrel of a man in a black sack suit, the only brightness on it his badge. He had a froggish face and a sloping forehead. His eyes pretty much always looked angry, unless he was in the first flush of drinking. He shaved every day but never seemed to get all the bristle off.

"I get back in town, first thing I hear is how you're shooting at Phil Kelso!"

"I didn't shoot at him," Hiram said coolly. "I shot at his hat."

Queenie put a hand over her mouth to cover a giggle.

"Knocked it off his head without putting a scratch on him," Hiram went on.

"Now, why the hell did you do that? He rides with Fletcher, and they bring cash into this town!"

"He was drunk and come at me, saying he was going to shoot out my lights. Just how he said it, too. He was trying to pull out his gun, so I shot his hat off to keep from having to kill him. Besides—it made me laugh. I pure needed a laugh. I disarmed him and sent him back to the saloon. That was last night—he still talking about it? I'm surprised he remembers."

"He remembers. You're going to pay for the hat and buy him a drink!"

"Oh, hellfire, Greer—"

"Just do it! Right away!" With that, Greer went back into the building, shouting at someone to bring him a drink.

Hiram muttered a few profanities. Then he said, "You know what, Miss Queenie Amaryllis Jones?"

"What?"

"I think I'd like to see New Orleans with you. Never been there."

She threw her arms around his waist. "When!"

"Oh—I'll want some money of my own. I have some notions as to that. So let's say—early June. What do you say?"

"I say go and buy that man a hat, and I'm going to write a letter to my sister in New Orleans!"

FIFTEEN DAYS ON the trail. Seven of them north of Fort Worth.

"Lord, but I need my bedroll," groaned Harry Duff, carrying his tin plate to the washing tub.

"Don't forget you've got night guard in four hours," Mase reminded him, setting his plate aside.

"Oh, I ain't forgot, boss!"

Mase smiled, watching Duff stagger off to his bedroll. There weren't enough of them to take shifts, with all these cattle to drive. That meant they were all working even longer hours than normal—and any drive offered wearisome hours.

Pug was out watching the cattle; Ray Jost, always ready for a chin wag, was smoking a pipe on the other side of the fire and telling Vasquez a much-worn tale of a cattle drive where a lightning bolt had struck three cows at once and cooked them to such perfection that the drovers dined on them for a week just as they were found.

It had begun to drizzle again, and it might go to a full rain in the night. The weakening campfire was smoking, sizzling with the drops of rain. The moon showed through the clouds from time to time, but just as often hid itself away. Dollager was scrubbing the big iron Dutch oven out with pumice and water, there being plenty of water to hand with the overflowing creek but twenty yards off. The herd was a mile off the trail, in case some other early, ambitious herd came up in the night; two herds jostling could lead to a stampede and the confusion of property. The Durst Ranch cattle, however, were branded, each one showing the proper ear notches and the mark of a “D” over the shape of a “Y” turned on its side, representing San Vincente Creek and its tributary, the Little Vince. It was a confluence that took place on Durst property.

Mase got up, put his tin plate in the tub, and strolled over to the remuda. It was a peaceful night, with a weak breeze driving the thin rain. Now and then frogs called from the creek and an owl hooted.

He selected a horse, saddled it himself, removed its hobble, and drew it by the reins over to the staked rope that served to keep the horses penned. Of course, the remuda horses could trample through the rope if they chose, and might if spooked, but most times their training kept them in place; they were dozing now, heads drooping. Mase pulled up a stake, led the horse over the rope, replaced the stake, and mounted up.

He cantered to the herd, fifty yards off, signaling Pug that he’d take his place. Pug’s dinner was waiting in a covered pan by the fire. Vasquez would soon be coming out to spell Jacob.

The herd was mostly bedded down, Mase saw, though a few bawled edgily, ogling the northern horizon where clouds curdled blackly and flickered. Ray Jost might have a new lightning story to tell after tonight.

Circling the herd, Mase swung the end of a lasso rope at the steers who looked like they were thinking of peeling off. “Ho, cattle, easy now, easy!” he called. Maybe the stock didn’t understand the words, but they were soothed by the tone.

He soon came upon Jacob, riding one of the remuda cow ponies, singing low and easy to soothe the cattle.

"How they look tonight, Jacob?" Mase asked, reining in beside the black cowboy.

"They was most asleep. Now some is waking up, Mr. Durst. It's that storm coming."

Mase peered again at the horizon. The black clouds seemed a long way off. "You sure it's headed here?"

"Oh, yes, sir. We're not careful, this herd'll go catawampus quick."

"Your talk sometimes don't sound Texas, Jacob. Alabama?"

"North Georgia, sir, born and raised, a slave nigh to thirty years. Worked for a master who raised cattle and horses."

The wind was picking up from the direction of the storm front. Lightning flickered more brightly that way. Mase watched it as he said, "I've heard there's good ranching up in the north of Georgia. How'd you come to Texas?"

"The Yankees killed the master when he tried to keep them from the stock, and they sure lay waste to his spread. They gave me my walkin' papers and a yearling mule. I come out here, looking to make my way. I know'd cattle and horses, so there was always work for me."

This impressed Mase as the biggest speech he'd yet heard from Jacob. What mattered was Jacob was a hard, efficient worker. "Crane talked you up, and he was right. You're a good hand."

"I thank you, sir. And I thank you for something else, too."

"What's that?"

"Paying me the same as them other boys. Usually I get half what a white man gets."

"If you worked half as hard as you do, you'd get half as much!" Mase said, grinning. "But that goes for every man in the outfit."

Jacob smiled. Then his smile was quickly erased as he stared off into darkness to the west. "You see that, Mr. Durst?"

"What is it?"

"I swear I saw a man afoot, or a boy mebbe—see that patch of brush out there?" He pointed. "Saw it move in there. Coming at the herd. Could've been a wolf fooling my eyes. It was on the east side of that brush."

"We don't want wolves nor men prowling here. Let's have a look."

Driven by the rising storm wind, the clouds cracked open, and the moonlight shone through as they trotted their horses quietly up to the west side of the brush. Going slowly to minimize noise, they moved along the brush line, peering into the shadows.

"There, sir!" Jacob whispered, pointing.

Mase saw it then, about sixty feet away: one of the shadows taking on the shape of a slim man moving out of the brush a few yards from a group of cattle. The shape firmed up in the moonlight, creeping in a squat toward the herd, rope in hand. It was a figure in buckskin with an unmistakable profile. An Indian.

Taking up his lasso, Mase coiled its loop for a cast. He dared not shoot at the man; the shot could scatter the herd.

"Jacob," Mase whispered, "head quiet as you can back behind the brush, circle him to the south. I'll take him from the north."

Jacob nodded and turned his horse, trotting off so

as not to make much noise. The wind was picking up, the storm clouds rushing now, looming over them. Lightning flared not far off; thunder rumbled.

Mase secured the lasso with a half hitch around the saddle horn and nudged his horse with his knees so it moved quietly ahead.

The Indian had picked out a yearling, was already whirling a loop to throw over the steer's head. Mase wondered how the rustler hoped to control the beast after roping it, seeing as he was on foot.

The rustler threw his loop—and at the same moment, Mase cast his own. It settled over the Indian's head, shoulders, and arms, all the way to the elbows, and Mase tugged it tight as he backed up his horse, dragging the man off his feet. The rustler lost his grip on the yearling, which ran off, dragging the rope, as Jacob rode up, jumped off his mule, and flipped the thief over on his belly. He pressed a knee on the struggling rustler to hold him.

Mase untied the lasso from his saddle horn, jumped down, drew his knife, and cut a yard of rope off. He hurried over and, after a short struggle, tied the rustler's arms behind his back.

"Turn him over," Mase said. The clouds parted, and he and the Indian regarded each other in the moonlight. "Why, he's but a boy!" Mase exclaimed.

The Indian boy might be at most fifteen. He was starveling skinny, his belly sunken toward his backbone. But his onyx eyes glared back at Mase with flinty defiance. Thunder rumbled in the distance, getting closer.

"Where are the others, boy?" Mase asked.

He got no response. The Indian teen only clamped his mouth more tightly shut.

"Could be there ain't no others," Jacob suggested.

"His band's got to be somewhere around here."

"Haven't seen no others. Nor their sign. I don't see any horse in that thicket either. Look at his feet—all tore up. No moccasins, nothing. No knife on him."

Mase nodded. While the Apaches and the Comanches in the area might at times be a little hard up for food, he'd never before seen one quite this starved or poorly equipped. He looked him over, and it seemed to Mase the buckskin garments were more Plains Indian than Texas.

"If he's Apache, I don't see the signs of it."

"Ain't Apache!" the boy hissed, spitting the word as if he hated Apaches.

"You speak English, boy?" Mase asked.

"What if I do?"

"Where'd you learn it?" Most of the Indians in the area spoke but a pidgin English, mixed with Spanish and Natchez.

"You untie me. Then maybe I tell you!"

Mase snorted. "Not likely."

"What we do with him?" Jacob asked. "Hang him?"

Mase shook his head. "Have to take him prisoner, I expect. Maybe give him to the Army up the trail, let them decide. Or turn him over to his band if we can find 'em. Take hold of his wrists. I'll pull him up."

He dragged the Indian to his feet—and the boy instantly tried to run. Jacob yanked him back. "You'll do yourself a mischief, boy!"

Lightning flashed a few miles away, and thunder

growled. The cattle lowed, most of them up now, milling restlessly.

"You got a horse or a mule, boy?" Mase asked. "I'll get it and put you on it, if you do. Otherwise you'll ride with a lot less dignity."

The boy angrily shook his head and looked away.

"I didn't see no stock tracks in that brush when I rode around it," Jacob said.

The rain was coming thicker now, lashed down by the fiercer wind.

"Throw him over your cantle, ride him into camp," Mase said. "Untie him under guard, tell the coosie to feed him."

"Feed him, sir?" Used to more hard-bitten trail bosses, Jacob seemed genuinely surprised.

"That's right. Tell Dollager to keep a shotgun on the boy while he eats. We'll tie him up when he's done. You send Vasquez, Jost, and Pug out here—Duff is to saddle up between the camp and the herd." He looked at the angry sky. "Get a wiggle on!"

"Yes, sir!"

Jacob lifted the boy as if he were but a sack of grain, carried him to his horse, and dumped him over the cantle. In a moment Jacob was in the saddle; one hand holding the boy down, the other on the reins, he galloped off toward camp.

Mase retrieved his lasso, mounted up, and set about skirting the herd, calling out to the cattle, heading off their nervous shying, and looking for Ol' Buck. If the herd threatened to scatter in the storm, maybe he could get Buck to lead them back.

The wind rose still more; lightning cracked nearer, and he had to gallop to intercept a big steer running away from the storm; it had been leading a dozen others off to the south.

Mase succeeded in turning them and saw Vasquez and the others riding hard around the herd, trying to keep it roughly in place.

Half an hour of fevered riding passed as they fought to keep the cattle contained, before Mase spotted Ol' Buck pounding to the south, with a bawling, frantic line of perhaps a hundred steers following after.

Mase drew his pistol, rode to intercept the lead steer, and fired in the air to get Ol' Buck's attention. Buck half stumbled, confused, then turned and the others followed as Mase kept riding, firing once more to drive Buck back toward the herd.

In a flash of moonlight, Mase saw the Indian boy, somehow astride Jacob's mule. The Indian was about forty yards away, reined in and watching. "What the devil!" Mase muttered.

A moment later lightning struck just to the west of the herd. He smelled ozone, and electricity sizzled blue across the wet ground; he glimpsed sparks arcing between the horns of a steer, the maddened longhorn rushing directly at him: head lowered, nostrils smoking, the whites showing around its eyes, hooves pounding.

Mase turned his horse, but it was too late; the horse screamed, deeply gored by the onrushing steer. It sunfished and fell, and Mase just managed to jump free before it could fall on his leg. He struck the ground hard, the air knocked out of him, and struggled to get up, seeing the stampede come right at him.

He got up, gasping, and turned to run but knew it was too late—then a horse was suddenly there, right in front of him. It was one of the remuda horses, unsaddled but harnessed—and it was led by the Indian boy on the mule.

"Get on!" the boy shouted.

Mase clapped onto the horse's rump and leapfrogged on as the steers rushed up to them, one of them trampling the spot he'd been in a moment before. The remuda pony galloped in panic with the steers, Mase with his arms wrapped around its neck. He caught a chaotic look at the Indian boy riding off on the mule. Cattle streamed by on every side.

Then he was in the clear, grabbing the horse's mane, digging his heels in its ribs, shouting, "Whoa!" It was a full minute before he was able to get the panting animal to stop.

Mase turned to see the Indian boy at the mouth of an arroyo. The boy who'd saved his life. The young Indian paused and looked back at him—Mase raised a hand in salutation. The boy raised his hand and then rode into the arroyo, passing from sight.

CHAPTER FIVE

THE STORM BROKE up quickly, but it took Mase and his men the rest of the night and some of the morning, riding through mud and sporadic rain, to gather up the strays. About four hundred fifty head had scattered past the drovers into the surrounding arroyos and plains. Four of the horses had run off, too. Those they located fairly quickly, as they were tame enough to stick closer, but the cattle were hiding from the storm in gullies and brush brakes.

So exhausted they could barely sit their saddles, Mase and Pug drove the last of the strays back into the herd, then returned to camp, finding the others there already eating breakfast. Dollager had pulled enough dry wood from storage in the canvas "possum belly" under the wagon to get the campfire going. The sky was clear now, and the sun was just warm enough to be welcome. Every drover had red eyes, and they were all glumly silent as they ate, but no one spoke a word of complaint. Mase knew that if they'd had enough hands, they'd have gotten the gather finished twice as quick. But he wasn't one to lash himself with regret.

He took a plate of food and sat on a log beside Jacob. Dollager brought him a cup of coffee.

"Sorry about your mule, Jacob," Mase said after a long pull at the coffee.

Jacob was silent for a while, then said at last, "I reckon she's still alive anyhow. I don't expect the Indian killed her for food, being as he got his feed."

"His tracks probably washed out after that storm."

"Yes, sir."

"Well, you've got a remuda horse, though we lost one. I suppose we should take some meat from that dead horse. I was never one for horsemeat, though." He ate some sourdough biscuit and bacon. Hungry as he was, he thought he'd never tasted better fare.

He looked out at the herd, saw some of them peacefully cropping grass, many others lying with legs folded, comfortably dozing. The night had worn the cattle out, too. "Dollager, you get some rest last night?" he asked.

"More than you did, Mr. Durst. Of that, I'm sure," Dollager said, walking up with a warm pan in his hand. "Jacob—I must confess I took my eyes off that Indian for a moment, and he ran away with your mule. I do apologize."

"It's all right, Mick," said Jacob. "I'll get 'er back."

Dollager held the pan out to Mase. "I've made some fritters from the dried apples and blackstrap, if you fellows would like some."

"I could eat the apple tree, bark and all," said Mase as Dollager spooned the fritters from the pan onto their plates. "Being as you slept some, coosie, hows about you just sit on a horse for us for a little while and watch the herd from over here? Those cows are as tired as we are. I doubt they go anywhere. I'm gonna catch a couple hours' sleep. You others do the same. Then I'll get up and take Dollager's place. Just roust us if there's any trouble, coosie—or if you see any Indians at all."

"Very good, Mr. Durst."

Mase finished his meal and went for a lie-down. It was four hours before he woke—he checked by his railroad watch—and he sat up annoyed. "Why'd no one wake me?"

Dollager looked up from a griddle, where he was frying the next meal. "Pug said to let you sleep, sir. He and Vasquez and Jost are keeping an eye on things. The boy Duff there is yet asleep. I've got Jacob off looking for dry wood."

Mase stood up and stretched—and then went stock-still, staring out at the plains. There, on a low hill a hundred yards away, was the Indian boy sitting on Jacob's mule. Just watching them.

"There's that boy, coosie! See him? You find out anything when you fed him?"

"He said his name's East Wind Blake. He's a Sioux. He revealed nothing else I'm afraid, sir. Not a loquacious lad."

"A Sioux! He's a long way from home. And there he is, watching us."

"Are you going to take a shot at him, Mr. Durst?" Dollager asked, peering at the boy. He sounded a little worried. "So as to get the mule back?"

"That boy saved my life last night. I will not be shooting at him."

"The men know he pulled your chestnuts from the fire," Dollager said. "Pug saw it happen. I expect that's why they're reluctant to go after him, despite the larceny."

"We'll just see. I might have to buy Jacob a mule."

As he watched, the boy turned the mule, rode her over the hilltop, and vanished from sight.

KATIE WAS PITCHFORKING hay in the barn on an overcast Saturday afternoon when she heard swift hoofbeats approaching. She looked up to see Jim ride his pony into the barn. His face was flushed with excitement, his eyes wide.

"What're you doing here?" she demanded. "You're supposed to be helping Curly and Hector fix the fence!"

"Curly sent me to get you! And he sent Hector to get his gun! There's three men saying they want to pull down our fences!"

"What men?"

"They're from Circle H! They put rope on the fence, and Curly cut it with a knife and now he's waving that knife at 'em!"

"What! Did he ask them what they were about?"

"Yes, ma'am. He sent me here, and he was talking to them a whole lot when I left."

He's trying to stall them, she thought.

She leaned the pitchfork against the wall and went to get her saddle. "I'll saddle Bonnie. You can take me to the spot. Water that pony some and rest him while I'm saddling up. You've got him blowing from the gallop. It's the Lord's mercy you didn't fall off and break your neck. . . ."

A hard ride brought Katie and Jim to the northeast corner of the property, where it abutted the Circle H's north pastures. Curly and Hector were watching helplessly as two men finished attaching heavy ropes to a fifty-foot-wide section of wooden fence. Andy Pike sat on his horse, with a shotgun laid across the cantle, watching Curly and Hector. Curly now had his repeating rifle in hand.

The other Circle H hands she knew by sight: Red Sullivan, a sunburned face to go with his ginger hair and mustache, and Wurreck, a small, tense man with a thick black beard.

Beyond the hands, on Circle H land, about two hundred cattle were grazing. Katie suspected they'd been brought here as part of this show of force.

"Curly—you threatened those men with a knife?" she asked, walking over to him.

"They said they were going to pull the fence down, senora! I had nothing else to stop them with! *Estúpido!* I should have brought a rifle! Hector, he bring it to me, and I try to talk to them—"

"It's okay, Curly. Nobody expected this foolishness."

"I didn't want to shoot without asking you."

Katie nodded as she took her rifle from its saddle holster. "You did right."

"Mama," Jim whispered, "what do we do?"

"I'm going to find out." She smiled at Jim, sorry she'd let him come out here with her. "You wait here with Curly."

Fingers tightening on the rifle, she walked down the fence a little till she was opposite Andy Pike. He sat on his horse, watching her, about ten yards away. Katie was a fair shot—her parents had taught her how to use a rifle and a shotgun—but this was no time to open a gunfight.

The men at the fence had paused in their work. They looked uncomfortable, staring at her, as if it had just now occurred to them that they might have to fight a woman.

Pike spoke, low and drawling. "You boys going to pull that fence down or not?"

Sullivan and Wurreck went back to tightening the knots. Their horses waited behind them, the other ends of the ropes attached to their saddle horns.

"Someone going to tell me what this is all about?" Katie demanded. She looked at Pike. "How about you, Andy Pike? Anything to say?"

Pike cleared his throat. "Ma'am, Mr. Harning says you've built a fence across his property."

"Now, how can he do that? It isn't his property! It's Durst land!"

"Well, he says it's his, and the court will prove it! Says to tell you he'll pay you something anyhow, if—"

"The hell you say!" she interrupted, shouting the words. She put the rifle to her shoulder and centered it on Pike. "Back 'em off!" She had the drop on him. But she'd never killed a man. She wasn't sure she was ready to do it—or if she'd be arrested for it even if she was ready.

Pike eyed the rifle. Then he shrugged. She could see in his eyes he was going to call her bluff. "I don't think you'll shoot me, Mrs. Durst," he said. "I can't see you wanting to go to prison."

She had to make some kind of move. Suppose it brought on a general gunfight? What about Jim and Hector?

"Jim!" she called. "Head on back to the house!"

"No, ma'am!"

She glanced at him. Defiantly he came up and stood by her. "Papa said I was to take care of you!"

"Jim—"

But then Pike was yelling, "Do it, Red! Go on. You too, Wurreck!"

The two cowboys at the fence ran to their horses, climbed on, and backed them up, tightening the ropes on the fence posts. The posts grated, coming loose in their sockets. Katie hesitated, still not sure which way to jump.

"Stop!" was all she managed—and then the section of fence came apart with a squealing, crunching sound, and the horses dragged the boards back onto Circle H property. A wide gap showed in the property fencing now.

"Let's get those cattle moving!" Pike called out. "Right through the fence!"

The cowboys loosed the ropes from their saddles and galloped off toward the small herd.

"No, that I'm not going to permit!" Katie shouted. "Curly—aim at the ground. Keep those cows back!"

She swung the muzzle of her rifle and fired at the ground in front of the Circle H cattle. Curly fired, too, his rounds striking close to hers. The animals bawled and milled restlessly, backing away.

"Mrs. Durst—!" Pike began.

"Shut up, Pike!" she snapped, reloading her rifle. "You listen to me! I'll shoot the cattle who come across that fence line!"

She fired again, feeling the kick of the rifle butt more now; more dirt sprayed, kicked up near the cattle. "Curly, get those ropes. Use 'em to block the fence line!

"Mister, unless you plan to kill us, you got to move that herd back!" Curly called. "I'm going to block up this hole! I'm coming over on your land!"

Pike gaped at Katie, then at the cattle, then back at her.

Curly trotted over to untie the ropes, and to Katie's considerable exasperation, Jim and Hector followed him and began to pull the ropes back toward the fence. Now her son was right in the line of fire!

She could see Pike's mouth moving, could read his lips as he cursed her, but he turned his horse and rode toward his men. Katie watched tensely. Was he going to help them run the cattle her way? She'd have to shoot some of those cattle. She had to make some kind of stand.

But then Katie saw him waving his hat at the other men, sending them back toward the Circle H ranch house. She figured he was going to ask for further orders from Harning.

She waited till the three cowboys had ridden off and then went to help stretch the rope across the gap in the fence. They'd be shoring up that fence the rest of the day, she supposed.

Katie seethed with anger. Tom Harning had reckoned that without her man there, she'd back off and let him claim some of the Durst land. Maybe scare her into leaving the ranch.

She had stopped the intrusion. But there was not much hope it would end here. She turned to Jim, who was dragging a rope along toward the fence line. "You, Jim!"

"Yes, Mama?"

It was in her mind to give him a tongue-lashing for refusing to go back to the ranch. But he had done only as he thought his father would want him to. "Jim"—she kept her voice gentle—"next time I tell you to go back to the house, do it."

"If I can, Mama."

Now how was she to argue with that?

"What we going to do after we rope up the fence, senora?" Curly asked, pulling a rope free from an uprooted post.

She bent to work and said, "I'm going to bring Sheriff Beslow in on this. We'll just see what he has to say."

But Katie didn't have a lot of faith in Beslow. She had a feeling she was going to be fighting this land war on her own.

TWENTY DAYS INTO the drive. Not real close to Denison, and not real far from it.

It was a hot midday, the sun glaring in a cloudless sky, as Mase rode out to the low ridgeline with Ray Jost at his side.

"That where you saw him, up by the oaks?" Mase asked, pointing.

"Yep. Just sitting cool as a cucumber on that stolen mule, watching me when I brought those strays back this morning. Maybe thought he was going to get one for himself before I come along. Wasn't you wanted that Indian left alone, Mase, I'd have tried to lasso him off that mule, too. That old mule can't outrun this horse."

"Your first job is drover, Ray. You can't be out chasing after that boy."

"Stolen stock matters, don't it?"

"It does."

"And he got a saddle, too, and a rope, and Jacob's saddlebags! He tells me he had a knife in there, and a shirt, and some varmint traps."

"Yeah. I'm asking myself, why is he riding along with us?"

"Looking for a chance to steal beeves of course!"

"Could be. Not so sure. But why let us see him like this? It's no accident." They reached the copse of oaks without sighting East Wind Blake, but Ray pointed out the tracks. "Those are the tracks of Jacob's mule, sure!"

"You're in the right of it there," Mase said, looking at the tracks. "These are fresh tracks." He looked north along the ridgeline and saw a little hollow of brush spotted with trees big enough to hide a mule and a man.

"He could be in that brush there—see it?"

"I wouldn't bet against it," Ray said, nodding.

Mase dismounted and reached into his coat where the telescope Katie had given him was tucked against his bosom. He placed the spyglass to his eye and fixed it on the thicket. He could just make out the mule's head within the foliage, lifting up a little to sniff at the air. "Yep, I see the mule. That boy is in there. He's watching us, sure." He took an oilcloth package from his saddlebag and rode up to the nearest oak. He lifted the package in the air, waved it, and hung it on a broken-off snag sticking out from a branch.

"What you got in there?" Ray asked.

"Food—salted meat, bread, some wild onions."

"You really going to feed that thief, Mase?" Ray asked in disbelief. "What for?"

"He saved my life. That's one reason. You know, he could have taken that remuda horse with him, but he brought it to me, and he risked his life doing it." Mase looked down at the herd. "Let's go down and get some chuck. Then we're movin' out. I hope to be in Denison day after tomorrow. . . ."

HIRAM DURST WASN'T looking forward to this job. There was something about these sheepherders that stirred him inside.

He was sitting on his horse, at dusk, looking down from the hilltop at the small procession of oxen-drawn wagons, seeing the young men, two women, and even some children accompanying their elders. There could be gunplay, because they were trying to get around paying Leadton the goods taxes levied by the town council, and he saw two of the young men walking beside the wagons with rifles in their hands.

There were several sheep ranches up in the high valleys in the hills west of Leadton. The ranchers had to bring their wool and meat animals through town—or blessed close—to get them up to Morrisville, some distance north, where their best market was found. Now and then those moving their goods tried to skirt Leadton and avoid the "toll tax," as the council liked to call it. He didn't blame the sheepherders for that. Might be, as some claimed, that the merchant toll tax was illegal in Texas, and that it was too damned big a percentage of the goods' worth even if it was legal. Collecting the money could be rough when Sheriff Greer got himself involved. And it was Greer who'd found out the sheepherders were trying to slip by without paying today.

They were driving their wagons on the eastern trail, two miles out of their way, and soon they'd pull up to wait till night. Then they'd slip by Leadton in the dark.

But they'd been seen, and someone had told Greer just for the ten-dollar reward. Now the town sheriff was waiting around the turn in the road, him and the Kelso brothers and Joe Fletcher, his supposed deputies. Hiram had been brought along partly to "make things official" and to work out how many wagons there were, get an estimate of their goods and their likely resistance.

Hiram had a sick feeling in his belly about this business.

He drew his stallion back from the hilltop and quickly rode down a game trail, through an arroyo, and out onto the main trail where Greer and the others were waiting on their horses.

"Is it like the prospector said?" Greer asked as Hiram rode up.

"It is," Hiram admitted. "They look like they could be ready to fight over this one, Mike. Let me go parley with them."

"We'll start it that way," Greer said. He had a big bullwhip coiled around his saddle horn, and now he reached out to run a long contemplative finger over its hard leather. "How we finish depends on them. I'm not going to dicker."

"Better to just up and teach 'em a lesson right now," said Joe Fletcher. "They're taking this eastern trail to give us the slip!" Fletcher dressed sharp and kept a pleasant expression on his bland face; he wore a long blue coat, a white shirt and a vest, and a string tie. He tried to affect the look of a banker and claimed to be a "loan agent." More like a confidence agent, Hiram figured, when he wasn't playing deputy for the sheriff. Always had a smile that looked as if he was about to crack a joke—but the joke never came out. Queenie said, *Joe Fletcher? He seems friendly till you look in his eyes.*

"Joe's right," said Rod Kelso. "Put the fear of God in 'em." Rod was a crafty-eyed man, with slick black hair, a bitter set to his thin lips, and pitted skin.

"How much firepower they have?" asked Phil Kelso.

Rod's shorter, younger brother looked almost handsome compared to him, except his eyes were a little too close together. Both men wore striped pants, English riding boots, and frock coats, but—thanks to Hiram—Phil had that new brown high-crowned hat to go with his tan coat. It'd make such a good target. . . .

"They have rifles and shotguns," Hiram said. "And they've got the look of men ready to use those firearms."

"Go on, then," Greer said grudgingly. "See if you can get them to lay down the simoleons peacefully. But do it quick. I don't want to sit out here all damn night."

"Durst is liable to get himself shot, doing this fool thing," said Phil, chuckling as Hiram rode around the turn in the trail.

Good chance of that, Hiram admitted to himself.

The first of the four covered wagons pulled up short when Hiram blocked their road. He drew his mount to a halt in the midst of the trail, with his right hand up, trying to look friendly. The steep hills were gathering shadows in the thickening dusk, and Hiram couldn't see the sheepherder's faces clearly, but he saw light gleaming on the weapons of the two walking toward him. Beyond them a big older man with a spade beard and the cast of a patriarch was up on the wagon, his hands on the oxen reins. He had a shotgun propped within reach.

The two men with the rifles came striding into the dimming light, and Hiram recognized them. He'd run into them in Leadton when they were there buying supplies. They were the Marcheson cousins, Johan and Sid Marcheson, both of them with close-shorn blond hair, scant beards intended to make them look more manly than they were. They wore overalls and heavy boots. Sid, who seemed as scared as he was angry, was younger and thinner.

"Johan and Sid, I think. That right?" Hiram called out, still maintaining his smile.

"What you want, mister?" Johan asked.

"I'm collecting taxes for the city of Leadton. Toll tax on goods." He glanced past them, could see the bales of wool stacked in the wagons. There'd be mutton in there, too, probably in barrels, for they slaughtered some of their rams and lambs for butchers in Morrisville.

"This ain't Leadton," said Johan.

"Close enough according to town rules," Hiram replied, shrugging. "I'm afraid the sheriff and the town council are firm on the matter."

"We ain't paying it. Now, get out the way."

Hiram sighed. He sat back in his saddle and let one hand fall to rest on the butt of his Colt. He kept himself relaxed and retained the smile on his face.

But they saw where his gun hand was. Till now he'd never had to do more than bluster and shoot into the air to get the tax money. And one time he'd had to engage in fisticuffs with an outraged farmer. Luckily Hiram had come out on top.

This time he wasn't so sure he could get away without shooting one of these young men. There was a look in Johan's eyes. . . .

"We've got to insist, boys," Hiram said. "You'll still have most of your profit."

"What's the price this time?" Sid asked, licking his lips.

"We estimate—four hundred dollars."

"What!" Johan burst out. "You have taken leave of your senses, mister!"

"Just the messenger here. Now, you can provide equivalent goods, or you can find the cash—"

He broke off as Sheriff Greer, the Kelso brothers, and Joe Fletcher rode up, guns in hand. They had the drop on the sheepherders. "Drop those weapons, or die where you stand!" Greer shouted.

"Hold on, damn it!" Hiram said. "Let me talk to them, Greer!"

Greer pointed his pistol at the old man in the wagon. "You young fellas drop those guns, or I kill the old man!"

The Marcheson cousins looked at each other—and dropped their weapons. The old man put his hands up.

Fletcher and the Kelsos kept their guns on the cousins as Greer got down off his horse, taking his bullwhip with him. He got a good grip on the handle of the whip and shook it out to full length. "I hear something about how you're not going to pay up?"

"Now, listen, mister," Johan said. "We just want a fair—"

Greer slashed the whip through the air so it looped around Johan's calves. Greer pulled him off his feet with a jerk of his arm, dragged the bullwhip free, and commenced using it. Johan Marcheson screamed in pain.

"Stop that, Greer!" Hiram shouted.

Phil Kelso turned his gun toward Hiram. "You failed to get it done. Now the sheriff's seeing to it. You can get out, or you can get down off your horse and stand with them sheepmen."

The whip rose and fell, snapping, snapping, snapping, and the boy shrieked and tried to crawl away. The old man shouted something Hiram couldn't make out.

"I'm going back to town, Kelso," Hiram said. "Point that gun somewhere else."

Phil gave him a yellow-toothed grin and holstered the gun.

Sick to his belly, Hiram turned his horse and started back for Leadton. He was done with this job. He had no choice but to simply ride away.

But the sounds pursued him. The whip cracking over and over, echoing in the ravine, and the boy screaming . . . women weeping, the old man begging Greer to stop . . .

Hiram got maybe fifty feet down the trail. Then he

reined in the horse and turned around. He drew his gun and fired into the air and then aimed the pistol at Greer. "Sheriff Greer!"

Greer stopped what he was doing and turned to glare at Hiram. The Kelsos and Fletcher were looking over their shoulders at him.

"Sheriff! Just needed to get your attention. Hold on, will you?" Hiram swung the gun toward Sid. "Boy—you people got two hundred dollars with you?"

"We do! That's about all we got! We was going to buy some supplies—"

"Just get it and give it to the sheriff."

Sid ran back toward the wagon.

"What the hell you doing, Durst?" Greer snarled.

"I'm quitting my job, Sheriff." He tilted his gun hand back so the pistol was pointed at the sky. "But I'm getting you something to take back to the town council. Now, if you want to bring all this up with me later in town, you surely can."

"Was you pointing that gun at me?" Greer demanded.

"Sure looked like he was!" said Phil Kelso.

"Like I said—needed to get your attention." Hiram kept his gun loose in his hand, still pointed up. But they all knew he could drop it down and start shooting if he needed to. "You were getting carried away, Mike. Might've got you into trouble—there's a deputy US marshal up in Morrisville."

Greer grunted and coiled up his whip.

Sid came running back with a bag in his hand, panting. "This is all we got!"

Greer snatched the bag of money and climbed on his horse. He rode up next to Hiram and said, "Don't you ever point your gun at me again. You came to town with a reputation. But it's not going to help you if I want you gone. Just stay the hell out of my way."

Then he rode past, the other three men following him, all of them eyeing the gun in Hiram's hand.

Hiram waited a while, making sure the sheriff, the Kelsos, and Fletcher were gone.

Then he holstered his Colt, rode past the sheepherders tending to the sobbing Johan, and found a trail back to Leadton.

CHAPTER SIX

THEY WERE ABOUT eight miles from Denison when Mase spotted the Indian kid again.

A cold wind was blowing from the north so that the cowboys turned up their collars and pulled their hats lower, but the cloudless sky was a sharp blue, and there were yellow and red wildflowers on the low hills. The Indian boy was riding alongside the herd, about two hundred yards off. He was carrying what looked like a string of game dangling from his left hand.

Mase had just returned to the herd after scouting a few miles north. He'd discovered they were about to overrun some farmer's fences, so they had to move the herd west about half a mile. He was riding back to give this news to Pug when he saw the young Sioux approaching on Jacob's mule.

Mase turned his horse and rode slowly out toward the boy, careful to seem unthreatening and in no great hurry. The boy pulled up, seeming to hesitate as Mase approached.

Mase raised his right hand, palm outward, signing peace.

The boy held out the string of game, two jackrabbits and a grouse—it seemed he'd caught the animals with Jacob's game snares—and then dropped it on the ground. Some kind of offering, in return for the food Mase had left him, probably.

The Sioux lad turned to ride off, and Mase called out, "East Wind Blake! Wait!"

East Wind turned toward him, holding the mule in check—but seeming tense as Mase approached, as if he might spur her away at any moment.

Mase halted his mount about ten yards off. "Is that game for us?"

His face expressionless, the boy nodded.

Mase smiled. "I thank you. Tell me this—you had no mount, not even a knife with you. What were you going to do with that yearling you were roping?"

"Find a way to kill it or sell it." He shrugged. "I was starving. Lost my weapons, my snares. Eating beetles. Mice. Had to try something."

Mase nodded. "Come on into the herd, ride with us to camp, and we'll all share in that game. My cook will make a good stew out of it."

East Wind looked at him, then looked toward the herd. He shook his head.

"Why'd you help me in that stampede, boy?" Mase asked. "We should've been at odds."

"You fed me. You talked like you was a fair man. There ain't many of those."

Mase looked into the boy's eyes and weighed him.

He made up his mind. It was taking a chance, but he thought it would probably be all right. "You want a job?" Mase asked.

A flicker of surprise showed on the boy's face. "Me?"

"That's right. We can loan you a remuda horse, and you can give Jacob back his old friend there."

"You will hang me."

"If we wanted to kill you, we could've shot you by now. You saved my bacon back down the trail. That gets you a job. And we'll let the rustling go. You'd have to work hard, but I'll pay you fair. If you don't know cattle, we'll show you."

East Wind seemed to digest this. At last he said, "I know 'em. My father worked for the government agent, herding the cows and sheep for tribal food. I helped him for two years."

"Your father still alive?"

"No. Killed by Apaches. I joined some other Sioux to hunt Apaches. The government said we were renegade. They're all dead now. All but me."

"You get stuck out here alone, eh? Well, sounds like you need a job."

"Them men"—East Wind nodded toward the cowboys at the herd—"what do they say?"

"They do what I tell them. But I'll sure look like a fool if I don't bring that mule back. You want the job or not? You'll be paid same as everyone else."

East Wind gave him a long, slow look. Then he nodded.

"Take up that stew meat there, and let's ride over to the chuck wagon. You can leave the mule at the remuda and ride with Dollager. Help him out where you can today. Starting with skinning those rabbits and plucking that prairie chicken. We'll start you working with the herd tomorrow."

"No mail for you yet, Senora Durst," said Mr. Sanchez, smiling sympathetically from the other side of the counter in Tomas's Mercado General.

"The Butterfield stage came in yesterday?" Katie asked.

"*Sí*, senora. Only some mail for Mayor Greenwald and for Father O'Bannon. Oh, and something for the bank."

She glanced at Jim. He was looking over the hard candy, affecting a kind of scientific disinterest. "Well, next time, then. The herd may have gotten delayed on the way to Denison."

"Every trail drive—much delay. *Demorar!*"

"I'll just take the coffee, then, and the kerosene, and a bolt of the gingham there, and two pounds of flour, and a half pound of baking starter, a quarter pound of salt, a pound of sugar, and two pints of the strawberries, a spool of the brown thread . . . and let Jim pick out a couple of the hard candies."

Jim's cheek was bulging with a cherry jawbreaker when they carried the packages out into the midmorning drizzle. They put them in the buckboard, and the boy asked, "Can I give Bonnie a strawberry, Ma?"

"Just one. I'm going to make a pie."

Katie watched him feed the horse a strawberry, appreciating his kindness. He was like that with all the stock. He grieved, in his quiet way, when she had to kill a chicken or a lamb. Sometimes she thought he was too tenderhearted to be a rancher.

"Can I see if Lucas is home?"

"Go ahead. I'm going to the sheriff's office and then to see Father O'Bannon. You meet me at the church at lunchtime, and we'll have a little something at the café."

"Yes, ma'am!"

He turned away and she said, "Hold it, Jim!"

"What is it, Mama?"

"I know you'll tell Lucas about what happened at the fence. Just keep the story . . . small. Don't puff it up none. Don't make it sound like we're in a war."

"No, ma'am, I won't!" Jim was running off as he said it.

Katie smiled. But her mind was mostly on Jim's father. Probably shouldn't have gotten up her hopes about a letter. Mase had Pug and Lorenzo looking after him; he'd be fine.

But you never knew. They had so few men with them, and sometimes the Comanches ranged southeast. . . .

Sheriff George Beslow was just coming to the office when Katie got there. "Morning, Mrs. Durst."

"Can I have a word with you, George?"

A troubled look came into his eyes, and she suspected Tom Harning had gotten to him first. "Come on in."

Beslow opened the door for Katie and followed her into the small, stuffy office. An odor of sweat and vomit from the holding cell in back was overlaid by a veneer of old pipe smoke. The sheriff took off his hat, revealing his mostly bald pate. He had a thick brown mustache that hid most of his upper lip, and muttonchop whiskers. She knew him to have been a provost marshal for the Confederacy; and after the surrender, he'd come home to find that the Yankees had taken most of his father's land for slavery reparations, leaving him impoverished. Katie guessed this accounted for the bitter cast to his expression. She had never seen a smile on him that didn't seem to have been a lot of work to hoist.

Beslow tossed his hat on the desk and gestured to the wooden armchair across from it. "Will you sit, ma'am?"

Katie took a seat as he tamped tobacco into his pipe and then poised himself on the front edge of the desk, almost looming over her. She found it vulgar. But she said, "You might already know that Tom Harning sent his men to bust down a section of our fence. They tore down sixty feet of fencing, and they were fixing to drive cattle through right onto Durst land."

Beslow nodded. "Tom spoke to me. He says the property lines have been wrongly drawn. He says your fence was on his land. He's going to request a new survey."

"A new survey!" She hadn't anticipated that. "But the property lines are clearly described in the deed! That line goes from Coyote Rock due south to Jumpoff Ravine!"

"That kind of hearsay description—"

"It's all there written down on the deed, Sheriff. It's in no wise hearsay!"

He made a rumbling sound in his throat and puffed out a harshly aromatic blue cloud of tobacco smoke. She coughed and waved the smoke away. Someone groaned from the holding cell, probably just waking up from a long drunk.

"Nonetheless," the sheriff said, looking past her to

the street window, "Tom Harning is making the representation to the county."

"He destroyed some of my property, and I want him held responsible for it! That fence costs money and time to repair!"

Beslow shrugged. "When your husband returns, perhaps he'll take it up with Justice Crosby."

"I can take it up with him myself! Don't you see Harning is trying to intimidate me! He's trying to pressure me to get out!"

"That is not the way he described the matter."

Katie caught his gaze and held it. "Sheriff, they destroyed Durst property. Are you going to do anything about it or not?"

Surprised by her icy firmness, he rocked back a little on his perch. "Mrs. Durst, it's my understanding that you threatened Harning's men with a gun. And your man threatened to cut them with a knife! You fired shots at his herd, too!"

"I fired at the ground, George! Those cattle might've trampled me and my son! They were driving them right at us!"

Beslow stood up and went around the desk. He sat down with the air of a judge about to make a determination. Pointing his pipestem at her, he said, "If you had not fired your weapon, you might have a case! But"—he shook his head—"anything else you have to say on the matter will have to be done in court. And . . . Katie . . . there is another matter."

A certain sympathetic note had crept into his tone. She found it worrying. Pity from Sheriff Beslow was a bad sign.

He opened a desk drawer and drew out a folded document. "The bank has asked me to serve you with this notice." He passed it to her. "They are calling in the loan. You have forty days to pay it, or they will foreclose on the ranch. And you will be evicted."

THE LITTLE TOWN'S muddy roads had dried out in the warm morning sun, and now the wind off the plains was beginning to raise drifts of dust as Mase rode into Denison with Pug Liberty and Harry Duff. Lorenzo, Ray, and East Wind were looking after the herd to the southeast of town. Mase was here hoping his new hires were waiting for him.

Denison was a small, nascent settlement along the Red River; it had been officially founded just two years earlier, when the MKT Railroad—which folks called "the Katy"—had built its bridge across the watercourse. The Katy was mostly for minor freight and passengers. It could take but few stock animals, certainly not a herd of any size, so it was of little interest to Mase, but Duff gawked at the engine sitting at the station, its gold-and-black engine trembling, the inverted cone of its chimney puffing great clouds of gray smoke.

"I've been waiting a long time to ride one of those," he said.

"You'll wait a good deal longer," said Pug. "We have no business with the train."

Duff sighed. "Where we meeting those men?"

"At the stockyards," Mase said. "You're going to the general store over there." He handed him a list. "Fill that, put the goods in those canvas bags, and sling 'em over your horse." He handed him the purchase money. "While you're there, see if you can get some boots that'll fit that Indian boy. His feet are maybe an inch shorter than yours. And a pair of stockings to go with 'em."

"You sure you don't want to get him a silk pillow, too?" Pug asked dryly.

"I'll stop the cost from his pay."

Duff peered at the list. "I ain't much of a hand for reading."

"Just give it to the merchant. Can you count money?"

"That I can do!"

"Then make sure he gives us the right change. Now, go on with you. Pug, come along with me."

Mase and Pug rode off toward the stockyards—but Mase stopped partway there, seeing a Butterfield stage office. "Hold on, Pug. I'm just going to mail a letter to Katie. You got anything to mail?"

Pug snorted. "To who? I'll wait here."

Inside the Butterfield office, a fussy, plump little man in a checked suit stood at the counter; he had cheeks like round red apples and a head equally round.

"Well, sir!" he called in a squeaky voice. "Headed south or north? That's all we got for now."

"Neither one, leastways not on the stage," said Mase to the man's evident disappointment. "I need a stamp that'll get this letter to Fuente Verde." He brought out the envelope, addressed to Katie Durst care of Tomas's Mercado General in Fuente Verde, Texas. "How much for the stamps and to carry it there?"

"Just the price of the stamps. The government pays us to carry mail." He looked at the envelope. "I'd make it a fifteen-cent stamp. Only got the Daniel Websters just now."

"Daniel Webster will do fine." Mase paid over the money, watched the man put the stamp on the envelope and cancel it. "When's the next stage?"

"Day after tomorrow or so, we hope. Take about three days after that to get the letter to Fuente Verde."

"Much obliged."

When Mase returned to his horse, he found four men gathered afoot around Pug. Turned out, they were the drive hopefuls; they'd run into Pug on their way to the stockyard.

Pug introduced Mase. "This is my boss, fellas, Mase Durst. They're his cows, and he's the one who hires you."

One of them, declaring himself Denver Jimson, had recognized Pug from back in Missouri. Pug's brother owned a saloon in Augusta, Missouri, where Jimson had been a regular for poker.

Mase looked Denver Jimson over with considerable doubt. He was a clean-shaven man with dark blond hair, likely in his late thirties, and seeming silently amused about something. He wore a silver-gray Stetson, a gray suit, a silver-threaded vest with a gold watch chain stretched across it; his black boots were more for a town than for work on a cow pony. On his right hip was an ivory-grip, silver-plated Smith & Wesson .44 caliber Model 3 revolver. Mase had seen a gun just like it once before when he'd encountered the gunman John Wesley Hardin in a saloon at Ellsworth, Kansas. Hardin had put the gun on the bar and said, "I'm buying a drink for everyone, and I'll use this on any man who will not drink with me." Mase had the drink.

Of the four men there today, Denver Jimson was the only one wearing a pistol.

"That's a serious-looking .44 you have there, Jimson," Mase said. "You know how to work it pretty well?"

"Tolerably," said Jimson with that slight smile.

"We don't carry that kind of iron much in our outfit," Mase said. "If we need a gun, it's likely to be a rifle."

"I'll leave it in my saddlebag, Mr. Durst."

"You ever work a cattle drive?"

"I have, just once. I won't pretend I'm a seasoned hand, but I've done a little bit of all of it."

"Suppose we need a steer cut from the herd. Can you do it?"

"Yes, sir, I believe so."

"How are you for long hours in the saddle?"

"Mr. Durst, I suspect you have me picked out as a townman. You are not mistaken. But I'm no stranger to hard work and long hours. I grew up with it. Any skill I don't have, I will learn."

"He's all right, Mase," said Pug. "I can vouch for him. I'll be . . . responsible."

Mase looked at Pug, sensing more unspoken history between these two men than Pug had let on. He needed hands, and he suspected he was not going to find a replacement willing to take the Red Trail in this town. "Your judgment's always been good, Pug."

He turned to the other three. Karl Dorge, wearing a cowboy's denims and chaps, was a tanned, blue-eyed man with flaxen hair and a stocky but muscular physique. His grip revealed the calluses and strength of hard work.

"Karl Dorge is my name, Mr. Durst."

"Where you from?" Mase asked.

"South Pennsylvania," said Dorge.

From "Germantown" folk, Mase guessed.

Dorge didn't seem inclined to elaborate, so Mase pressed him. "How'd you get from there to here?"

"I was in the Navy for a while when I was young, able seaman elevated to bosun. The war ended, and I was discharged in Houston. Hired on working cattle down there. Last year I came to Denison on a job and got married. Not enough work hereabouts."

"So you're a sailor, and you've worked cattle. Experience on a drive?"

"Yes, sir. Three times."

Mase nodded. He turned to the next man, a wiry, weathered older cowboy, maybe midforties, face marked by a frown that didn't seem in any hurry to leave. "What's your name?" Mase asked.

The cowboy hooked a thumb at himself. "Ike Vinder," he said.

"You know the job?"

"Worked with Charles Goodnight more'n ten years. Got tired of the pay and the hours, tried my hand at railroad work, and I did some cooking, too. You got a cook already, boss?"

"I do."

Vinder sighed. "Well, I need a job, and I know cattle drives. You need it, I expect I can do it."

"Don't seem too high on the idea."

"I do what needs getting done," Vinder said. "Is it true you're making for the Red Trail?"

"We are. Unless something better opens up in the next few days."

Vinder shook his head sadly. "Way I hear it, Shawnee Trail is nothin' but Indians that's mad as wet hens, and floods. Can't hardly go that way. The Red Trail now . . . that's not much better. Got a bad reputation."

"You don't want to ride my route, don't sign on, Vinder."

Vinder shrugged. "I'll ride your trail, boss. You tell me to jump, I'll ask you how high."

Not a top hand, Mase decided, but he would do.

He turned to the last man—or maybe just a boy. He looked even younger than Harry Duff. The boy's grin was so wide, it near split his face as he stuck out his hand and said, "Rufus Emmer, sir."

"How old are you, boy?"

"Why—eighteen. Just."

"You know what you're called on to do on a trail drive?"

"Yes, sir. I grew up on my uncle's ranch—just a half day's ride south of here. Cattle, dairy cows, and horses. Things have gone askew there, as my aunt Bedalia says, so I'm pokin' round for other work."

"Can you cut out a steer?"

"Yes, sir, I can. I can rope, and I can shoot."

Mase already regarded Harry Duff as a handful. This boy was even greener. Well, he could always let go of anyone who showed they couldn't do the job.

"Boys," said Mase, "the trail we're taking is a hard one right enough. It's rough country for a drive, and there may be renegades and badmen. But if you're willing to ride it without whinin' about it, I'll tell you the rules, and I'll tell you about the pay. And if you're *still* willing—you're hired!"

* * *

SUNDAY MORNING KATIE stepped out of the chapel and was surprised to see Gertie Harning apparently waiting for her. Both women wore bonnets and light jackets against the thin rain.

The sight of Gertrude Harning brought Katie's troubles back to her—she'd done her best to put them out of mind in church, except for a quick prayer when she lit a votive candle—and she was suddenly dreading the meeting with the bank manager to take place on the morrow. Mr. Fuller wasn't a bad sort, but bankers were notoriously difficult to persuade once they'd made up their minds.

Jim came out behind Katie, hat in his hand. He said "G'morning, Mrs. Harning," and, squinting up at the rain, quickly put his hat on his head.

She gave him a sad smile. "Good morning, Jim."

"Is Len here?" Jim asked, looking around for Mrs. Harning's son.

"No, Tom didn't want . . . That is, Lenny had work to do today. With his father. And Mary wasn't feeling well. I've heard you are for the time being the man of Durst Ranch, Jim. Is that so?"

"Yes, ma'am," said Jim solemnly. After a moment he added, "Curly and Hector help me out."

Katie smiled at that. She glanced at Gertie, considered raising the matter between the Dursts and the Harnings, and then dismissed the notion. There was no point in holding Gertie responsible for her husband's ways. She had always seemed friendly, despite all. All Katie said was "Gertrude, how are you?"

Gertie smiled wanly. "Well enough." She seemed to

want to say something more—Katie could see her hesitating, searching for words.

Curly's wife, Maria, and their son, Hector, came out of the church. Their elder child, Consuela, had died two years previously of diphtheria. Maria adjusted the scarf on her head against the rain, murmured greetings, and hurried past them.

Hector paused and asked, "Jim—you going to help us finish that fence tomorrow?"

"Now, the question is," Jim said, "are you going to help *me*?" Then Jim grinned.

Katie laughed. Hector chuckled and said, "We'll get it done, Jim." Maria and her son waved and went out to the main road.

Gertie licked her lips, then said in a soft voice, "Katie—will you be sending letters on to your husband?"

"I can try to send a letter to Leadton—but there's no post office there, or stage office either. If I send it to Denison, I'm likely to miss him, and he won't ever see it. I am writing him a kind of diary letter to send on to Wichita."

"You have no way to contact him . . . ?"

Katie frowned. Was Gertie going to suggest she ask her husband to sell out to Tom Harning? "Is there something you want me to say to him?"

"I . . ." Gertie seemed to be struggling with herself. Clearly there was something she wanted to say. But there was fear in her eyes. "Just . . . wanted to send my . . . my good wishes for his enterprise. And my hope"—she gave Katie a look that seemed obscurely significant—"my hope that he's *careful* out there so that he can come safely home to you. Have a blessed day now."

Katie watched as Gertie hurried off toward her buggy. Puzzling over Gertie's behavior, Katie was struck by an unsettling thought. It had really seemed as if Gertie was trying to warn her of something.

And it was a warning Gertrude Harning was afraid to speak aloud.

CHAPTER SEVEN

MASE WATCHED THE herd crossing the Red River with a mingling of satisfaction and trepidation. Most of the herd was across, but there were four hundred to go. It was a cloudy afternoon between the red clay banks of the broad river. The cottonwoods and the brush on the far side showed a high-water mark from some previous flood that had deposited driftwood in the branches. Mase couldn't help noticing that the mark was higher up than his herd was, by far. And he'd noticed, too, on a low hill overlooking the south bank, the graves of three drowned cowboys.

The herd was twelve miles west of Denison, crossing where the river widened so that it was close to shallow. It was ideal under normal conditions. But last night a rainstorm had rushed in, dumping "the makings of a biblical flood," as Mick Dollager put it. The storm had moved off to the east, continuing to deliver its watery freight upstream, and this morning the Red River was running high and fast, under clouds running almost as rapidly as the water. The trail's ford across the river was awash at the edges. Still, the herd was so far willing to wade through it and to swim when they came to the trough in the center.

In last night's rain, the men had had a wet time of it, sleeping under their slickers as best as they might, and they were having a wetter day, forced to ride over and over into the river to guide the herd. Mase could still feel his own wet clothing rasp against his skin with his every move. He trotted his stallion on the south bank of the river, helping to urge the cattle into the water and keeping an eye on the new men. They were all doing a serviceable job of cow punching this morning, even Denver Jimson, who'd sometimes seemed at loose ends the day before. Afeard that his precious .44 Smith & Wesson might be water damaged in his saddlebags, Denver had given it over to Dollager's keeping.

They'd taken the chuck wagon across the river first, towed by the oxen and three horses: Ray Jost, Karl Dorge, and Ike Vinder had ridden ahead, pulling the wagon against the current with ropes tied around their horses' chests. This kept the wagon from being swamped and dumped over. The oxen had been forced to swim part of the way, and Dollager had had water up to his waist, but he'd kept his head, driving the oxen on till at last the chuck wagon reached the far bank.

Moving twenty-four hundred cattle across a swollen river was not speedy work, and the day was moving on faster than the herd was. They would keep moving once across and find a good spot for the noon meal, in an hour or two. . . .

Looking wet and uncomfortable, Ray rejoined Mase on this side of the river.

"Maybe I should've stripped down," said Ray, shifting miserably in his saddle, "like we done when we crossed before with the Richfield drive."

Mase nodded. Cowboys swimming their horses across a river often rode the short distance nude to keep their clothing dry. "Too cold here," said Mase. "That was my thinking."

"Me, too, but now I wished I'd done it." Ray swung his rope at a straying steer and whooped, "Huh-*whup*, hu-*whup*, ease on in!"

The steer rejoined the herd, and Ray rode up beside Mase, where they could watch Jimson, East Wind, Rufus, Lorenzo, and Harry driving the cattle across the ford.

"Kind of wonder if that skinny boy Rufus is going to finish this drive," Ray said. "Best of times seems like a gust of wind would blow him off his saddle."

"He's got a feel for staying in the saddle," Mase said, watching the boy. "But I do worry on him some."

The wind picked up, coming down the Red River valley from the east, and brought with it a grumbling sound that in a few moments filled out to a deep rumbling, a sound so elementally powerful, it sent a chill through Mase.

Mase looked east and saw the source of the noise: an immense surge of water, like a tidal wave crammed between riverbanks, was coming hard at them.

"Get out of the river!" he bellowed, spurring his horse into a gallop that took him along the bank to the west. Only Pug and East Wind and Rufus Emmer were out there now.

Pug grabbed East Wind's reins and tugged him toward the bank behind him. "Come on, boy!"

Still about seventy-five feet from the bank, Rufus turned and gaped in confusion at the oncoming wave. Pug and East Wind reached the bank a second ahead of the flood.

"Rufus Emmer, get out of the river, ya damned fool!" Ray called. Rufus turned toward the south bank.

A series of storms upstream had created the flood surge now roaring down at the remaining cattle in the river, driving debris ahead of it like pellets from a shotgun. Suddenly Rufus wasn't there, smashed from his horse and engulfed by the thundering river. As the wave crashed, the horse thrashed to the surface, neighing in terror, spinning in the current—and Rufus Emmer was missing from the saddle.

Mase was guiding his own horse with his knees, forcing it to race against the flood surge as he spun his lasso over his head; he watched the water, desperately hoping—and there! It was Rufus bobbing to the surface, flailing his arms, spitting water, his shouts muted by the roaring of the flood. He was coming to a whirlpool, and Mase felt sure that once the boy was sucked under, he wouldn't come out alive.

Mase angled the stallion into the water, casting the loop, bellowing at Rufus with all his strength. Rufus was grasping at a spinning log, missing it, when he saw the loop falling toward him. He snatched at it, caught the rope with one hand.

"Hold on!" Mase shouted though the boy couldn't hear him, and he spurred his horse back onto the southern bank; he wound his end of the rope around the saddle horn, quickly taking up the slack, feeling the line go taut.

He drove the horse up a steep slope so that its hooves sank deeply into the clay. The stallion was almost vertical, close to tipping over backward. Then it got purchase on a graveled ledge and dragged itself up, its eyes wild, its coat foamy with sweat.

Mase looked over his shoulder and saw the rope at the farther end vanishing into the water. The horse stumbled—and Mase had to jump free. He landed on his feet, dug in his heels, grabbed the rope, pulled hard, and drew it toward him hand over hand, fighting the current. He could feel the rope biting into his hands. The rope was still taut—but Rufus was nowhere to be seen.

Mase roared at himself, "Hold hard!" And he backed up, pulling, pulling . . . and Rufus bobbed up again, still grasping the rope, spouting water as he broke the surface.

The stallion was on its feet now, and Mase managed to get enough slack so that he could hitch the rope more tightly around the saddle horn. He slapped the horse's rump, and it moved awkwardly along the bank.

Mase let go of the lasso, and the stallion pulled the boy free from the rushing water and into the shallows.

Then Pug was riding up to Rufus, with East Wind close behind, the two of them jumping down to drag the boy onto the bank.

Still breathing hard from the effort, black spots flickering in front of his sight, Mase made his way down the bank and looked down at the gasping Rufus Emmer.

A few yards away, the river roared furiously along, flinging chunks of trees—and several dead steers.

* * *

"WHY, I NEVER saw anything like it," said Vinder wonderingly. "Any other man would have given that fool boy up for dead. . . ."

"I've known Mase a long time," Pug said. "It's natural enough for him."

Mase was dozing by the fire, his head on his saddle, his hat down over his eyes. He could hear them talk, but he had nothing to say.

They'd eaten supper—he'd had to eat with care because of the bandages on his hands—and he was in sore need of rest. Sore indeed, in most every muscle.

Rufus was even sorer. Badly battered but unbroken, he was snoring nearby.

What really hurt was losing eleven beeves. Most of the cattle at the tail end of the drive had been able to swim free, though farther downstream. But of the eleven dead ones, most of them had drowned, their carcasses washed up on a sandbank downriver. A couple more had been injured so badly, flung onto rocks and struck by debris, that they'd had to be put down. Dollager had saved some meat from them for the trail and given some to a passing farmer and his wife—there was too much to take along in the wagon—and Mase told the man to go ahead and come back with friends and butcher the rest of the dead cows.

They'd had to spend a good piece of the day getting the rest of the stragglers back into the main herd, and now all but the night guards—East Wind and Dorge—were gathered around the fire, sitting half slumped on the ground in their weariness.

Mase sighed and pushed his hat back to look at the sky. The clouds had passed, and the stars shone in great sweeping profusion as if luxuriating in the sky. Mase just lay there, listening to the men and wondering what Katie was doing right then. Was she looking up at those stars? Most likely she was reading to Jim about now. . . .

"Rufus sure got a reason to be grateful to Mr. Durst," said Duff.

"'And so there grew great tracts of wilderness, Wherein the beast was ever more and more, But man was less and less, till Arthur came,'" intoned Dollager as he worked at scrubbing the Dutch oven.

"What's that you said?" Duff asked in puzzlement.

"'Twasn't me, young man," said the cook. "It was Alfred, Lord Tennyson. *Idylls of the King.* A poem concerning King Arthur and his knights. Like our Mr. Durst, Arthur brings civilization by caring for his fellow man."

"Sí!" Lorenzo called out. "Mase, he is a man like my father." He sighed. "I have displeased my father. I must get back to him and ask forgiveness."

"What'd you do to get on his wrong side?" Jimson asked.

"Oh, I ran away with my second cousin. A beautiful woman but—too young. We tried to be married. But we did not succeed. I only succeeded in making everyone angry! Even she is angry with me. And I struck my uncle when he cursed at her. So—my father, he sent me away. But someday . . ."

Still scrubbing, Dollager recited, "'And the son said unto him, Father, I have sinned against heaven, and in thy sight, and am no more worthy to be called thy son. But his father said to his servants, bring forth the best robe and put it on him, and put a ring on his hand. . . .'"

"That the Fred Lord feller again?" Duff asked.

Pug snorted. "Why, you damned fool, that's from the Bible."

"Oh, sure, I knew I heard it somewhere."

"You are a good hand at recitation, Mick," said Denver.

"I was a stage actor in England as a young man," Dollager said as he dumped a bucket of water into the Dutch oven to rinse it out. "A fine figure of a young man, too. I fear I was as prone to drama offstage as on. That offstage drama led me here."

"How's that?"

"One day a man offered me an insult relating to a lady, and I called him to meet me."

"That's all? Just to meet you?" Duff asked.

"He means a duel," said Denver.

"I am sorry to say, the gentleman died in the encounter," Dollager went on, dumping the rinse from the pot. "As he was a baronet and I but the son of a cook, I was, as you say, in hot water. The law against dueling is rarely enforced but"—he chuckled dourly—"it was soon to be enforced for me! I joined Her Majesty's Army so as to escape England. After the Indian war—"

"Which tribe?" Duff asked.

Mase grinned at that but said nothing.

"He means the kind they have in India," said Pug.

"After two years of service, a colonel in the Army who was a cousin of that baronet pursued me in the courts. And so I was drummed out of the Army and made my way in haste to this land of plenty."

"Plenty of trouble, you mean," said Vinder. "That's what it's the land of."

"Vinder, you sourpuss," said Mase, sitting up, "go on out and relieve East Wind on night guard."

Vinder frowned like he might object, but thought better of it. He got up, brushed himself off, and went to the remuda for a horse.

"We drive west tomorrow, Mase?" asked Lorenzo.

Mase nodded. "I expect to run into the Chickasaw that way in a day or two. We're likely to lose a few beef to trade our way through. Then it's north on the Red Trail. Any coffee left, coosie?"

MR. FULLER, YOU know it's not only unfair—it's irregular," said Katie Durst. "Everyone knows the bank waits till the crop or the herd or the wool is sold before expecting its loan repaid! And that wait gives the bank even more interest to collect!"

The banker squirmed in his seat. "Now, the realities of banking, Mrs. Durst, are not always easy to explain to a lady. . . ."

Katie was thinking, as she looked at Ralph Fuller, that everyone she spoke to lately seemed worried by the encounter. The sheriff, Gertrude Harning, now the banker. She knew what Fuller was squirming over, sure enough. No one wanted to tell a settler that they must become unsettled, that they were to be evicted.

"This business of 'not easy to explain to a lady' is hogwash," Katie said. "Are there unmentionables involved? Or do you think a woman hasn't the savvy to understand?"

Fuller's cheeks reddened. "No, no, I ah . . . It's just

that . . . Well, what is policy one year may not be the next! The bank has its own finances to consider. Depositors are few, Mrs. Durst. We have not been growing at the rate we'd like. We sometimes need to call in notes."

"We told you the money we borrowed was to add to our herd so we could sell it up north, and you said that was a fine idea, being as how so many ranches are filling their purses that way. Now suddenly it's all chancy? Why is that, Mr. Fuller? My husband has not failed in his enterprise! He is well on his way to selling those cattle and at a top price! We already have a deal with a stock buyer! You have only to wait at most till mid-June—"

"We . . ." Fuller closed his eyes and took a deep breath. She noticed his hands trembling on the desk. "We are foreclosing in forty days."

Katie shook her head. "I will see this bank in court. My uncle is a lawyer, and I have already written to him. Tell me, Mr. Fuller. Has Tom Harning been in to see you? Has he got a hand in all this?"

His eyes snapped open wide. He went from blushing to pale in an instant. "Now, why . . ." He cleared his throat. "No, ma'am."

"He wants our land. He's been pushing for it. And he's a pretty powerful man around here. Seems like a mighty big coincidence."

"Mr. Harning— No. He's . . . this is the bank's decision. And I must . . ." He cleared his throat again. "That is, I have to bid you farewell for now, Mrs. Durst. I must see Mr. Gaffell now about a . . . on a certain matter . . ."

Sensing that the bank wasn't going to budge—that Mr. Fuller was about to squirm right out of his chair and rush out of the room—Katie stood up and said, "This isn't going to do your reputation a speck of good, Ralph Fuller, or this bank's either."

She turned and walked out, wondering what Mase would have done if he were here. Maybe just what she was going to do. Head for a lawyer. There was none in town, but there was always Uncle Forrest.

She crossed the street, stepping over the copious droppings of a team of oxen, and went to Tomas's general store. He would see her letter to Aunt Lizzy was put aboard the Butterfield stage tomorrow.

It could well be that Lizzy would be of no help. Her husband, Uncle Forrest, had moved away from her. Lizzy lived on money Forrest earned from his lawyering—a law practice that mostly involved traveling from town to town, but Katie had heard from her aunt that the two of them scarcely spoke. It was hard to know where he could be reached. She had to hope Lizzy would know. Uncle Forrest had a kindness for her and Mase and Jim. She thought he might help . . . if she could find him.

ARE YOU DONE drinking yourself to perdition yet?" Queenie asked. She was standing in front of Hiram's table, fists on her hips, looking at him with her head cocked and her eyebrows raised. He knew that look. Women took on that aspect with him after a time.

"Why, I'm past perdition and on the way to the next place after it," said Hiram.

He was sitting in a corner of the Stew Pot Saloon, with a bottle of brandy and a deck of cards, playing solitaire. It was a moderately busy night in Leadton.

He glanced around the smoky room, saw miners and merchants and a handful of drifters lining the bar. Three men played cards nearby and a couple of out-of-work cowboys were betting on who could spit into a spittoon at ten feet distance. "I'll tell you what it is, Queenie. . . ." He slapped down a card and said, "I'm out of a job, and I'm pondering my next move."

"I thought that was going to be New Orleans—the two of us?"

"Don't have enough money."

"I have some saved. A pretty good pile. We can use mine."

"I thank you kindly, but I'll make my own."

She snorted. "Men and their pride!"

"I don't think you'd like me much if I didn't have that kind of pride," he said. "Truth is"—he slapped down a card—"it's the only kind I have left. Got a good look at myself out there on that trail with those sheep-herders. Didn't like it. Don't know that Hiram Durst fella."

"Now you're talking drunk."

"Not so drunk as all that." He put down the cards and poured a drink. "Just you wait. One more hour and I'll be talking drunk for true. Why don't you get a glass and join me?"

"I've got to get the girls up, start 'em to work the bar, sell some spirits." She looked around and shrugged. "Leastways it's peaceful in here. The Jack of Hearts, now, is like to run wild with those rustlers coming through."

"Which rustlers are those? You mean the Kelsos?"

"Never heard the Kelsos were rustling."

"Whenever they have nothing else to do. If it's not them, who is it?"

"Man named Cleland and a couple of pals—they look like saddle bums. They've got some kind of understanding with the sheriff."

"Do they?" Now he found himself interested. Anything to discommode Mike Greer. "Hal Binder still running the place? I thought Sanborne was going to run him out." There was a long-standing rivalry between the two saloonkeepers, and Murch Sanborne had been trying to force Binder out of business for close onto a year.

"Truth is, I'm suspicious that Sanborne put those Cleland boys up to hurrahing Binder's place," she said.

"Now, that's a point of interest," Hiram said. He set his drink down with a clack. "I think I'll have a word with Binder. Might ask for a job . . ."

"What!"

"See you later."

"Don't make any damned-fool drunk's decisions, Hiram!"

He winked at her and went up to his room, fetched his double-barrel ten-gauge shotgun, and descended the outside stairs to the street. Across the graveled road, a few doors to the left, was the Jack of Hearts. The winking harlequin figure of the jack, sporting five hearts held in his two hands, was painted across the big false front of the building, now scantly lit by a few streetlamps and moonlight.

Hiram crossed the road, went through the double doors into the dance hall. There were surprisingly few customers. Just four at the bar, a couple of men standing at the faro table in the corner, a few near the stage. Two half-clad girls were gyrating on the small stage to an accordion player and a man beating a bass drum. The girls were singing something impossible to hear.

Carrying the shotgun as casually as a man can carry one into a saloon, Hiram went to the bar and signaled Stanley, the black bartender. "Glass of beer!" he called, leaning the ten-gauge against the bar.

As Stanley brought the beer, Hiram assessed the three men sitting close in front of the stage, each with his own bottle of whiskey to hand. They were all dressed like cowboys, with buckskin vests and well-worn broad-brim hats; they were unshaven and dirty as if they'd just come off the range. The taller, big-nosed one in the middle had an old Confederate rifleman's cap and a Colt Dragoon pistol on the small table in front of him; he was chewing on an unlit cigar and gawking at the shapelier of the two dancers. There was a flicker of fear in the girl's eyes when she glanced at the man in the Confederate hat.

Hiram paid for the beer and asked, "Say, Stanley, who are those three?"

"That's Niall Cleland in the Reb hat," said Stanley, bending near to be heard. "Those other two—I don't know their names. They follow him around like puppies. They've been raising hell in here every night. Boss is scared of them."

Cleland chose that moment to stand up, grab the accordion player by his instrument, and shove him hard offstage. The man fell on his back, his accordion caterwauling as he went. "This music is hell on a man's ears!" Cleland shouted.

"There I have to agree with him," Hiram said.

"Dick's all right. He don't deserve that!" Stanley said.

"I expect that's true," Hiram said, nodding.

Cleland was taking a swing at the drum banger—who ducked and ran for the door, drum tucked under his arm. The girls were cowering back against the wall.

"You girls—sing!" Cleland shouted. "That's my music! Purty girls a-singin'!"

Cringing, the dancers began to sing "My Old Kentucky Home" in frightened voices.

"Why doesn't Binder kick them out, Stanley?" Hiram asked.

"Cleland's known for killing, is why. Killed two men in Morrisville. The sheriff should chase him out, but the story I heard is . . . Well, it's not my place to say."

"Where's Binder?"

"He's in the back."

Hiram fished in his pocket and came up with a silver dollar, slipped the coin to Stanley. "Be obliged if you could ask him to come and have a quick word with me."

Stanley tossed the dollar in the air, caught it, and nodded. He went through the door behind the bar. Cleland was dancing around, clapping his hands to make rhythm for the song the girls sang so raggedly, and his men were laughing.

Hal Binder came out from the back room, followed by Stanley. Binder was a round-faced man with a handlebar mustache, a pair of Ben Franklin spectacles, and a small whiskey-reddened nose. He wore a pin-striped suit and a string tie. He glowered toward Cleland, then turned to Hiram. "What do you want, Durst?"

"I'm just surprised you put up with those yahoos there, Hal." Hiram nodded toward Cleland.

"Sheriff won't back me up, and I'm not going to fight 'em myself!"

"I need a job, and you need this place protected. Suppose I can get rid of those idiots for you?"

"You mean a full-time job here?"

"That's right. If folks are going to come in here and try to drive you out of business, you need someone to nip that in the bud! I'll watch over the place. Sit in the corner with my shotgun. You won't have a lick of trouble."

Binder gnawed a knuckle, eyeing Cleland, who was now manhandling the shapely copper-haired girl. Cleland had one hand around her neck and the other on her bosom. "Long as it's legal."

"It'll be legal—but it might be a mess. Might need a mop after."

Binder shrugged. "Hell, I got a mop."

Hiram nodded, scooped up his shotgun, cocked it, and, holding it pointed down at his side, strode across the room to Cleland.

"Hey, muttonhead!" Hiram yelled.

The man in the Reb hat spun around and stared, blinking at him. The other two men gawped as if Hiram were a ghost. The two girls used their chance and scurried to cringe behind the bar.

Hiram raised his voice so that everyone in the room could hear. "My name is Hiram Durst, Cleland, and I have decided that you disgust me! You disgust me like an overflowing privy! You disgust me like a pig eating its offspring! You wear that hat like you're proud of it, but no son of the South is proud of you! Bullying musicians and women—acting the drunken buffoon. I look upon you, Cleland, and I feel nothing but disgust!"

"You son of a—!" Cleland blurted, reaching for the pistol on the table. He grabbed it, swung it toward Hiram, who was raising the shotgun.

Hiram braced and pulled one of the two triggers.

The shotgun blast threw Cleland back into the table; it shattered as he fell on it, twitching and bleeding atop the splintered wood.

"I've still got one shell in this shotgun," Hiram said, swinging the muzzle toward the two other men in the gang.

"No!" yelled one of them, raising his hands.

"Don't!" cried the other, holding his hands out as if to block the shotgun.

"You two run through that door, get on your horses, and ride!" Hiram snarled. "And don't ever come back to this town!"

The men turned and bolted through the door. Within seconds Hiram heard the clatter of galloping horses. Hiram laid the shotgun across a table and wiped cold sweat from his forehead.

That was when Sheriff Greer came stalking in. "I heard a shot—!" He stopped, staring at Cleland's body.

"Had to shoot him, Mike," Hiram said. "He was going to kill me. Just for telling him he disgusted me."

"It's true!" Binder said, hurrying over from the bar. "Cleland went for his gun!"

"It is!" the copper-haired girl shouted. "We all saw it! Self-defense!"

Everyone in the bar chimed in with the same tune. Greer took one more look at Cleland. "I'll get the undertaker," he growled. He headed for the door. He stopped there and turned to Hiram. "Looks like you've got this one covered—but you'd better not put a step wrong, Durst! You'd better step right careful!"

Then Greer walked out the door, and Binder yelled for a mop.

CHAPTER EIGHT

TWENTY-EIGHT DAYS ON the drive to Wichita.

The sun was settling toward the horizon, coloring the low clouds and the misty hills a rusty red as Mase rode back to the herd. He waved his hat at East Wind, who waved back and cantered his horse to meet him alongside Pug, who was riding swing.

"There's a band of Chickasaw, about forty warriors, camped up ahead about a quarter mile," Mase told them. "They're right in our way, and I figure they're waiting for us."

"They were out in the open?" East Wind asked.

"They were. Doesn't look like an ambush. You speak their lingo?"

East Wind shrugged. "I speak Siouan. But I've got some Choctaw, too, and it's close to Chickasaw. And there's signs we all know. Most know some words in English and Spanish, too."

"You come along, then. I'm looking for a Chickasaw

round here named Cloudy Moon. Find out if he's there, and if he is, we'll parley with him."

"Just you and this boy?" Pug asked, rocking back a little in the saddle. "You loco, Mase?"

"I'll bring Lorenzo and Denver, too."

"Now, hold on," Pug said, frowning. "You need more men along than that!"

Mase shook his head. "Suppose it's all to keep us distracted while they raid the herd?"

"Could be," East Wind said.

"That's why I need you and the other men to watch the herd, Pug," Mase said. "East Wind, can you fire a rifle?"

East Wind gave him a snort of disgust. "'Course I can."

"We'll loan you one. I'm going to get my pistol. You go and get Jimson and Lorenzo. Tell Jimson he can bring his six-gun. We're going to avoid trouble, but it's best to look like we're well armed. We'll meet up at the chuck wagon. Pug, let's go ahead and make camp here. Have Dollager start a meal—better make it big in case we have guests."

Half an hour later, the four drovers were riding up within twenty yards of the Chickasaw camp at the base of a low hill crowned with a granite outcropping. The camp had a spur-of-the-moment look, with men sitting about on blankets laid in the grass near a small campfire—that seemed more smoke than fire—with a few pottery jugs and baskets about it.

"They could be on a picnic," Jimson muttered.

Ponies and mustangs, their flanks painted with hand circles and hand imprints, were picketed nearby.

The Chickasaw warriors wore breechcloths, short jackets of deer hide, and thigh-high boots of the same leather. Every bare spot on them was painted or tattooed. The sides of their heads were shaved; their only hair, apart from colored scalp locks, was cut down to a flattened ridge running front to back, and from it drooped the feathers of eagles and hawks.

The first impression of a complacent camp was deceptive: Mase saw about twenty warriors ranged about the rocks above, some squatting, some standing, and he counted seven rifles among them, the others with bows and arrows. All of them were watching him and his companions. Mase figured if there was any trouble, those men on the rocks would open fire and shoot the drovers off their horses without a second thought.

"Hold here," said Mase, reining in.

The drovers stopped, and Mase raised a hand to show they'd come in peace. East Wind gave a more complex series of hand signs. An Indian of about forty-five, with a mien of authority about him, stood up and spoke to the others. Three of the warriors near him stood up, with rifles in their hands.

"That older one has the look of a *minko*," East Wind murmured.

"What would that be?" Lorenzo asked.

"A Chickasaw war chief."

The *minko* strode toward the cowboys, his escort following with rifles held at ready but not aiming at anyone. The Chickasaw deputation stopped about twenty feet away, the war chief raising a hand in greeting. He spoke in his own dialect, pointing past them back along the trail. He had an aquiline nose, high cheekbones, and a diagonal scar that slanted through part of his forehead and across his left eye socket; the milky eye was blinded.

The chieftain made a fairly long speech directed at East Wind, mostly in Chickasaw. Then he fell silent, waiting. East Wind responded in a mix of Indian lingos, with a few English phrases, including the words "plenty guns" and hand gestures. Once he pointed at Mase.

The war chief spoke again briefly and nodded at Mase.

"This man is Cloudy Moon," said East Wind. "We're talking pretty good because he knows some Siouan and I know some Choctaw. I told him you're our leader. He says you will make a decision to go back to where you come from, to fight, or to pay."

"Now we're getting to it," said Denver.

"What does he want for safe passage?" Mase asked.

"Says he wants twenty steers, five pounds of coffee, five pounds of sugar, a hundred dollars in gold—too much of everything, boss."

"Offer him two steers, one half pound of coffee, one half pound of sugar. Let him bargain us up to three steers and a little more of the goods. And I've brought six good hunting knives and five blankets for trading."

East Wind set to bargaining with a lot of discourse and hand signs, showing two fingers for two steers. Cloudy Moon scowled and made a slashing motion with his hand and gave a great speech with such expressive hand gestures that Mase almost understood him.

Back and forth it went till at last they struck a deal: three steers, a pound of coffee, a pound of sugar, a jar of blackstrap, four knives, five blankets, and forty dollars in gold.

They shook on it, and then East Wind arranged a deputation of Indians to come to the herd to receive their barter goods.

Five Indians, including Cloudy Moon, fetched their painted ponies and came along with the drovers. All of the warriors were armed with rifles; they talked in blithe tones, sometimes laughing.

Mase was tense the whole way back, but the Chickasaws made no hostile move. Pug and Rufus rode up, hands on their holstered pistols, to meet the party. "Mr. Durst—you need us to fight you out of this?" Rufus asked, looking at the armed Indians with wide eyes.

Since Mase had saved the boy's life, Rufus had been his shadow, whenever it was allowed, trailing after his boss as if he were the foreman and not Pug.

"We're just fine, Rufus," said Mase. "We've made a deal. We'll let 'em have their pick of three beeves."

"There's one going lame we could give 'em," Pug said in a low voice.

"It was part of the deal that they'd pick their own. But we might have a use for that lame cow later."

The sun was almost gone, and the shadows had merged by the time the Indians had selected their beeves and received their goods. Now they were all gathered around the cooking fire.

"Should I offer them a dram of liquor, sir?" Dollager asked. He had a carefully guarded bottle of whiskey secreted away in the wagon.

"Not on your life, Mick," Mase said. "Just coffee with sugar, beef stew, and a biscuit. Me, Jimson, and East Wind will eat with them." He turned to Pug. "The rest of our people will eat afterward—I want them circling the herd, keeping watch for the rest of the band."

Pug nodded and went to issue orders. Rufus heard the orders but hesitated. "Go on, boy," Mase told him. "Watch the herd. Keep an eye out."

"You sure you got enough men to watch your back, Mr. Durst?"

"I reckon we'll be all right."

Reluctantly, Rufus followed Pug to the remuda.

Mase, East Wind, and the Indians sat around the fire, eating, the Indians muttering to one another, East Wind sometimes answering a question from Cloudy Moon. Mase noticed the chieftain eyeing the chuck wagon.

"What's he asking you about, East Wind?" Mase asked.

"How many cattle we have. And what's in the chuck wagon."

"You think they're going to make some kind of play?"

"No, I don't think so. This chief has medicine. I can feel it. It's the kind that says he's a man of his word."

"Hope you're a good judge of medicine."

After the meal, Mase drew out the map that Crane Williams had given him, and with East Wind's help, he conveyed to Cloudy Moon that he wanted to know how to reach Red Trail most directly and what he could expect on the trail.

Cloudy Moon made a speech, and East Wind snorted and said, "Long and short of it is, he'll be glad to tell you all about it. But you got to pay. Then tomorrow he guides you to the entrance of the canyons. He wants two more steers."

"Well, I'll tell you what. . . ."

The lame steer was accepted as payment for the information, and Cloudy Moon told them just what they needed to know. Some of it was good news.

And some of it wasn't.

KATIE WAS JUST bringing a jug of fresh milk from the barn when three men rode up to the ranch house. She put the jug down on the porch and shaded her eyes to look at them. The sun was rising behind them, and she saw mostly their silhouettes as they trotted up. After pondering them a moment, she made out two of the men, Andy Pike and Red Sullivan. The third man, sitting on a gray horse between them, was taller, gaunter, paler than the others, and clean-shaven; he wore a duster and a wide-brimmed gray hat. There was a six-gun tied down on his thigh. He just sat on his horse, looking at her, seeming amused.

If this man worked for Harning, he was new; he was surely no ranch hand, and that tied-down holster was like a business card. Feeling a chill go through her, Katie realized he was most likely a hired gun.

She felt his expressionless gray eyes watching her as she called, "Curly!"

He came out of the barn, horse tackle in his hand. Curly wore his gun belt as always since the breach of the fence. He saw the men reining in a few yards from Katie, and he dropped the tackle in the dirt, hurrying over to her as Jim came out of the house.

"Ma?"

"Back in the house, Jim!"

"Ma—!"

"Go!"

Katie heard him moan to himself as he retreated into the house.

"What's your business here, Pike?" she asked.

"Delivering a message from Mr. Harning," he said. "There will be men this side of the fence to do some surveying. They've got the papers from the county."

"They can show me those papers," Katie said. "Maybe I'll allow them on Durst land."

"Ma'am," said the man in the gray hat, his voice a lazy drawl, "you'd better have yourself another think on all this." He rested his impudent gaze on her face and never took it off.

"What's your name, mister?" Katie said.

"It's Adams, ma'am. Clement Adams."

She'd heard the name somewhere. Maybe in an old newspaper. "You work for Mr. Harning now?"

"That's right."

"You say, think on all this—all what, Mr. Adams?"

"They're foreclosing on you." He leaned back in his saddle a little, moved his shoulders as if stretching. His smile was as impudent as his gaze. "Your property lines aren't even legal. And there's only so much Mr. Harning can put up with."

"The foreclosure isn't going to happen," she said, and hoped she sounded as if she believed it. "That scheme with the property lines isn't going to hold water in court. The deed shows the property lines. And as for what Mr. Harning can put up with, I guess we'll find out just how much that is. Or he can pull his horns in and give himself a rest."

Red Sullivan chuckled. "She's about got you buffaloed, Adams."

Adams frowned at that. Pike said, “Mrs. Durst, the point is, you need to pull out. This place will be taken by the bank before your husband comes back. You should be looking for a home for him to come back to.”

“Lies!” growled Curly. He put his hand on his gun, and before he could draw it, Adams had his six-gun pointed at him.

“Go on ahead. Pull it,” Adams said easily. “Save me some time and trouble.”

Looking down Clement Adam’s gun muzzle, Curly froze.

“Get away from here!” Jim yelled, stepping out on the porch. He had his mother’s pistol in his two hands, pointing up at Adams.

Adams stared at the boy—and before Katie could act, Curly stepped in front of Jim.

“You have to kill me if you try to hurt this boy!”

Katie reached down and snatched the gun from Jim’s hand. She pushed him back behind her; getting a grip on the gun, she swung it toward Pike.

“Who goes first, Pike?” she demanded.

Andy Pike and Red Sullivan exchanged looks. “This ain’t going so well, Andy,” Red said, grinning.

Pike nodded. “Adams, put the gun away. We delivered the message.”

“The message I got is that you men are snakes who’ll do anything for a dollar!” Katie said. “Get off my land!”

Adams holstered the gun, tipped his hat to Katie. “I learned a long time ago, ma’am, when the train comes down the tracks, you got to get out of the way. You need to clear out. Simple as that.”

He turned the horse and rode off at a leisurely pace, followed by the other two.

"Curly," Katie said, her voice hoarse, "would you keep an eye on those three from a distance till they're away from here? Don't challenge them. Just make sure they're gone."

"Yes, Mrs. Durst." He gave her a sad look as if he wanted to say something else, but he turned on his heel and strode to the barn for a horse.

Heart pounding, mouth dry, Katie went into the house, pushing Jim ahead of her. The man Adams had a hair trigger to him. He might've killed Curly or Jim.

Katie was deeply angry. She was angry at Adams and those other men; she was angry at Harning; she was angry at Jim; and she was angry at Mase Durst. She had warned him there would be trouble with Harning. But he had left them alone, anyway.

She spun the boy around and snapped, "Boy—you could've gotten Curly killed! Or me! That man had his gun in his hand! You can't go . . ."

Katie saw the tears in his eyes then. She knelt down and pulled him to her. She was shaking, almost sobbing. But she kept it down, not wanting him to see her cry. Best he thought she could handle anything that came along.

"Jim . . . you were brave. But you have to leave the fight to me and Curly and your pa when he comes back. There'll be ways you can help . . . if it's needed."

"What ways?"

"You'll see. But you will not be using a gun. Do you promise me?"

"Yes, ma'am."

She kissed him on the cheek and wiped his eyes. "Go on now. Check the chickens. See if they've left us any eggs. Will you do that?"

"Yes, Mama."

She watched him go out to the chicken coop, and then she went to her bedroom. Folded on the little table by the bed was the one letter she'd had from Mase so far.

She sat on the edge of the bed and read it again. She needed to hear his voice. She did hear it in her imagination as she read.

Darling Katie,

Well, we are outside Denison, and the drive is moving along just fine. We're doing ten miles a day at least, sometimes more. The cattle are fat and sassy. We haven't lost any stock, but we sure came close. We caught an Indian boy, no more than fifteen, stealing one of our yearlings! He had no horse, no shoes, not even a knife, and he had lost all his people. He'd made his own lasso from grass. Well, he was more than half starved, so I had Dollager feed him, but then he got away with Jacob's mule! There was a lightning storm, and we had a stampede that same night and I had some trouble getting out of the way and up comes this Indian boy, bringing me one of my own horses. Then he rode off on that mule. It took us a whole day to get the herd back together. Come a couple or three days more and the boy started following us and bringing us game. We ended up hiring him onto the drive! Can you beat that?

Katie smiled. She wasn't surprised. It was just like something Mase would do. It was also just like him to not give her enough explanation of what exactly had happened. She was sure he was leaving out some of the danger he'd been through.

We're shorthanded, but the men are shaping up good. The Duff kid and Jimson are learning. The food's fine for a drive. Dollager's a good hand with chuck. He's got me liking that yellow spice. Curry, he calls it. But it's your cooking I hanker for. More than that, I sure miss you, the sight of you and the touch of you and hearing your voice. I think of you more than a busy man should. I miss Jim, too. I can't say I don't worry about him. I guess I just have to trust you and Curly and Hector to take care of everything.

You can tell Jim the story about that Indian boy. He'll like that. The boy is a Sioux who wandered far south. His name is East Wind.

With luck we're going to hire some men in Denison tomorrow, and we sure need them. I'll post this then. Then we're across the Red River and west to the trail. I wish I could hear from you. But since you're the best woman in Texas, I know you've got everything in hand. I love you, my darling, and will write again first chance I have.

Tell Jim all is going well, and I'll see him in June. Tell him I said to do every one of his chores.

Mason Durst

Katie felt a little better reading the letter again. She'd known it would help her anger seep away. Anger was a burden she couldn't afford to carry. There was too much else on her shoulders now. . . .

The best woman in Texas . . . everything in hand.

Katie didn't feel she measured up. But she knew that she had to act like it was true.

CHAPTER NINE

THIRTY-ONE DAYS INTO the drive.

Mase, East Wind, and Pug rode along with Cloudy Moon, just the three of them under the noon sun in a wide grassy basin between high cliffs of sandstone. The curving red stone bluffs would have converged if not for the mouth of a canyon cutting due north.

They rode across the high grass, seeing spoor of deer and antelope, and halted at the entrance to the canyon. The floor of the canyon before them was rubbly with fallen stone, patchy with brush. The passage was about sixty feet wide, opening up to around eighty feet inside.

"Well, Mase, that's a narrow run for herd and men to push it," said Pug, shaking his head. "And over that ground, too."

"We'll clear it some," said Mase. He turned to East Wind. "Ask the chief if it's like this all the way along."

East Wind used signs and two languages to ask the question.

Cloudy Moon shook his head and spoke for a time, gesturing to show the route of the trail ahead and its rough spots.

East Wind nodded and said, "Boss, it's pretty bad for a mile, and then it smooths out and becomes sandy. There's water along the way, and there's a canyon cutting across . . ." He slashed his hand horizontally. "Like that. And it has a stream in it, sometimes runs hard and fast. There's not much forage till you get close to Leadton."

"This the only route to Leadton, Mase?" Pug asked.

"Nope, there's a road that runs northwest to Leadton, but it's off to the east, and it's past country we can't get through." He looked down the canyon, picturing the herd going through. "It'll be slow for a while. But we'll get there." He turned his horse and pointed at the grassland. "We can graze the herd here, fatten it up some, and move it north through the canyon."

"And the chuck wagon on such terrain?" Pug asked.

"We'll clear the way for it, ease it through as we can. Add horses to the oxen where we have to. Crane Williams got through with his herd. We can do it, too."

"Crane's herd was smaller, and I misdoubt he had a chuck wagon," said Pug.

"You knew before we came it'd be tough," Mase said. He was wishing Pug had a sunnier outlook on the venture.

"I ain't complaining, Mase. I'm just thinking about what we got coming. I expect we'll get 'er done."

Cloudy Moon spoke again, and East Wind translated.

"Says he goes now. Will go east to the wickiups of his people. Gives you his blessings."

"Glad to have any blessings I can get," Mase said. He reached out to the chief, and they clasped forearms as brothers.

Then Cloudy Moon rode off to the east and Mase, Pug, and East Wind rode south toward the herd.

But on the bluffs overlooking the grassy basin, four men watched the riders depart. Joe Fletcher, Sawney Tine, and the Kelso brothers, rifles in hand, were pondering what they'd seen.

"You figure they're crazy enough to take a herd and a wagon on that trail, Joe?" Sawney asked. A part-time rustler who worked for the feed-and-grain store in Leadton, Sawney was a chunky, half-shaven man wearing a floppy brown hat that'd seen too many rains, and a buckskin jacket over an old blue Cavalry shirt. He claimed the Cavalry shirt had been left over from serving in the war, but Fletcher figured him to be a deserter from the Indian-fighting troops. Leadton attracted deserters, seeing as it was so far from any Cavalry fort.

"Don't seem they have any choice with their herd so close," Fletcher opined. A rising wind from the north gusted cold over them, and he buttoned up his coat collar. "They'll move up here, likely graze the herd before they go on. We'll hit the herd tonight, see if we can peel off a good three hundred to the south and Kerney Canyon, off east. It'll be a good dark night for it. We'll wait till round four in the morning. They'll be scarce watching out by then."

"I wish we could sell them cows," said Rod, "instead of the other way."

"We'd never get 'em there. Too easy to find. This will pay off nicely, boys. You'll see."

MASE AND HIS crew were camped near the mouth of the canyon, and as the sun went down, Rufus, Karl Dorge, Jimson, and East Wind worked to clear big stones and small boulders, sometimes using a pickax to clear a place, sometimes having to swing an ax at mesquite to open the way for the wagon and make it easier for the herd.

Mase and Pug oversaw the job for a time, sometimes lending a hand, but it soon got too dark to work at it effectively, and he sent them to relieve the hands watching the herd.

Smelling coffee and stew cooking, Mase went to the chuck wagon. "Hey, cookie, is that coffee ready?"

Dollager poured him out a cup. "How fares the canyon trail, sir?" the cook asked.

"We opened it up a piece. I don't think Crane had a chuck wagon when he came through. Everything was on pack mules, as they did it then. But we'll get your wagon through. The trail opens up about two miles in." He wasn't actually sure of the distance—two miles? Three? Four? Cloudy Moon didn't think in terms of miles.

Pug came in and sat down on a supply crate near Mase. Lorenzo, Ray Jost, Harry Duff, and Vinder rode in, glad to dismount after hours in the saddle.

"Mase, those beeves are loving this grass round here," said Ray, coming over to the coffeepot. "Been a while since they had water, though."

"They drank up plenty at that watering hole this morning," Pug said.

"There's water a few miles into the canyon," said Mase.

"Sure, if we can get to it," muttered Vinder, once more annoying Mase.

"We got a good start clearing the trail," Mase said. "Some places we'll just have to rough it."

"Thus far it has not been roughing it?" asked Dollager, smiling as he poured a cup of coffee for Ray.

"Why," said Ray, "that canyon is nothing! One time I was on a drive, and we had an earthquake, and we all slid down to the bottom of a big hole two hundred feet deep. Well, I had to climb up the cliff and pull each cow up with a rope myself."

"Now, that's a heap of bull—" Vinder began.

Ray poked him in the chest and said, "Don't you call me a liar, mister—even when I'm lying!"

That got a good laugh, even from Vinder.

"Pug," Mase said in a quiet aside, "how has Jimson been doing?"

"Denver's holding up his end just fine. 'Course, he's slower than some of the men working with the cattle. Doesn't know much about roping. But he's got sand, Mase."

"You saw him show sand yourself?"

"Well . . ." Pug lowered his voice, glancing at the other men, who were laughing at some story Ray was telling. Something about a prairie dog so big you could ride it. "I was working on Jeff Bolton's spread. Denver heard that Joe Fletcher and Kell Tremaine had signed on to the Whiskey Creek Ranch, that they was going to try to move the WCR herd onto Bolton land. Being as he was a friend of my brother's, he asked if we needed a hand. We were outgunned by those Whiskey

Creek boys, so we said okay, and Denver came in just as Fletcher and Tremaine and four others was raiding our line camp. They pulled over our wagon, tossed some torches at us—and then Tremaine shot Danny Wells right out of the saddle. I was mad as a wet hen, and I come at Tremaine, and he shot me and wounded me pretty good. He was about to finish it, and Denver shot it out with Tremaine, killed him, and scared off those others. Then he bandaged me up and took me to the doc. Hell, he didn't even get paid for any of that. . . ."

Mase nodded. "So he mixed in out of friendship?"

"That's how it was."

"Sounds like a good man to have around."

"I won't say he's never been in trouble. He has. But he's a decent man, Mase."

That made Mase think of his brother, Hiram. *I won't say he's never been in trouble. . . .*

Was Hiram a decent man? Mase thought he was deep down. But who knew where his trail had led him over the last five years? Hiram had always cast a wide loop. He could be in a territorial prison now, for all Mase knew.

Harry Duff, sitting by the fire, was using a small knife to carve a figurine from a piece of pine wood and whistling to himself under his breath.

"What you carving there, Duff?" Mase asked.

The cowboy held it up: an image of a Chickasaw warrior. The head was the most detailed part, and Mase recognized Cloudy Moon. "Why you've even got his scarred eye on there! Where'd you learn to carve like that?"

"Oh, I reckon I learned some from my pa but mostly by wasting a lot of wood on my own."

"You said you'd only been eighty-five miles from your home till you come with us, Duff," Pug said. "You're farther than that now. Seen anything new to you?"

Duff nodded. "Never been so up close with a passel of Indian warriors before. Not so many left down round our place. And that Red River floodwater—never saw nothing like that. Saw a locomotive, too. Seen 'em in pictures, never myself."

"You'll see the elephant sure enough when we get to Wichita," said Pug.

"This business of seeing elephants puzzles me," said Dollager as he brought the tin plates for the first dinner call. "I am quite sure there are none on this continent."

"It's a way of speaking," said Mase. "Means a man has a chance to see something new—see what there is to see. But there are a couple of real elephants in this nation. A fella I knew saw 'em at P. T. Barnum's circus up in Chicago. Never saw one myself."

"I've not only seen elephants," said Dollager, ladling stew onto a plate. "I was nearly trampled to death by one!"

"Listen to him!" Lorenzo said, shaking his head and laughing. "He is as bad as Ray!"

"I neither engage in mendacity nor hyperbole, gentlemen!" Dollager declared, handing a plate of stew and biscuits to Pug. "It was in India in the jungle out west of Calcutta, and a herd of wild elephants came at the file of Her Majesty's soldiers with which I served! Each one was big enough to step on one of your longhorn cattle, and wipe it off its foot! We were in the jungle there seeking the rebel camp, and the rogues used torches to drive the herd directly toward our column! I managed to get my wagon, but it was badly jostled by an elephant and I was thrown to the ground—whereupon a great bull, the biggest I'd ever seen, came right at me in raging fury, making the very ground shake in its thunderous charge!"

Mase was amused to see the cowboys silent and rapt as they listened, wide-eyed, to the story.

"As I rose to my feet," Dollager went on, waving his ladle in the air, "the bull came straight for me, trumpeting madly, its eyes blazing red as it lowered its head to thrust its tusks at my brisket! Gentlemen, I never moved so fast as I did that day! I outstripped the fastest sprinter of the fastest footrace! I bolted off the trail and dove under my wagon!" He shook his head and ladled up a plateful of stew. "But not before the bull came so close with those tusks that he took one of the tails of my coat with him as he passed, tearing my coat from my back and carrying it away with him!"

THE FIRST GUNSHOT brought Mase instantly out of his bedroll. By the time he got his boots on, he was wide-awake and reaching for his rifle.

He could hear Pug shouting orders and the pounding hooves of running cattle. He ran to his horse—seeing Rufus and Denver doing the same—and regretted not having a horse saddled already. As fast as he could, Mase slung a saddle on, buckled it, stuck the rifle in its rig holster, and jumped aboard, kicking the stallion into action.

He could see the starlight glistening off the horns of the cattle as the herd milled and bawled, many on the south end stampeding away. A muzzle flash showed from down that way: a gunshot. Was that one of his men trying to drive the cattle back into the herd? Or someone trying to split up the herd? Another muzzle flash showed in the same spot, and an unfamiliar voice warbled a Rebel yell. Rustlers breaking off part of the herd, heading it south!

Mase considered firing his rifle toward that muzzle flash; he might hit a rustler, but firing in that direction he'd only add to the fear and confusion in the cattle, driving more of them away from the main herd.

He could see the silhouettes of his own men over to the northwest, trying to control the herd.

Mase skirted the herd toward the south, shouting at the cattle, snapping a rope to head off steers beginning a run. He heard another crack of gunfire—and felt a sting as his right hip was grazed by a bullet. But the sensation, and the sound of the bullet, told him it had come from the northwest. Wasn't that where his own men were?

A mass of cattle was breaking from the herd, moving off to the southwest, lost in the darkness. If the Durst Ranch riders set off after them, they'd lose control of the greater mass of the spooked herd. Pug would be closing that part of the herd off from the south, cutting their losses till the herd was under control and daylight would give them a chance to bring the runaway beeves back. And maybe confront the rustlers.

Mase heard Pug's voice shouting at the cattle, and he rode that way, along the lower edge of the remaining herd. "Pug!" he called.

"Over here, Mase!"

Mase spotted Pug, lasso in hand, riding his way.

"You get a look at those men?" Mase asked, riding up to Pug. "Indians?"

"Not Indians. I saw that much. Didn't see any faces. Look out!" He drew his gun and fired in the air, seeing Ol' Buck coming his way. "Get back, damn you, Buck! Go on!"

The steer skidded to a halt, tossed his horned head in confusion, then turned and trotted back to the main herd.

"Pug, did you boys fire shots? Or just the rustlers?"

"I fired a couple. Vinder and Rufus fired, too—heading off some bunch quitters."

"Anyone shoot at the rustlers?"

"Not that I saw. I fired in the air."

"Everyone should've been firing in the air or at the ground. But someone over there, where you men were, fired toward me—skinned my hip!"

"How bad you hit?"

Mase touched the spot, found a bit of fabric had been shot away on his pants, but felt no blood. "Just a graze. No blood."

"Hell, a few inches difference and they could've gut-shot you!"

"I was thinking that, too. Hee-*yaw*, longhorns, get on home!"

But maybe they were firing at the rustlers, Mase thought, *and their aim was wild.* Still—someone had been stupid, unless they were *trying* to hit him.

Even if he'd made some drover angry along the way, why would anyone try to kill the man who'd be paying them? Made no sense . . .

* * *

AFTER THREE HOURS in the saddle, herding till just after the dawn lit the basin with blue-gray light, Mase decided the cattle were calmed down enough and stabilized in one place. He rode up the line, picking out half the drovers to head for a quick breakfast. He'd get that shift fed, then put them back on the herd while the others ate. Once the breakfasts were done, he'd pick out riders to bring back the beeves that had been run off. A little more than four hundred missing cattle had to be rounded up. That would require more than a couple men.

And he would be going with them, Mase figured, as he rode into camp to get his own bacon, biscuits, and coffee. It'd take time and men to locate the runaway cattle and a good deal more to get them back here, and there might well be a fight. He'd take Jimson along, too, since Pug made him out to be a gunhand.

It was an hour more before they were ready to head out. The sun had risen well over the horizon and clouds were blowing in from the north, bringing a faint mist that wasn't quite rain, when Mase, Dorge, Jimson, Jost, Lorenzo, and Duff rode out to the south. Rufus and East Wind seemed disappointed they hadn't been invited along, but Mase didn't want to risk the youngest riders here, both of them pretty much just kids, on a mission that might involve a gunfight.

The gathering team rode out six abreast, every one of them wearing a gun belt as they followed the tracks of the runaways. Cattle being herd animals, they had mostly stuck together, and the tracks showed them heading south and east. On the way here up to the Red Trail canyon, Mase had seen a draw down that way that led into a canyon. Looking through his spyglass, he had glimpsed water back in that canyon. Maybe a spring. The cattle might be following their noses to the water.

Up ahead, the ground rose to a low ridge covered with grass, little more than a thirty-foot-high ripple in the prairie, and Mase said, "Hold on a second!"

As the others reined in, he tugged out his rifle and spurred up to the top of the rise, rifle propped on his hip, to get a quick gander at whatever was on the other side. He didn't want to lead his drovers into an ambush.

About two hundred yards ahead, down the shallow slope, four men were riding toward him in a tight group. They looked like rough characters to Mase, but they might have been from some local ranch.

They saw him at the same time and slowed their horses.

Mase backed his horse down the slope till the strangers couldn't see him, and called to Jimson. "Denver! I need you to post yourself over to the right. You saw that brush down there? Use that for cover. You're going to flank some men when I call you. Don't kill 'em unless you have to. But get their attention."

Denver touched his hat in acknowledgment and rode off to the right, under cover of the rise.

Mase rode up the slope, a little below where he was before, and stopped just high enough to see over the top of the rise. The four men were sitting on their horses, just waiting. Two of them had rifles in their hands, but they didn't seem ready to bring them into action. Mase urged his horse up to the top of the hill and said, "You other men come up behind me and then stay on top of the ridge. Hands on weapons but don't jump the gun."

He heard their mounts moving up behind him as he rode over the low ridge and down into the lowland area. Mase's Winchester was ready to fire, a round in the chamber. He stopped at the bottom of the rise and shouted, "You men want to parley, come on over here."

The four men rode slowly forward till their horses were about thirty feet from Mase's stallion. The man on the right was a chunky, greasy-looking fellow in buckskin. On the left were two men wearing black frock coats. One of them had a high-crowned hat; his eyes were close together, his teeth crooked. The other, without a hat, had pitted skin, smallpox marks, and his hair greased back.

The man in the middle had an air of authority, the look of being in charge. Clean-shaven, he wore a long blue coat, a white shirt and vest, a string tie, and a low-crowned black hat. A townsman's look. Yet there was an arrogance in the way he held himself that suggested he was a man who made his own law. He had a light, pleasant smile, but his eyes were hard as flint.

"You men lose some cattle?" he asked, his voice mild as if just curious.

"That's right," said Mase. "Someone raided us, drove a piece of our herd down south here. We'll be taking them back come hell or high water."

"It happens we saw something over four hundred

cows stampede through here this morning," the man said, shifting in his saddle. "We had nothing to do with any raid. But we know just where those cattle run to. It's off a piece to the south. A man has to know the way. And we do."

"You're saying you're not the rustlers?"

"We are not! But we saw 'em. Chickasaw, I reckon. When they saw us coming, they run off. Now, it's a long way from here to there. But if you are willing to pay us five dollars a head, we'll take you there."

"Five dollars! That adds up to around two thousand dollars. That'll come up to about five hundred dollars for each of you four men. Not bad! What makes you think I've got that kind of money with this drive?"

"Just a guess. If you don't, you can buy as many back as you can afford from us."

Mase almost laughed aloud at the man's nerviness. "And the rest fall to you?"

The rustler shrugged. "We found 'em, didn't we?"

"What's your name, mister?"

"It's Samuel Clarke."

"I surely doubt that. My name is Mase Durst. And that at least is true. You see those men on the ridge above me? They're all good shots. Here's my offer: you drop your weapons and lead us to our cattle, and we won't have to kill you for rustling our beeves. I'll give your description to the US marshal and let it go at that."

The chunky man in the buckskin jacket and floppy hat snarled, "Damn it, let's just take them cows and sell the whole bunch! This is a lot of foolishness."

"Shut up, Sawney!" the rustler boss snapped, glancing over at the speaker. Then the man who called himself Clarke turned to Mase. "Don't care for your deal. You pay up, and we'll find those cattle for you. We can shoot, too, mister. You don't want to lose any of your men, do you? But hell, you'd probably catch the first bullet."

"Denver!" Mase shouted.

Denver rode out of the brush to the right, his pistol in his hand, and shouted, "Joe Fletcher!"

Startled, the man in the long blue coat turned to stare at Denver. "Jimson!"

"I've got the drop on you there, Joe! And those men on the ridge are aiming at you other boys!"

The rustlers looked up to see that the drovers on the low ridge had their guns trained on them.

"It's been a while, Denver," Fletcher said.

"Put your hands up, or I'll kill you, Joe! You know I won't miss!"

Fletcher hesitated. Then the man he'd called Sawney growled to himself and pulled out a big Dragoon revolver, swung it toward Denver—even as Mase dropped the muzzle of his rifle and fired. At thirty feet he easily hit Sawney, the bullet cracking into the man's chest so he jerked back in the saddle, firing his pistol spasmodically. The Dragoon's bullet hit the ground, and Sawney's horse ran off, its rider slumped over its neck.

"Fletcher—drop it!" Denver yelled. "Last warning!"

Fletcher dropped his pistol and put his hands up.

"Now, you other men, throw down those weapons!" Mase shouted, swinging his rifle at the other two rustlers. They looked at each other—in that moment, Mase guessed that they were brothers—and dropped their pistols in the grass.

"Ray," he called out, "see if you can catch that horse that run off, will you? See if that man's dead."

MASE WAS SITTING by the fire that evening, listening to his men talk and holding the map Crane had given him up to the light to peer at it yet again. There wasn't much to it. Just a man's hen scratchings barely making sense. But it did look like there was water partway up the trail. He would have the same hands clearing some more of the canyon trail tomorrow morning at first light as the other men moved the herd up to where it was already cleared. The chuck wagon would go first. . . .

He remembered Ray's worry that the rustlers might be waiting for him somewhere up the trail. He glanced up at the cliff tops. He saw nothing but a vulture circling up there.

Suddenly he had a sharp mental image of the rustler Sawney rocking back in his saddle under the impact of the Winchester's bullet. It bothered Mase . . . that the killing didn't bother him. Not much, anyhow. Sawney had without a doubt been planning to kill him or Denver—Mase had acted instinctively. But shouldn't he be feeling some remorse for killing a man?

No. He was all in on this drive. That meant fighting to the death to defend it. Mase realized that if so much wasn't riding on this drive, he might not have been so quick to kill. He had sunk pretty much everything into this cattle drive. The Durst Ranch was in debt to the bank, too. He had to make good—for Katie and Jim as well as for himself. It was Wichita or bust. He felt the burden of it every waking minute—just as he felt the weight of his responsibility for the lives of his drovers. All that pressure had concentrated in his hand to squeeze the trigger of his Winchester. . . .

"The boss made them use their knives and their hands to dig a grave for the dead one," said Ray Jost as the drovers sat around the fire. The men who hadn't been on the gather with him listened raptly. "They had them cows herded in that southeast canyon, just like Mase figured. He made 'em do all the work. Then he found seventy-four dollars on them, and he took that, all their guns, and Sawney's horse as a fine and sent 'em on their way. That horse looks just fine in our remuda."

"I'm kinda surprised he just let them ride out," Rufus said, shaking his head. "My uncle Chet would've hung 'em!"

"Hung 'em from what?" Ray asked, tossing a mesquite twig into the campfire. "A mesquite bush?"

"Furthermore," said Dollager, eating his own meal now that the others had finished, "best not hasten to bloodshed, young man. It weighs heavily upon the soul. Mr. Durst was indeed more generous than many would have been. Why, my old captain in India would have consigned those scoundrels to a firing squad! But as Aristotle said, 'At his best, man is the noblest of animals, but if he does not cleave to law and justice, he is the worst.' Hanging men outside the law is bestial indeed."

"Wouldn't have bothered me none," Ray admitted as he rolled a cigarette. "But maybe this Aristotle knew a thing or two." He turned to Mase, who was standing up, stretching, preparing to put in a few hours watching the herd. "Mase—what troubles me about letting those owlhoots go is we may meet 'em sometime on the trail. Maybe get ourselves bushwhacked."

"It's a chance I took," Mase admitted. "But I am no executioner, so it was that or drag them along with us till we find a court. From what I hear, the law in Leadton is as crooked as a Virginia fence. So we might've had 'em with us all the way to Wichita."

"You did the sensible thing," said Pug, nodding.

HE MADE A mistake letting us go," said Rod Kelso. "He'll pay for taking money from my pocket—and my gun! That was a damned fine gun!"

"He kilt Sawney, too," Phil pointed out. He waved at the dance hall girl who was ferrying drinks around the Jack of Hearts.

"Hell, I never liked Sawney nohow. But my gun! And fifteen dollars! And then having to herd cattle—I hate that kind of work! Plumb degradin'!"

"As if you know a stitch about work," growled Fletcher.

He was mad at more than Durst. He was mad at the world. It made him angry just to see another Durst sitting across the room, at the table beside the stage, his shotgun propped on his leg, one hand holding it the way a king held a scepter as he watched the big crowd of drinkers in the saloon. The place was going great guns since Hiram Durst had taken over as guard here. Hiram nodded his head with the fiddle music played by the old one-legged prospector seated on the little stage, just like a king listening to his music in court.

Durst. Was he related to Mase Durst? He seemed to see a resemblance in their faces. Seemed likely they were kin.

Hiram Durst was a dangerous man. And a very alert one. Not a good man to challenge face-to-face.

But at some point, there would be a chance, if it worked out as Fletcher hoped, to set things up so that Hiram Durst could watch his own brother die—before dying himself.

That would balance the accounts all right.

CHAPTER TEN

THE GUN SMOKE rose from Katie's pistol, curling blue in the morning sunlight. Holding the gun with her right hand, she aimed—catching the tip of her tongue between her front teeth and closing one eye—and fired once more at the old flour-starter tin on the stump. She missed, but not by far. Katie was out in the nearest pasture to the house, bereft now of stock, thinking she'd better just shoot six more rounds and then get back to her chores. Jim was out riding the fences with Hector, but he'd be back soon.

She had tried firing the Colt Army pistol Mase had given her with two hands, the way Mase had suggested, and with one hand. Two hands felt awkward. She found that she could manage with one despite the kick, and it seemed to aim better. She didn't know if she was ready to get in a real fight with the likes of Clement Adams, but practicing with the gun gave her a feeling of strength she needed right now.

"Senora!"

She turned to see Curly waving to her from his horse as he walked it up. "You have a letter! They send it from town!"

"Oh! Is it from Mase?"

"No, senora. The name on it is Malley."

"It's my uncle Forrest!" she said, holstering the gun. She tore open the envelope and read it then and there. It was the merest note.

Dear Katherine,

Your letter has been forwarded to me by Elizabeth. I am most concerned to hear that your homestead is in jeopardy. I shall have to look at the agreement between you and the bank, but it is quite possible they are within their rights. However, the matter can surely be delayed until the loan is repaid. That may not resolve the matter, but it may be our only recourse as yet. I am obliged to complete the representation I have undertaken in the defense of a worthy man, but will make my way to you as soon as possible when that is concluded. I hope it may be within a fortnight.

Affectionately
Yrs,
Forrest Malley, Esq.

THIRTY-FOUR DAYS INTO the drive to Wichita. They'd been two of those days eking their way slowly up the canyon, pushing the reluctant cattle into the stone chute of the trail, but not too hard. It would have been easy for the cattle to split their hooves or break their ankles on this uneven, rubbly ground.

Mase and Pug were standing to one side, watching the chuck wagon clatter and rumble as Dollager, leading the oxen on foot, tried to get over a moraine, or ancient glacial rock deposit. The bank of small boulders and gravel was only about five feet high, but it was steep and supported by an uptilt of the stony canyon floor that could not be cleared away. There was no way around; it stretched from one canyon cliff to the other. They'd taken most of the supplies out of the wagon to reduce its weight, but it was still too heavy. Straining and bawling, the oxen had at last gotten themselves over, the tongue of the wagon scraping over the stone behind them, but the wagon seemed stuck now. Dollager roared commands at the oxen, urging them on. The wagon tongue screeched across stone. The front wheels rose, slipped over the impediment—then came a raucous crackling sound, and the right rear wheel of the chuck wagon snapped off its axle. The wheel had caught awkwardly on a big rock atop the blockage.

"Hellfire!" Pug growled.

The chuck wagon's left rear wheel went over, the broken axle of the right side dragging through rock as it followed. Then the wagon slammed to a halt.

"Hold it, Dollager!" Mase shouted. But there was no need for the order. The wagon wasn't going to move much from where it was without the fourth wheel.

Dollager joined Mase and Pug to inspect the damage. The wheel was more than broken; its iron rim was warped and half its wooden spokes shattered.

"Well, we've got spares," said Mase. "We'll set up a lever and put it right. Let's start taking the rest of the supplies out to lighten 'er up. . . ."

He turned to shout at Karl Dorge and Rufus and Denver, who were working to clear brush. "Yo, boys, come on back! We've got us a new job!"

Pug called out to the drovers pushing the herd up. "Hold on now. Keep 'em where they are!"

A few pieces of extra lumber had been brought along for chuck wagon repairs, and Mase pulled two long oak boards out of the wagon bed, as Pug and Dollager detached one of the spare wheels and rolled it over to the axle.

"We shall need a fulcrum," Dollager said.

Mase looked around, spotted a boulder in the moraine that was about the size of a bushel. "Let's you and me dig that one out and roll it over. . . ."

Pug called Dorge, Duff, and Jimson over. East Wind was sent to keep the oxen steady. Using the small boulder as a fulcrum and the two boards, stacked, as a lever, the four drovers tilted up the back corner of the wagon as Mase and Dollager lifted the replacement wheel onto the axle.

The wagon was soon moving on, bumping across the stony ground, and the cattle were following, the sheer press of them pushing those in the front over the barrier.

The trail was clearer now, though occasionally the drovers had to clear rocks that might have proven dangerous to the herd. It was slow going in the narrow passage, the cattle pressed together, steers sometimes angrily jabbing at one another with their horns. The cowboys had to keep chiefly in the drag and in front, for fear of being gored in the tight confines of the herd, or of getting crushed against the stone walls of the beetling red cliffs.

Onward they went, as a damp wind picked up, wailing as it came down the canyon. Toward evening, riding out a short distance ahead, Mase heard the cattle making an excited mooing he recognized, and looked back to see their muzzles lifted to sniff at the air. Likely they smelled water.

The canyon jogged to the left, and around the curve, a quarter mile on, they came to a sizable pool of clear water. It was coming from a spring in a clay layer of the cliff walls.

As Dollager moved the chuck wagon into place, Mase once more scanned the tops of the cliffs. He knew the drive was in a bad spot in this canyon if the likes of Joe Fletcher took up a position on those rocks. They could pick off a number of men before the drovers could get under cover. There were game trails up there, maybe from mountain goats, and a man could move around those trails for a better shooting angle.

All they could do was keep a watch on the cliffs. Mase got off his horse, led it to the pool, and let it drink. He waved Ike Vinder and Rufus over to him. "You two set yourselves to watch those cliffs. Keep an eye on the cattle but mostly watch those cliff tops till it gets good and dark and you can't see anything else."

"You expecting that Fletcher bunch to come after us from up there?" Vinder asked.

"Expecting—nope. But prudence is a virtue, boys. Now get to it. Post yourself over there, Vinder—Rufus, you go on over there."

They went to their posts, and looking around, Mase

spotted a small dead tree, half crushed by a boulder. Mase went to the tree and started breaking off branches for the campfire, thinking the while that the crushed tree was a reminder that there was some real risk from falling rocks here. He dropped the wood at the ring of stones Dollager had arranged for the campfire, and that wailing wind chose that moment to whip down the canyon again, mischievously flipping Mase's hat right off his head. He caught the hat by the brim in midair, just as it was about to blow into the pool.

"Mase," said Pug, riding up, "there's a yearling with a broken ankle. Stepped in a hole in the rock."

"Well—I guess we'll have fresh beef. Go ahead and shoot it, and I'll send the coosie to cut the meat off."

Pug rode back to do his bidding. Arranging the wood for the fire, Mase shook his head in disgust. How many cattle had he lost? Eleven at Red River. More to the Chickasaw. He suspected that a few of those the rustlers had driven off were still out on the range somewhere. They needed to do an accurate count.

He shook his head. Each lost beef was a loss in income for Katie and Jim. . . .

"Dollager!" he called, standing up. "I'll start the fire and the coffee! You've got some butchering to do!"

"MIZ DURST," TOR Oliver said, "I sure appreciate the pie and the home brew, but, ma'am, I'm not sure what any of us can do for you."

"It's not for me—not only!" she protested. She was standing at the stove, underscoring her words by tapping a finger on the cold iron. "It's for your own selves, too!"

There were three neighbors gathered around her kitchen table that evening. None of them seemed convinced they should band together with her against Harning. Not even in court.

Tor Oliver was a widower, white haired and bearded, who kept to himself at his ranch bordering the Durst land to the southeast. Beside him was Marty Smole, a stern, darkly tanned cotton farmer with a deeply lined face, and his wife, Gwendoline, a shy little woman with gray-streaked black hair and big brown eyes.

"Now, how's it going to help people to get in a fight with Harning?" Oliver said, shaking his head with incredulity. "He's a powerful man, and he's mighty friendly with some big men in the state! He's got half a dozen hired hands who carry guns! I have two men working for me who carry nothing but sheep shears!"

"Standing up to him doesn't have to need guns," Katie insisted.

"Hmph!" snorted Smole, raising his bushy eyebrows. "Do you say so, now? Why, ma'am, Harning's the kind who'll fight anyone who defies him! He'll force a fight!"

"That's right," Oliver said. "That's him to a T."

Katie shrugged. "Mr. Oliver . . . you'll have to face him one way or another. San Vincente Creek runs through my land and then down to yours. And that's what he wants—along with all the good grazing on Durst Ranch. He wants to control that water, don't you see? And if he takes my land from my husband and me, why, he'll block up the creek so you can't use it for irrigation!"

Mr. Oliver blinked—and blanched. "You—you don't know that, ma'am."

"Wouldn't surprise me," said Mrs. Smole softly.

Her husband looked at her with surprise. "Why, Gwennie!"

She blushed but went on. "I think we should listen to Mrs. Durst. This man will stop at nothing. It's not right what he does—we've all heard the stories. And he treats his poor wife like an old rag. Have you heard how he talks to her?"

"Hmph!" said Smole again. "That's none of our business."

"How is it you think we can be of any use without picking up a gun?" Oliver said.

"By testifying to anything you see that you think is wrong," Katie said. "And if I send a message—then you might choose to come to be a witness to what is happening. You don't have to mix in a fight."

"That sounds to me like the right thing to do!" declared Mrs. Smole almost boldly.

"Suppose he's coming onto my land with armed men, threatening me. . . ." Katie suggested. "He's done it before! Now I've barred him and his men from my ranch. I've let it be known. If you see them on my property—if you see him breaking any law—speak up! Talk to the sheriff!"

"The sheriff?" Smole smirked and shook his head. "That man will dance a jig if Harning asks him to."

"If enough people speak out, the sheriff will have to do something," Katie insisted.

Oliver picked up his hat and stood up, staring at the floor. Then he shoved the hat on his head and said, "I've got to head home. But I'll think on what you said."

Smole nodded. He took his wife's hand and drew her to her feet. "That goes for us. We'll think on it."

Gwendoline Smole gave Katie a shy smile. "I've

always admired you, Katie Durst. I hope you whup that man one way or the other. I surely do."

Then she took her husband's arm and they all went to the door, leaving Katie alone in the kitchen.

"Mama?"

She turned to see Jim in his red long johns, standing at the entrance to the hall. "Can I have some pie—and home brew?" he asked.

"You're supposed to be asleep!"

"All the talking woke me."

"So you were listening, were you?"

"Yes, ma'am. I think you said it right. Everything that you said."

She opened her arms, and he came to her hug. "You can have pie," she said, hugging him. "But no home brew."

MASE WAS SITTING on his bedroll near a lantern with a piece of paper laid over his knee, trying to work out how much money the ranch had lost in missing cattle. . . .

He heard a crackling from somewhere above, then a rumbling sound, and he looked around—to see a boulder about seven feet in diameter bouncing past him, whooshing through the air and missing him by a few inches. It flew on with meteoric intensity over the campfire, making the flames flutter and sparks fly, and straight at East Wind and Rufus, who were standing together near the chuck wagon. Both of them saw it coming and threw themselves to the right and left. It struck the ground between them, rolling on to shatter against the cliff face with an echoing *crack*.

Dollager, standing at the Dutch oven nearby, gaped after it and then said breathlessly, "Truly there's an angel keeping watch!"

Mase jumped to his feet and turned toward the high rocks the danger had come from. He could see faintly a small cloud of dust up there. "Anyone see that thing start down?" he called.

"Not me," said Rufus, getting up.

"Nor I!" called Dollager.

"What the devil's going on?" Pug asked, trotting up to them, breathing hard. "Why, I was just pulling up my britches in the shrubs and comes a sound like a cannon!"

"A boulder came down from there," Mase said, staring up at the cliff. His mouth was dry, his pulse pounding, though nothing more was falling from the canyon wall. His fear was all about what had almost happened. "Came within a hair of busting me flat, Pug! Rufus and East Wind, too!"

"That is a hell of a thing!" Pug said, taking off his hat and slapping it against his thigh. "Could've killed you easy!"

Mase looked toward the cattle bedded down about two hundred feet away, too far off to be disturbed by the noise of the boulder.

He reached down to the saddle lying by his bedroll, picked up his gun belt, and strapped it on. Then he caught up the lantern and started toward the cliff the boulder had come from.

"Where the dickens you going?" Pug called, hurrying after him.

"Just want to have a look," Mase said.

"I'm coming with you, boss!" Rufus said, running up behind them.

"Just stay out of my way, then," Mase said. "I want to see any tracks there might be."

"You think someone was up there," Pug asked as they traipsed toward the cliffside, "and . . . done this a-purpose?"

"I don't know," Mase said. "Could be. Kind of a big coincidence, that rock deciding to come loose while we're camped right below . . ."

"The cattle could've done something to shake it loose."

"They're not butting that slope, Pug."

They reached the bottom of the cliff, which was clumped up with a mound of old rubble and eroded soil, spotted with prickly pear cactuses. Vinder was standing by the mound, staring up at the cliff, scratching his head.

"You see anybody, Vinder?" Mase asked.

"No, sir, boss—I heard the dang thing comin' down, and it passed me by. About made me jump out of my boots! I was walking by right here on the way to the camp. Trying to see if anything more's coming down—or anybody's up there." He shook his head. "Not a thing."

Mase held the lantern up over the ground, found an old animal trail and mountain goat tracks. "Could be some old ram knocked that chunk of rock loose . . ."

"Haven't seen any of the critters hereabouts," Pug said, looking at the ground. "Those goat tracks are old."

Mase started up the thin trail over the mound, looking for footprints of a different kind. He found some scuff marks that did look like they might've been left by boots. And it looked like they went up from the camp. But the ground was steep there, and the soil had come loose, blotting out most of the markings. He couldn't be sure they were the prints of boots.

How could they be coming from the camp, after all? They'd have seen anyone sneaking through. There was scarce any room to get past the herd.

He ascended a bit higher and saw a place where a shrub had been half pulled out of the cliffside. By a climber or some animal?

Looking up the thin, zigzagging trail, he lost sight of it partway in shadow. It seemed to him that even one of his own men could have gotten up to those high rocks without being seen.

Mase shook his head. Just didn't seem possible that it could have been one of his hands. Must have been the rustlers.

He turned and, half sliding, descended to the flat ground nearby. "Too dark up there to go any farther right now," he said, returning to Pug and Rufus. "But somebody sure could've been there."

"You think it was that Fletcher bunch?" Rufus asked.

"Could've been. Or maybe just a mountain goat. We'll increase the watch tonight. I'll join the first one."

He was pretty sure he wouldn't be able to sleep much tonight, anyway. . . .

CHAPTER ELEVEN

FORTY-ONE DAYS INTO the drive to Wichita.

The canyon opened up that morning, becoming several times wider and offering patches of graze for the herd. Mase and his drovers felt like a man with claustrophobia released from a locked room as they drove the herd into the broader trail. The red cliffs were still surrounding them but farther off, and it was possible to ride swing on the herd now. Bawling and mooing, hooves clattering and thumping, the herd moved on to the north.

But Mase had a fresh worry now. As he rode point, not far in front of the herd, he watched the hulking black rain clouds moving in from the northwest. He didn't see any clear signs that there were flash floods in this canyon in the past, but it was raining a dickens of a lot this year. Mase wondered if he had taken too big a chance on the Red Trail. Maybe he was going to have to dig some graves soon for men who'd drowned, for men crushed by a panicky herd in a storm. At the same time, he was constantly scanning the cliff tops for signs of bushwhackers.

Mase kept remembering that boulder flying past, those boot tracks on the game trail leading up the cliffs. *Had* they been boot tracks? He hadn't been certain. He remembered, too, the errant bullet that had skinned his hip the night the rustlers had struck. Had someone been trying to shoot him in the back?

And then he had Katie and Jim to think on. Were they safe? There had been that talk of Harning taking the ranch to court. Mase remembered Harning stopping him in the street one warm afternoon last year in Fuente Verde. The rancher had demanded to see the Durst Ranch deed.

Mase had stared at him in astonishment. "What put it into your mind that you've got the right to make that demand, Harning?" he'd asked.

"I've heard you're homesteading without a deed, is what," said Harning, scowling.

"The devil we are!" Mase told him. "You get a judge to tell me I've got to show you, and then I'll do it."

And Harning had indeed gone to court. Judge Murray, who was a lick too friendly with the big local landowners, had played along, and Mase had brought in the deed. Harning had scarcely looked at it. "Why, anyone could have cooked up that paper!"

"Looks legal to me," Murray told him a little regretfully.

Harning had snorted and stomped out of the courtroom. . . .

Mase shook his head. What would such a man be putting Katie through with her all alone back home?

* * *

THE GATE TO Durst ranch was an eighth of a mile away from the house. But the land between was flat and largely empty, and the day was bright and clear, so Katie could see the buggy stopping out there. The horse looked like one of the tall, high-stepping horses that the Circle H favored for its buckboard and buggy.

Curly, who was looking after the cows and their calves with Jim and Hector, had tied the gate shut with leather straps to discourage Harning's men from riding up to the house. Whoever was in the buggy seemed to be considering whether they should try to open the gate.

Katie had ridden with Jim along the fences this morning, and Bonnie was still tied up at the water trough nearby. Katie climbed into the saddle and rode out at a canter toward the gate.

As she got closer, she made out Gertrude Harning alone, standing by the gate. Mrs. Harning was wearing an ankle-length lavender dress with puffy sleeves, and a matching hat and gloves. Gertie waved, and Katie waved back. She could see into the buggy now. Harning wasn't there.

Feeling more relaxed since it was only Gertie, Katie reached the gate and dismounted. "Hello, Gertie. Would you like to come for some tea?"

"I would at that, Katie. I thank you."

Katie went to the leather straps, took a couple minutes unknotting them, and then opened the gate. "Just bring the buggy on down."

She remounted, and in a few minutes, Gertie was sitting at the kitchen table, and Katie was using the pump at the sink to fill the teapot. She'd already lit the kindling in the stove, and the water was soon heating up.

"Gertrude, how are Mary and Len?" Katie asked as she took her best china cups and saucers from the cabinet.

"Oh, they're hale enough," Gertie said, shifting uneasily in her chair. "And certainly they're full of beans and vinegar, always rushing. I do get Len to the school—it's a long ride for him, but he goes. But that boy needs a tutor. He's got a quick mind but doesn't take to reading easily. Mary's a scamp and a bit of a tomboy."

"I was a bit of a tomboy myself," Katie said, putting out the china, along with spoons and the sugar bowl—after she made certain there were no ants in it. "I've considered sending Jim to the school—maybe next year he might go. It would be good for him to learn how to be mannerly with a teacher. He doesn't much see folks except for us on the ranch, and he's what my mama would have called unpolished."

Katie badly wanted to ask what had brought Gertie here, but she held herself back. Their husbands being at odds, social calls between the two ranches simply did not occur. They knew each other only from church and the occasional chance encounter at the milliner. Today, a certain pensiveness in Gertie suggested she was here on a personal errand.

An uncomfortable silence grew as Katie watched the tea water seething. Gertie glanced around the kitchen.

"It's a nice bright kitchen," Gertie said at length as if searching for a compliment.

Katie smiled, stirring the tea in the kettle with a

wooden spoon. She'd seen the Harning ranch house and knew it to be two stories and five times the size of her four-room home. "I insisted that Mase put two windows in the kitchen. I will not abide gloom in a room where I must spend so much time."

She poured the tea and sat down across from Gertie. "Well, Gertrude, I am glad you've come." She passed over the sugar bowl. "But I must say it's your first time here. Was there anything bringing you today?"

"Why, I thought . . ." She took a deep breath and said, "I don't quite know how to explain, Katie." She gave Katie a look that was almost imploring. "Can I confide in you discreetly?"

"Of course, Gertrude! I am many things—but no gossip!"

Gertrude sighed. "There is a great distance between myself and my husband. I feel as if I have fallen into a trap in marrying him. Is that wicked to say?"

Katie shook her head. "It's scarcely a novelty. I've known many a woman to feel the same. I'm lucky to have found Mase."

"A woman normally takes her husband's part. But I cannot always do so. I know that Tom is on the—on the wrong side of the fence in this matter between him and your husband. I know, too, that he's hired a man who seems to do little but laze about, waiting for an order to use his gun. That man . . ."

"Clement Adams?"

"Yes." Gertie's eyes widened. "You've met him?"

"He came here with Andy Pike and that Sullivan. Adams came out with some pretty sharp warnings and pointed a gun at my hired man. I think if things had gone a whisker different, he might have killed Curly on the spot."

Gertie closed her eyes and compressed her lips. "Mother Mary, preserve us!" Then she looked at Katie with a new determination showing in her eyes. "Katie. I am sorry!"

"No harm was done." *Except to my peace of mind,* she thought. "But it made me wonder how far your husband would go!"

"I don't know myself," Gertie said, almost whispering. She took a sip of the tea and then said, "But, Katie—I am afraid for you. And for your husband."

Katie leaned toward her. "Is there something you want to tell me about that, Gertie? Something particular, like?"

"I . . . cannot. I don't want to lose my children. . . ."

"Lose your children!"

"I cannot explain fully. But, Katie—I *am* looking for ways to help you. And while there are certain kinds of testimony I dare not give—the time might come when there are other things I can speak of. Yes, and to a judge! The moment would have to be right. But I want you to know that if I can help you . . . I will. For I cannot rest at night for fear of what Tom might do. And not only to you and Mase . . ."

They drank a little tea in silence, Katie giving thought to how she might persuade Gertie to reveal more.

But then Gertrude gave out a soft little moan, pushed her tea cup away, and stood up.

"I thank you for the hospitality. It has been a joy. Perhaps we can talk again after church sometime. If we have something to say on this matter . . ."

"Gertrude—wait."

"I cannot. I cannot trust myself to . . . not yet, Katie."

She went to the door, almost too rapidly for courtesy, opened it, and turned back just long enough to say, "If I can help—I will. I do want you to know that. God bless you now!"

Then she almost ran to her buggy, urged the horse into motion, and drove quickly away from the house.

IN THE LATE afternoon, Mase shot a small pronghorn antelope up the trail. He let its carcass bleed out and tied it over his stallion's rump. He figured on handing it over to Dollager.

Mase rode back to the herd, smelling rain in the air. He knew the storm was coming. He looked up at the sky and saw the lowering dark clouds and was surprised they hadn't yet cut loose.

He rode up to the chuck wagon and saw the oxen released from their yokes grazing contentedly nearby. Dollager had already stacked up a good deal of wood within a fire ring and had the sense to drape a large piece of canvas over it in case the rain started. But where was the cook? Mase cut the antelope loose, dropping it close to the fire circle, and rode toward the herd.

The cattle were settled down in a circular field of grass scattered with coneflowers and sumac shrubs, with here and there a cluster of Jerusalem artichokes. Close to the herd, Dollager and East Wind were sawing into the large spiky wild plants. Beside them was a leather bag stuffed with other greens.

"I brought you an antelope, coosie," Mase said. "What have you there?"

"Jerusalem artichoke. Grows wild about here but I hadn't noticed till East Wind pointed it out," Dollager said. "He has also shown me the uses of prickly pear, which I shall use in a goulash, and rock cress."

"Was a time before I started with you, I'd had-a died without the prickly pear," said East Wind, sawing away with a serrated knife.

"Best start on the meal soon, for it's going to rain," said Mase.

East Wind nodded. "Rain for true and certain. Big rain."

"Right you are, Mr. Durst," Dollager said, tossing artichokes into the bag. "Come on, East Wind. You can assist me."

"Unless I am to watch the herd," East Wind said, looking up at Mase inquiringly.

"A good meal is what I want," said Mase. "You can butcher that antelope."

Mase rode off to the tail end of the herd to find Pug and Jacob mounted up and running a couple of stray yearlings back into the bunch.

"How's the trail look up ahead?" Pug asked, reining in beside him.

"Wild and rugged and starting to narrow some. And there's a river up there—a narrow one but deep looking. Looks like it's only there part of the year."

"Can we swim the herd over, you think, boss?" Jacob asked, rubbing his chin.

"Maybe. If it doesn't start raising hell after the rainstorm." He looked up at the sky—just in time to get fat drops of rain right in the eyes. "Damn it!" He wiped his eyes. "Here it comes, and the herd will get twitchy, Pug. Let's circle round 'em, keep 'em contained till it lets up some."

The rain became steady, lashed by a rising wind, and soon became a deluge as the men circled the herd, Pug calling out all the drovers except East Wind to help, shouting at them to put on their slickers. Heads bowed against the steadily drumming rain, they called out reassurances to the cattle, and drove the few bunch quitters back to the herd.

The rainfall kept coming, sheets of it sweeping over them; the herd was jumpy, and it was continual work to hold it in place. Every drover had to change horses at the remuda after a couple hours, the animals exhausted by the constant activity and the endless weight of the riders. The men were drooping in their saddles, muttering to themselves—the drumming of the rain on their hats was making them as twitchy as the herd. Mase was watching the ground, afraid the camp would be washed out. They might even get a flood surge. But the ground was slanted enough that it shed the water downhill from them, though sometimes it came up past the hooves of their mounts.

After almost four hours, the rain let up, becoming a wind-whipped drizzle, and Mase started taking men off the herd, sending them to the chuck wagon for rest and food. With the rain's letup, Dollager had started the fire but he was still cooking, so at first the cowboys only got hardtack with blackstrap and salted beef. Mase tried to send all the men in, while he kept watch on the herd, but Rufus refused to go till Mase had his turn.

Mase thought about giving Rufus a stern order but

decided against it. He didn't want to discourage loyalty or self-sacrifice in a young man.

Limp with fatigue, Mase rode into camp, just as the goulash was being served out. It was late for supper, but the men were glad to get it. Antelope meat, spiced with salt, pepper, and prickly pear, filled out by rock watercress, the edible parts of the artichokes, wild onions, and the few remaining potatoes. Mase was amazed at how good it was.

"Coosie, you sure have outdone yourself," he said.

Everyone looked at him with astonishment. Mase rarely gave out shiny compliments.

Dollager chuckled. "Glad to be of service, milord."

"It surely is fine vittles," said Jacob, nodding.

East Wind finished his meal and said, "I'll go out and relieve Rufus." He didn't ask for permission. He just jumped on Jacob's mule—they had an understanding about that—and cantered out to the job.

"He's run off with your mule again, Jacob," Ray observed.

"Why," said Jacob, grinning, "she's taken a shine to him. He's a good 'un, that Injun boy. Haven't ridden with a better."

Ray nodded. "I expect that Mase figured right on him after all. And he helped us out with that Cloudy Moon. But of course he can cowboy—them Indians learn to ride and rope pretty young. I knew one was still a papoose who used to ride a foal and catch rabbits with a string—"

The men groaned and shook their heads. Then they laughed.

The next morning dawned clear and blue, and Mase declared they'd have a morning for drying clothes, mending, and grooming. Some of the men needed a shave and a haircut badly; he was sorry he hadn't made a rule about grooming, since long hair and beards increased the risk of lice in the camp. Cleaning up was good for morale, too.

Dollager discovered that he was expected to be the camp barber. Shears in hand, he took up the additional post cheerfully enough, explaining, "Why, I was company barber in India before I was a cook."

The drovers stripped to their drawers so they could dry their clothes, spreading the laundry over shrubs and wagon wheels and saddles, a display of motley colors against the dull red and green backdrop of the canyon. As he waited for his clothes to dry, Ray brought out a mouth harp, and Dollager pulled a fiddle from his trunk, and they improvised together, a curious but strangely fitting mesh of Celtic tunes and cowboy songs.

"We'll move the herd on to the river now," Mase announced after the noon meal, "and we'll just see what we have to do to get across it. . . ."

He had a powerful hunch it would not be easy.

Taking up his post with the ten gauge at his usual seat in the Jack of Hearts, Hiram Durst was not pleased to see Joe Fletcher coming toward him.

"Hiram, how's business?" Fletcher asked.

"Haven't got any. That's how I like it."

Fletcher grinned. "Just getting paid to sit there?"

"That's right," Hiram said, meeting Fletcher's eyes. "Just getting paid to sit here."

"I don't expect he pays you much for that."

"Not so much. Enough to pay for my room and board and a few drinks."

"Can I buy you a drink?"

"Maybe after my watch is over. What can I do for you, Joe?"

"Seems like you might want to make some more money. I need another man to help me out on a job. Just work for a day or two. I understand Binder is planning to shut down for a couple days."

"Later in the week. He's running out of liquor. They're slow to bring it down from Morrisville. And nobody's even got a good still going. That's where you should make your money, Joe. Moonshine. Cut the sheriff in and you've got a gold mine."

"Not a bad idea. Right now I'm looking at cattle. There's some coming up Red Trail canyon. I intend to take a share. I figure he's crossing my land."

"What outfit is crazy enough to come that way?"

"Oh, I don't know who they are," Fletcher said, looking away.

Hiram was pretty sure Joe was lying. He knew. Strange thing to lie about. Hiram wondered why Fletcher bothered. "So you have land down south of town?"

"Depends on how a man views it. That land's mine if I claim it."

"I reckon there's a whole tribe of Indians that'd disagree with you on that matter. We're in the Indian Nations here, Fletcher."

"Indians got no say in it."

"You plan to take a toll?"

"I plan to take twenty-five percent of their herd. I'll need men to help me stand up to them—and to herd the cattle to the holding pen north of town. I'll find a buyer in Morrisville."

"'Stand up to them'—now, I wonder what you mean by that."

Fletcher glanced around, then leaned closer to Hiram and whispered, "There's a place where the canyon narrows, not so far south of here. Devil's Head it's called. They've got to bring those cows through right there. There are rocks either side for cover. They'll have no choice but to give in and pay the cows over. We'll be under good cover. I'm not expecting to lose a man."

Hiram snorted. "I understand you already lost a man a piece back. Sawney, it was. Most likely it was from tangling with that same outfit. I knew him. I did not care for that man's company, but it seems to me his getting shot just proves there's fight in this cattle outfit. Doesn't sound like folks who're going to hand over any part of their herd."

Fletcher straightened up, his jaw working in subdued anger. "It'll work this time. You want the job, or don't you? I'll pay you top dollar."

Hiram wasn't tempted. "Nope. Not a chance. You'd best move on now, Fletcher. You're obstructing my view. My whole job is watching the place. I'd best get to it."

Fletcher's face reddened, and he opened his mouth to say something—and then shut it and strode off to the bar.

Hiram had the feeling there was a good deal more in this matter that Fletcher hadn't told him. He wasn't at all sure he wanted to know what it was.

* * *

THE DRIVE HAD made camp at the river the previous evening and found the current roaring along, surging madly from the recent storm. It wasn't possible to swim a herd across.

Now, in the early morning, Mase, Pug, and Dollager were standing near the bank of the narrow, roaring river, regarding it dolefully. It came into the canyon from a ravine that slanted across the trail, the water roaring through northeast to southwest. Mist from the powerfully rushing white water rose like white smoke.

"That's a helluva thing," said Mase. The river was running so fast and hard, he had to raise his voice to be heard over it. "That river's not here half the year—hasn't even got a name, and it's stopped us cold."

"Maybe we should name it the Helluva River," said Pug, shaking his head in disgust.

"Perhaps more aptly the River Styx," Dollager said dryly. "You might have to be deceased to cross it."

Jacob, Lorenzo, and Ray joined them as Mase said, "I guess we'll have to wait it out. Might take a week to get quiet enough to get the herd over."

"Seems to me, Mase," Ray said, "there could be a fresh storm. We could wait a week, and then it might just go to high and fast again."

"My father," said Lorenzo, "he like to build bridges. Sometimes even when there is no value in the bridge for him! He build for everyone."

"An admirable man," said Dollager.

"Yes, senor coosie, is true. Now, I build three bridges with my father. Sometimes, it's just the beginning of a bridge, but enough to cross. And you see? There are trees along the bank! We could build a bridge!"

Mase turned to survey the southern bank of the river. "There are some. I see tupelo and ash and cottonwood. Not a lot of them but maybe enough."

"How would you get the wood across that river?" Pug asked. "Why, it'd be washed away."

"Oh, there are ways, Senor Liberty," Lorenzo insisted. "I show you if you have the tools."

"We've got three kinds of saw with us," Mase said. "It's all in the chuck wagon. Got a big two-man saw, ripsaws, and a log saw. We've got a broad ax and two other axes; we've got mallets and chisels. We've got hand planes, hammers and nails, and extra rope. We have the tools, Lorenzo."

"I'm a fair hand with that work myself, Mr. Durst," Jacob said. "Just pick out a tree, and I'll get 'er felled."

"Already picked it out," Mase said, pointing. "The closest tree, right by the ford. That cottonwood's the biggest one on the river. And right where the stream narrows. Right there the river's about forty-five feet wide. We cut it proper, it'll fall across, and we can use it as a start. Pug, let's get out the tools and all the rope we have. . . ."

THERE ARE MEN on the property, senora," said Curly, coming into the barn.

Katie put the horse brush aside and said, "What sort of men?"

"They have, how you say, the *telescopio* for measuring. And the sheriff is with them."

"Is he!" She went to the tackle board, grabbed her

saddle, carried it back, and slung it on the mare. "Where are they?"

"Near the gate—you can see them if you go outside, senora." He went to his horse, already saddled, and led it outside.

The two of them were soon cantering up to the three men standing inside the southern fence. There was a buggy waiting on the other side of the fence, its horse scuffing at the ground near the sheriff's mount. It was a hot, sunny day, and as she squinted at the scene, Katie was sorry she hadn't put on a hat to keep the sun out of her eyes.

The two young surveyors looked up as the armed riders arrived. The surveyors had a clerical look to them, one in shirtsleeves and a cap with a green-shade bill, the other in a gray suit and small spectacles on his nose. They stood beside their tripod with its small leveling instrument.

Beslow, in shirtsleeves and a gray Stetson, stood nearby with his hands on his gun belt, trying his best to look both casual and in authority but seeming embarrassed. His badge flashed in the sunlight.

"George, you weren't even going to do me the courtesy of pretending to ask for permission?" Katie asked coldly.

Sheriff Beslow winced. "Didn't see any need to trouble you. We've got all the paperwork permitting the survey. Got it in my saddlebags. Judge signed it."

"I'm guessing that'd be Judge Murray."

"It is."

"We'll be quick as we can, ma'am," said the man in the green-shaded cap. "But it'll take a couple days to get it done. Maybe three."

"Whether it should be done at all is my question," Katie said.

"I told you they've got the right to be here," said Beslow.

"Maybe they have the legal right. But that doesn't make it fair," she said firmly. "It's all done at the behest of a man who wants to steal this land. And you know it, George. Harning's setting up his legal challenge. It's smoke he's using to cover up his real move."

"You'll have your day in court," Beslow said, sighing.

"I'll need to see those papers now."

The sheriff let out a grunt of irritation. Shaking his head, he stalked through the open gate and went to the quarter horse tied to the fence. He fished around in a saddlebag and came out with the papers and walked them back over, handing them to her with a flourish.

Katie shaded her eyes and looked over the court order. There was Tom Harning's signature as complainant, and there was Judge Murray's signature at the bottom of the order. She read through the two-page document, comprehending most of it, tried to find something she could use to challenge it, but came up empty.

"Is this copy for me?"

"Didn't make one for you."

"I'll bet you're supposed to."

"Well . . ." Beslow took the papers back from her. "This'll have to do for now."

"Why couldn't those men have shown me the papers on their own?"

"Their firm asked for protection, and the judge granted it. Being as how you fired your weapon at Harning's men over the fence business."

"I told you no one fired at them. Only at the ground."

"And your man there threatened the Circle H hands when they came visiting here."

Katie shook her head. "They weren't visiting, George. They were trying to scare me into leaving."

He looked at the ground, compressing his lips. "I wasn't there."

"I am a witness," said Curly. "It is as the senora says."

Beslow scowled at Curly. "Nobody's asking you about it, Mex."

"You ever hear of Clement Adams, George?" Katie asked.

He shifted his weight and let out a long breath. "I have."

"He was with Andy Pike. He's no ranch hand, Sheriff."

"Adams is no wanted man either."

"I expect he's right careful how he murders a man."

"Now that's a wild allegation you should not be making, Mrs. Durst."

"You should be ashamed, tolerating that man in this county, Sheriff." Katie turned to the two strangers. They looked sheepish and pretended to be focused on their surveying. "You boys were hired for a job, and you're doing it. I've got no fight with you. You can get water from my pump if you need it, for you and your horse, and you can freely drive your buggy on our land."

"Thank you, ma'am," said the man in the spectacles.

"Come on, Curly," Katie said. She turned her horse, and without another word, they rode back to the ranch house.

* * *

THE TREE TRUNK began to crackle, to tilt toward its back cut. Lorenzo and Jacob yanked out the two-man saw and stepped well back as the cottonwood toppled over.

Its upper bole struck with a crunch exactly where Mase wanted it to fall, branches snapping with popping sounds as it slammed down on the farther bank. Its lower branches splashed into the rushing water, but most of the tree trunk was clear, propped up by the rocky clay of the banks. As he'd hoped, the broken-off snags of branches had stabbed into the clay, which would help hold the log in place. Getting the contiguous logs across would be tougher.

"Good job, boys," he said, nodding as Pug and Rufus walked up to gaze approvingly at the fallen tree. "I'll get a rope across, and we can use that as a guide rope to keep from falling off while we move out there. . . ."

"You're going to walk out over that tree trunk your own self?" Pug asked, frowning. "The upper end of that tree is slim. Needs to be reinforced. Big man like you might crack that thin part. Then you're going to fall and get swept down that river."

Mase shrugged. "I'll have a rope around my middle."

"You'll still damage the bridge! And if you get swept off in that current, pulling you back won't be so easy."

"Let me go!" Rufus said, his eyes sparkling at the thought. "I don't hardly weigh nothin'!"

Pug looked at Rufus appraisingly. "By gosh you are the slenderest fellow here. But no, there's East Wind. He weighs even less than you."

To Rufus's disappointment, East Wind it was. A rope fastened around his waist, he began working his way nimbly across the river along the slippery, mist-wet trunk of the fallen tree. Mase paid out the rope, hand over hand, as East Wind slipped past the now vertical branches. He stopped from time to time to unhook the rope from a snag, trying to keep it straight over the trunk.

Mase was breathless as he watched, afraid the Indian boy would slip and fall to be dragged by the current under the trunk, where the rope could end up tangling him and keeping him underwater.

East Wind eked his way carefully across and stepped onto the bank, the drovers cheering.

East Wind immediately commenced tying the rope to the exposed roots of a blackened lightning-charred stump of a tree atop the riverbank. Rufus was sent next, a rope around his waist, too, using the first rope as a safety line. Next went Lorenzo and Duff, carrying tools to start cutting the branches out of the way.

Three of the other cowboys were taking turns cutting down an ash tree that would provide part of the wood for the finished bridge. They'd cut it down, remove the branches, and use the oxen to drag it close to the nearer end of the fallen cottonwood. Then they'd use chisels to split it down the middle, creating two flat surfaces on the split side.

Mase turned to look at the oxen cropping weeds by the camp. They seemed strong enough to pull a fallen tree. He saw Dollager giving Ol' Buck something to eat—the cook had made a pet out of the lead steer, talking to the beast as he gave it dried apples and hardtack with molasses. It was past time for the noon meal. Mase walked over to Dollager. "Coosie," he said, "you're feeding that steer before these hungry lumberjacks over here!"

"It's all ready to eat, Mr. Durst!" Dollager said, patting Ol' Buck. "It's in the pot there. Just call the men over, and I'll serve it up."

"Soon's that ash tree comes down."

"Planning to sink some posts on the banks to hold the bridge, sir?"

"We are. Once we make the posts."

"I'm rather good with a shovel and a sledgehammer, sir. I've got the tonnage to put into it. I can help drive them in."

Mase smiled. "You'll get your chance to prove it, Mick."

"Very good, sir." Dollager walked over to the pot—and Ol' Buck followed ponderously behind him, like a dog after its master. Mase couldn't help but laugh.

Duff came suddenly galloping up from the herd. "Mr. Durst!"

"Well? What's all this hurry about?"

"I spotted some men on the cliffs! Two of them, over to the east! They're watching us for sure!"

"Point 'em out!"

"Easier if you get on your horse and ride closer to the herd, boss!"

Mase went to his horse, which was tied to a wheel of the chuck wagon, and mounted. He followed Duff back to the herd. The cowboy pointed. "You see? Up by that notch!"

Mase dug in a saddlebag and pulled out the spyglass Katie had given him. He settled his horse and looked through the little telescope. At first he saw nothing. But slowly sweeping back and forth, he caught a glint of sun off metal. He homed in on it, focused, and within the wavering circle saw two men in hats, one with a rifle in his hands. The rifle wasn't pointed toward the drovers—not yet. He couldn't see their faces clearly, but he had little doubt that the one on the left was Joe Fletcher.

Mase toyed with the idea of opening fire on them. He doubted he could hit them from here, but it would be good to warn them off. Still, there was a small chance they weren't who he thought they were. Suppose he hit one—and it was just a random saddle bum or even a traveling lawman? Before he could make up his mind, they seemed to realize he had spotted them—they drew back from the rocks and out of sight.

But he knew they were close by. They would be watching, waiting, for the right moment to make their move.

"Duff," he said, "I'm going to tell you what I am going to tell everyone else. We're changing a rule. From now on we wear our gun belts all the time, and we keep 'em close to our bedrolls at night. Keep 'em loaded and be ready to use 'em. . . ."

CHAPTER TWELVE

THE DROVERS WORKED by lantern light till an hour past midnight, and everyone was aching with exhaustion before Mase called a halt. "I'll ride herd for now," he told Pug. "Tell the men to bed down." His hands were blistered from using an ax and saw, stripping branches from the fallen ash tree, then taking his turn with a sledgehammer and driving chisels to split the trunk down the middle. Yet most of the hardest work had been done by other men while he and Lorenzo supervised.

Mase climbed wearily into the saddle, then rode along the river for a few minutes, trying to figure out if its level was falling. It didn't seem so. And he noted gathering storm clouds to the northeast. They might be in for another deluge.

He rode out to the herd where Rufus was skirting it, absently whirling the end of a rope, though the cattle were settled down. He seemed to be nodding in the saddle as if he might fall asleep. A cowboy asleep in the saddle after a long day was no strange sight.

"Rufus!" Mase called, riding up.

The boy looked around, startled. "Mr. Durst!"

"Don't look so surprised, boy. You go on in and hit the bedroll."

"No, sir—I mean, if you don't mind, I'll give you a hand. I still got part of my watch to go."

Mase smiled. "You looked to me like you were going to fall on the ground, snoring. But suit yourself. When you do go in, get your slicker out. Might rain again."

Rufus looked doubtfully at the sky. There were a moon and some darkly scudding clouds and a wash of stars. "Don't see any rain, boss."

"Coming from the northeast. Let's drift around the herd, see what needs doing."

Mase led the way to the south, riding at a walk along the outer fringes of the cattle. Most of the herd was asleep. They turned east along the lower edge of the herd and then north, Mase starting a rough head count, then realizing he'd have a better chance to check as soon as the bridge was complete. When they drove the longhorns across the bridge, there'd be room enough for only three or four to pass abreast. That'd give him an easy opportunity to count steers.

"We're something like two-thirds of the way through the drive," Mase said. "What are you going to do with your money when you're paid off? Loose women and cards?"

"Me? No, boss. Why, I wouldn't know how to . . ." Rufus cleared his throat. "And cards—why, I never had any luck at that. Uncle Chet says I got a face you can read like a sunlit trail. I figure to go back and give him half to help with the ranch. I want my folks to know. . . ."

Mase nodded. Many a man had found himself at loose ends and signed up for cowboying just to prove something. "You're thinking wise with your money. Too many cowpunchers waste their money away before they even get home."

Rufus yawned. "Back home I got in a knucklebuster with my cousin—he seemed to think my uncle favored me over him. Like I was angling to inherit. He give me a pretty good drubbin'—but then again, I broke his nose. Anyhow, I heard you might be hiring, so I come and joined up just so they'd all know I could make my own durn way."

The clouds rumbled. The humidity was tangible. They were just completing their circle of the herd when Mase heard an eerie ululation echoing in the canyon. Some of the herd lifted their heads and sniffed the air nervously.

"That coyotes?" Rufus asked, looking even more nervous than the cows.

"Nope." The clouds parted, and moonlight shone down—and Mase saw three sets of golden eyes shining in the darkness about fifty feet off. He drew his rifle from its saddle holster and dismounted, figuring to get a better shot down on the same level, with his boots firmly anchored on the ground.

"What is it?" Rufus whispered.

"You never heard a wolf howl before?" Mase asked softly, putting the rifle to his shoulder.

"Not down where I live, no, sir," Rufus said.

Mase aimed between one set of golden eyes—but before he could fire, they flicked out along with the others. The beasts were turning away, dark slinking shapes pacing off to the north. He tried to aim at one of the shapes, but the dark seemed to deepen and he lost sight of them. They were planning to bring down one of the smaller cattle, Mase figured. If he opened fire they'd run—but it was a big herd, and they'd just run to another part of it.

"Had 'em and lost 'em, Rufus," Mase said, remounting. "Keep watch."

"How many?"

"At least three moving north." He glanced at Rufus and smiled, noting the boy seemed suddenly far more wakeful.

The clouds once more covered the moon, and Mase slowly paced his mount up the edge of the herd, thinking he might want to send Rufus to bring Jimson and some others who were handy with a gun.

Then the clouds once more released a little light, and he saw two of the wolves fifty feet ahead, canine silhouettes picking up speed, rushing toward a yearling. He shouted, "He-*yaw*!" and spurred his horse at a gallop toward the wolves, dropped his rifle's muzzle, and fired. His horse reared as the bullet kicked up the dirt between the wolves and the herd. Two sets of golden eyes turned his way as the wolves hesitated.

His horse settling, Mase fired again, and one of the wolves yipped, turning to run away from the herd. The other turned to follow its injured fellow. There were shouts from the camp at the rifle reports, and the cattle were getting up, milling, horns clacking, a few of them running from the main group.

Mase rode to cut the bunch quitters off—just as the rain began coming down in a slanting wall of wet.

Mase holstered the rifle and set to controlling the herd. A minute later East Wind galloped up from the camp, followed by Pug.

"We heard shots!"

"Wolves!" he yelled. "Gather the herd! Hold 'em!"

Then another shot sounded, a pistol cracking from the south, and he turned, knowing it had to have been Rufus who'd fired the gun. The rain was lashing down hard, and he couldn't see past it.

Mase cantered back along the line of the herd, shouting, "Rufus!" He coughed as rain splashed into his mouth. "Rufus!"

Then he saw a sprawled figure on the ground—two of them. One was a wolf.

Mase reined in beside Rufus, leapt off the horse, and crouched beside him. Rufus groaned and turned on his side, trying to get up.

"Hold on there, boy!" Mase admonished him, shouting to be heard over the pounding rain. "How bad you hurt?"

"Knocked me down . . . bit me . . . on my arm . . . shot him . . ."

Pug rode up with a lantern, climbed down, and held it over Rufus. "Got bandages in my saddlebag. Hold on now. . . ."

In a couple minutes they had a rough bandage stanching the wound on Rufus's left forearm. They helped him up.

"Got down for a better shot," Rufus said. "He run at me, knocked me down tolerable hard. . . ."

"He can take my horse back to the camp," East Wind said, dismounting. He looked at the dead wolf.

It was an adult red wolf, Mase saw. Stone-dead, shot

in the chest. The boy must have gotten off the shot as the beast leapt at him.

"Good shot, kid," Mase said as Pug helped Rufus onto the horse.

"He was standing on my chest. . . . I fired right in his neck. . . ." Rufus said, dazedly.

"Ride double with him," Mase told East Wind. "Get him back to Dollager. See he gets some alcohol on those bites. Send the other drovers out to me."

East Wind nodded, mounted behind Rufus.

"Rufus," said East Wind, reaching around him for the reins, "if you can kill a wolf who's trying to kill you, that's good warrior medicine. I'm going to skin that critter for you. . . ."

They rode off to the camp as Mase remounted and said, "Let's get the herd back in line and away from this here dead wolf. . . ."

The rain lashed furiously down. It was going to be a long night. . . .

THE RAIN QUIT a little before two in the morning. The clouds broke up enough to admit the glow of the moon and the stars. Bone-tired, Mase went to the river to see if new flooding had swept the cottonwood tree away. No, it still stretched across the river but water splashed over it now in places.

Mase shook his head and went to his bedroll—which was sopping wet. He laid his slicker over it, put on an overcoat, lay down, and listened to the roar of the river. He slept like a dead man.

Pug woke him at dawn. Mase had told him at the start of the drive to do that every day. Right now he wished he hadn't. But he got himself up and said, "Coffee?"

"Coming up."

Mase picked up his bedroll and carried it over to a wagon wheel to spread it out so it'd dry. The sky was mostly clear, though fog from the river was drifting around the camp.

Dollager was at the fire, humming to himself as he stirred an enormous pot of porridge. "Mr. Durst, help yourself to the coffee. It should be ready."

"How long before you can feed the camp, coosie?" Mase asked.

"Ten minutes, sir."

"How's Rufus?"

"He's well enough, sir. His head hit a rock, but he'll be fine if I'm any judge—long as that arm doesn't get infected. I fancy I cleaned it good and proper."

Pug poured coffee for them both, and Mase said, "Let's get the men up, Pug. Breakfast is about ready. Let Rufus rest, but roust all the others. Who's on the cattle?"

"East Wind and Duff. I sent them about an hour ago. He was up skinning that wolf when I woke up. Working by a lantern."

Mase grimaced. "Nothing like skinning a wolf first thing in the morning! I'll spell Duff after I've eaten. Let's get the men working on the bridge soon's they've eaten."

A few hours later, spelled by Jimson and Dorge, Mase and East Wind rode in to view the woodwork beside the surging river. The canyon was echoing with the clatter of hammers and the screeching of saws. Every man, including coosie, was working to prepare the split ash tree to be laid down beside the cottonwood. The trunk was stripped of branches, skyward side flattened out, planed smooth. It'd take every rope they could spare to stabilize the two logs till they could nail cross boards connecting them.

"How we get that ash wood across the river, boss?" East Wind asked.

"We're going to use the oxen to line it up with the cottonwood. Then we tie a rope to the north end, and every man is going to cross over and work in a team to pull it over along the top of the cottonwood beam. All of us pulling should do it."

"Maybe."

Mase glanced at him. He himself wasn't sure it would work. "You have a better idea?"

East Wind pointed across the river, a little west, where an apron of pebbly stone protected by an old tree stump stuck out level with the water. Water gushed shallowly over it. "Horses swim. The river will push them down west. But I think they can climb out there if we ride 'em to it. Some men go over the tree with ropes. . . ."

"With the horses on the other side, we can pull the logs across?" Mase shook his head. "They'd get washed downstream."

"Current's slowed by that cottonwood, boss. Now, we couldn't get the herd over that way. But horses . . . maybe."

"I'll think on it. You go ahead and help Dollager, and then you may as well finish with that wolfskin. If Rufus is up to it, he can help you scrape the hide with his good arm." East Wind wasn't much of a carpenter.

Mase went to pick up a saw. There was another tree to fell.

THERE WAS A strange, cold inwardness in Curly's face when he came back from town with the supplies. Jim was with him, jumping down from the buckboard and waving at his mother.

Katie, just done putting the laundry on the line, was about to take Bonnie out to check the fence line. "You want to go with me and check the fences, Jim?" she asked.

"Yes, ma'am!"

"You go on in the barn, lead Bonnie and your pony out of their stalls for me."

He ran off to the barn, and she walked up to the buckboard. "Everything all right, Curly?"

He avoided her eyes as he stepped down from the buckboard. "It cannot be true, senora. I'm sure it is not true."

"What? What has Harning done now?"

"It is not him. The sheriff, he say he has received a message that"—he licked his lips—"that Senor Durst was killed. Up on the Red Trail."

The ground seemed to ripple under her as if there had been an earthquake. She put a hand on the buckboard's wheel to steady herself. "That's . . . No. Can't be right."

"That's what I tell him. I say no! I don't believe."

"Where did he hear this?"

"A message from a Ranger who passes through, senora. He hears it in Leadton."

"How . . . how did Mase die?"

"Stampede, he said. Killed by the cattle."

Mase. Dead. It was as if someone had told her the world had been canceled.

How would she tell Jim? He needed to know soon. Because he'd have to learn to live with it, and that would take a long time for them both. She would have to keep going. She . . .

Something struck Katie then. *A message from a Ranger who passes through, senora.*

A Ranger . . . who'd happened to have been in Leadton. It was all just the word of a man passing through.

She took a deep breath. "A Ranger? Did the sheriff give that man's name?"

"No, senora."

A sudden realization took hold of her, and now she was steadier on her feet. The grief washed away. All she felt now was anger. "The sheriff is lying, Curly. You were right—it's not true. This is Harning trying to get me to give up and move away." She shook her head. "If Mase was dead—I'd know it."

Curly looked at her with his eyebrows raised. "Yes?"

She nodded. "Yes. I can *feel* him in the world, Curly. And I'd know if he was gone."

Curly's eyes widened. "*Sí!* My grandmother—she said something like this. She knew when my grandfather died though he was many miles away."

Jim came out of the barn. "They're waiting for us, Ma!"

"Jim—come here."

He came to her, and she put her arms around him. It was like hugging a part of Mase.

"You okay, Mama?"

"Sure I am. But Curly's going to take you for that ride around the fences, Jim. There's something I have to do. I'm going to town. I've got to see the sheriff."

WHY DO YOU do it, Harning?" Beslow leaned back in his chair, looking like he'd bitten into a rotten apple.

"Why do I do what, Beslow?" Harning asked. He was standing in front of Beslow's desk, wanting to get his business done and head home. It was late afternoon, and it was a long ride back to the Circle H. But then again, maybe he could stay the night in town. . . .

"Putting all this pressure on the woman won't work. Katherine Durst can't sell you that ranch. It's not only hers. Hell, it's in her husband's name. He'll be back in due course, and he'll tell you no. He won't sell no matter what she says."

Harning gave Beslow a dismissive wave of the hand. "My lawyer says that if she takes my money and leaves the place before he comes back, I can move some men in—then we can argue that I've got rights there. Maybe I'd lose. Like enough I would. But it'll tie Mason Durst up in court for a long time, 'specially with Judge Murray on my side. Durst won't be able to run the ranch till it's decided. And she'll be gone! She's part of what keeps him there. She'll have the boy with her, too. If he comes back to all that, why he might just give up—"

"Harning!" Beslow snapped.

"What?"

"Shut up. Just—stop talking."

"What's got into you? This deal with the man Chavez is bothering you? It's over. You gave him the message. You get paid. It's not your worry. You just decide what you want to do with a thousand dollars, Beslow."

He reached into his coat pocket.

He took the money out and froze when Beslow stood up and said, "Put that money back in your pocket. And get out of here."

Beslow's face was red. His hands, pressed to the desktop, were shaking.

"What's gotten into you, Beslow?"

"She was here." Beslow opened the drawer of his desk, took out a whiskey bottle and a glass, and poured himself a double. "Katie Durst was here." He drank off half the whiskey. "She knew, Harning. She just looked in my eyes—and she asked me. And I . . . couldn't keep pretending. She knows he isn't dead. She could tell just looking at me."

"Why, that's a heap of cow chips! You just lost your nerve, that's all."

"She knew, Beslow."

"What did you say to her?"

"Nothing. I just shrugged and said, 'Maybe he's not, ma'am. Maybe it was just a rumor.' It was all I could say. And then she told me what she thought of me." He licked his lips and said, "And it was what I was thinking myself." He drank off the rest of the whiskey. "She was right, Harning." He sank back into his chair, staring at the whiskey bottle. "You do what you want. But keep it all out of my sight because I'm not having anything more to do with this. Now, get out of my office."

Harning snorted and put the money back in his coat. "You think you're a better man than me?" He shook his head. "You're not."

Then he turned and walked out, thinking he wanted a drink himself. He'd stay the night. Maybe see Darlene. Why not? Why have a mistress if you hardly saw her?

It could be, he thought as he started across the street for the cantina, that the sheriff was right about the legalities. But he hadn't told Beslow all of it. If he put enough pressure on Katie Durst, she'd break—once she heard for sure that her husband was dead. When he was dead for real.

Harning nodded to himself. The man he had hired was still in place. With any luck, Mason Durst would never come back from the Red Trail alive.

IT WAS DUSK on the nameless river. Mase watched pensively as East Wind rode the horse across the plunging stream, wearing only his breechcloth. East Wind was the lightest of the drovers, so the horse could use most of its strength for swimming. The water was a little higher and faster now after last night's storm, though the current was a little weakened here by the cottonwood they'd felled. They'd had to start the horse a piece upstream close to the cottonwood log so as it was washed down, there was room to move diagonally toward that stony extension of the riverbank. If East Wind missed it, he and the horse could both be killed in the white water farther downstream.

The horse was near the landing place—but slipping downstream. East Wind leaned over and called something to the horse, kicking at its ribs with his bare feet—and the horse redoubled its thrashing efforts. It reached the bank and scrambled up.

"Maybe one's enough," Pug said, walking up to the riverbank to stand beside Mase.

But East Wind insisted he could get another horse across, and Mase let him do it. This time he got there even faster.

Mase sent Duff across the cottonwood log first, and he pulled the long length of towrope over. They already had the ash tree timbers lined up on the southern bank, ready to be pulled across. Big posts had been sunk in the bank at the south and north sides of the river to hold the fallen trees in place.

Vinder, Dorge, Vasquez, and Mase crossed the river on the planed cottonwood—slowly and carefully, for it was slick with the water that slopped over it—and helped rig up the horses to pull the ash across. Directed by East Wind, the horses pulled the rope attached to the ash, and the men added their own strength to the tow. The post on the south side held it in place as they slowly dragged it across the water, fighting the current and the sheer weight of the enormous length of lumber. But at last it was in place, snugged between the sunken posts on both sides and pressed against the cottonwood. Now the other half of the split ash would have to go. . . .

They got both split logs in place just as it was growing quite dark, and Mase called a halt for supper. Tomorrow, he figured, they'd nail down the cross boards connecting the planed logs and fill in chinks with clay and pieces of bark.

Mase mounted up and went to check on the herd. He found that Rufus was there already, driving bunch quitters back in place. "Rufus, what are you doing out here? Dollager say you could go to work?"

"Yes, sir, boss," said Rufus, riding up beside him. "He checked my arm. There's no kinda gangrene or nothin'. I got no fever. I can work."

Mase nodded. "You'll make a good hand yet. How's that wolf hide coming?"

"Well, sir, it was something to see—that East Wind busted in the wolf's skull, scooped out its brains, and spread 'em over the side that ain't got the fur on it. He says that's for curing it. He rubs it in there with some plant he pulled up by the river." Rufus shook his head. "Wolf brains for curing! Anyhow, he's got it stretched out real tight over some branches for drying."

"What're you going to do with it?"

"If it don't stink too bad, that fur is going to be my pillow for the drive. Then I'm going to build me a cabin somewhere and nail it up over the fireplace. When I come to courtin', I'll bring the lady in for a visit and show that to her. Tell her the whole story. I reckon that'll impress her."

Mase smiled. "Come on, let's take a turn around the herd. Keep a close look out in case those other wolves come on back. . . ."

They trotted their mounts off together. "How's the bridge coming, boss?" Rufus asked.

"We got the logs over. We'll do the cross boards tomorrow, cinch it all up good, and start the herd across. It'll take a considerable time, but we'll get them over, maybe three abreast."

But Mase was more worried than he let on. Would the bridge hold up to the current and thousands of cattle crossing it? Suppose the bridge collapsed? They'd lose beeves down the river, and there weren't enough trees around here for another bridge. They'd have to wait out the river. Supplies were low, and his cattle buyer was waiting.

And he wanted badly to return to Katie and Jim. He needed to see with his own eyes that they were all right. . . .

CHAPTER THIRTEEN

THE RIVER WAS running high and hard that morning, splashing at the bridge, some of the water swishing thinly over it.

The last of the stabilizing ropes and cross boards were in place. It was time to move some cattle across. In this case, the chuck wagon would go last. They'd had to move it fifty yards down the south riverbank to make more room for the herd crowded up to the riverbank.

They'd all been up at dawn, and now it was midmorning. Most of the drovers were in the saddle, keeping the cattle close to the river. Almost holding his breath, Mase watched Lorenzo Vasquez driving Ol' Buck toward the bridge. The big lead steer trotted forward—and stopped right at the edge of the riverbank. His eyes rolled as he took in the roaring river, the water splashing over the bridge. Then he turned around and butted back into the mass of the herd.

Mase let go of some cusswords and turned to Pug. "Let's move the other cattle toward it. One of 'em is sure to cross and get the herd started over. . . ."

The cowboys called out to the cattle, lashed them with rope ends, drove them toward the bridge—where they stopped just where Ol' Buck had stopped. They contemplated the loudly rushing water and turned back.

"Son of a—!" Mase burst out.

Dollager strolled up to him then. "Trouble with Ol' Buck crossing, Mr. Durst?"

"Seems to have decided to go back to Texas."

"I can hardly blame him. Well, sir, will you let me have a try with him?"

"You? On a horse?"

"Not at all, Mr. Durst. Observe, sir."

Dollager strode over to Ol' Buck, patted him on the snout, then reached into an apron pocket and pulled out a handful of sweetened biscuits. He broke off part of a biscuit and held it out. The bull ate it with gusto. He offered the animal another—but this time Dollager took a step back. Ol' Buck followed, taking another morsel. Dollager brought out another biscuit and began to walk backward toward the bridge, waving the sweet biscuits, the great beast tromping along after him. Dollager turned, took four long steps onto the bridge, and offered up the biscuits.

Ol' Buck stared at it. Then looked at the rushing water. Then again at the biscuits.

Dollager came a little closer and held the biscuit just out of the beast's reach but within sniffing range. The lead steer snorted and stepped onto the bridge. Dollager kept backing up, occasionally feeding Buck a morsel to keep him going. Soon the other cattle began to follow, a few at a time, and the men commenced to cheer.

THE GUNFIRE SOUNDED like it was coming from the northwest corner of the ranch. That was how Katie reckoned it as she finished saddling her horse. That would put it near the place the fence had been broken down.

"Senora Durst—do not go out there!" Curly protested, backing his horse from its stall. "I will go alone and see!"

Katie shook her head, led Bonnie out into the barnyard, and climbed into the saddle. When Curly brought his horse out, she said, "You come along, Curly, and keep your rifle handy. I won't get too close to whoever's doing the shooting. But by God if they're killing my stock . . ."

She was glad Jim wasn't home. Marty and Gwendoline Smole had swung by the ranch on their way to town for supplies to see if all was well. They had offered to take Jim into town with them. They were a childless couple and enjoyed the company of children. He had jumped at the chance.

More shots cracked, the sound echoing to them thinly across the range.

Curly mounted his horse, and they rode off quickly in the direction of the gunfire. Durst Ranch cows with young calves grazed out this way, and two horses, as well. When they got most of the way to the fence line, the cows and their young ones came at a half run to Katie and Curly; they were running from the noise of the gunfire. The stock ran past toward their pens by the barn.

Katie saw the rising gun smoke first, then the gleam of sun off rifle barrels. As they rode nearer, she made out Clement Adams and Andy Pike firing at the Durst Ranch's brand-new fence posts.

The rifles cracked, one and then the other, splintering the posts.

"Senora, this way!" Curly said, riding well out of the line of fire. She followed, and they reined in at the fence below the target shooters. The two men were standing about forty feet from the fence, on Harning property, splintering the tops of a post with their alternating fire. Their horses were tied to a mesquite shrub behind them.

Growling to herself, Katie rode up the fence line, stopping close enough to call out to them. "Andy Pike! Hold your fire! You could hit my stock, firing that way!"

Curly rode up beside her. "They know, senora. They do not care."

The shooters stopped, blue smoke drooling from the muzzles of their rifles. Pike turned his head to regard her, squinting against the sun, grinning crookedly. "Why, ma'am, we're just doing some friendly target shootin'! I got two dollars bet on it!"

"You miss half the time," said Adams. "I've already won that money. Maybe we *should* shoot us some stock. Take it back to the cook for supper!"

Katie drew the rifle from her saddle holster and rode closer. "You'll have to shoot me first, Adams!"

"Why, ma'am, there's no sense in that! But you have to understand, those animals are trespassing on Harning land!"

"You *know* damn well that's a lie!" Katie said. "You should also know by now you can't back me down!"

"Maybe it's time we see about that!" Adams said, turning to face them.

Curly muttered something in Spanish and slid off his horse, rifle in hand. He set it atop the nearest fence post and aimed it at Adams. *"Es suficiente!"* he shouted. "No more! I am a good shot, Senor Adams! If I go to jail—then I go! But first I kill you! Or you ride away!"

Katie's heart was pounding. But she climbed down off her horse and took up a position beside him, her rifle tucked against her shoulder. "Same goes with me! *Es suficiente!*"

Adams smiled and began to raise his rifle—but Pike reached out and pushed the barrel down.

"Hold it, Clement!" Pike raised his hat to Katie. "I reckon I've lost the shooting match. We'll see you folks soon enough!"

He turned and walked back toward his horse. Adams hesitated, then shrugged and turned to follow him. The two men mounted and rode off.

Katie rode over to look at the chewed-up tops of the fence posts. "They're getting mighty playful," she muttered as Curly joined her.

"It is soon to be no more a game, senora," he said sadly.

IT WAS A warm afternoon, fifty-two days into the drive to Wichita.

The trail was narrowing again as the drovers moved the herd to within a day's drive of Leadton. There was more rubble here, Mase saw as he rode ahead of the herd, and far less graze. Already their water barrels, filled at the river, were down to the dregs. They'd come across a few muddy puddles left by the rainstorms, but little else. After so long without a drink, the cattle were thirsty, bawling hoarsely, their tongues rasping out. For a week they'd come across no springs, no creeks, no water holes. The map marked a watering hole out east of Leadton, and graze, too. But that was beyond the pass that led out of the canyon. Mase needed to get the steers out of the canyon and to that water and grass. The remuda horses were thirsty, too. They shared in the drovers' water, but they weren't getting enough.

The rains had long since ceased, and the ground had dried and it was dusty here now. The men in the drag of the herd were wearing their bandannas up and wiping dust from their eyes.

Mase rode on, hoping to see the pass marked on his map that led out of the canyon. He rode another two miles through scrubland and dust, past occasional muddy spots with no water in them to drink.

As he went, the cracked red sandstone walls of the canyon narrowed more and more. Another quarter mile and the cliffs converged at two pillars of stone standing close together. Then Mase saw the landmark. The rough pillars, looking like stacks of heavily eroded blocks, were of uneven size. The taller one on the right was topped by the landmark. Crane had scrawled "Devil's Head Pass" by a crude drawing of a rock formation shaped like a head with two horns. There it was: a giant horned head of red stone—a misshapen head without a face. One of the horns was broken off, but it was in the right place at the northeastern side of the canyon pass. This was the canyon's end, leading into the open country on the southeast side of Leadton.

He drew out his spyglass and scanned the land visible beyond the natural columns. There was a tumble of boulders to either side of the rocky corridor's northern end, then open ground leading to low hills. The hills were covered with grass and cut by a clear trail north.

Mase lowered the spyglass, smiling with relief, and turned back toward the camp. Crane's woefully incomplete, bad scrawl of a map had proven itself.

He rode quickly back to Pug and said, "The pass is a few miles ahead! Let's get 'em through!"

Pug rode back, issuing orders, and the drovers increased their push on the herd, sending it stumbling faster on toward the shadow of the Devil's Head. The dust rose around the herd, cowboys coughed out their calls to urge the cattle on, and they moved slowly northward.

The day was wearing on, shadows stretching out, when they reached Devil's Head Pass.

Lorenzo was driving Ol' Buck up toward the opening between the stone columns—when a shot rang out.

"Hold up!" Mase shouted. He could see thin blue smoke rising from a tumble of boulders at the base of the right column.

Lorenzo halted in uncertainty. "Get under cover!" Mase shouted. Lorenzo rode back to the cover of the chuck wagon, followed by Ol' Buck.

Mase rode left, heading for the rocks under the western pillar, looking for cover himself. He waited for another gunshot, but heard nothing. *Must've been a warning shot,* he guessed.

Mase reached the pile of rocks. Grabbing his rifle,

he dismounted in the shadow of a boulder—when a familiar voice shouted to him, the words sounding eerie through the narrow stone pass between the pillars.

"Durst!" It was Fletcher's voice. "That was a warning shot! You've come to my land! You will pay a toll of half your herd to pass through!"

"Only half, Fletcher?" Mase called. "Why not seventy-five percent? Dream big!"

He heard Lorenzo and Dollager laughing from the chuck wagon at that.

"It's my land, Durst!"

"It's Indian land!" Mase shouted back. "You're a damned liar, and you're getting not one cow and not one penny!"

"I've got a lot of men here with me, Durst!" came the shout from Fletcher. "You can pay up, or you can go back the way you came! We control this pass, and there's no other way through!"

Mase heard hoofbeats and turned to see East Wind riding up.

"Pug sent me to ask what you want to do."

Mase turned and shouted, "We're gonna talk it over, Fletcher! Hold your fire!"

Then Mase said softly, "East Wind, you go back and tell Pug we're going to run the cattle through when I give the signal. And every man is to fire over the cattle through that pass! They don't need a target! The gunshots will drive the cattle hard and drive the rustlers to cover!"

"What signal, boss?" East Wind asked.

"I'll fire my rifle twice—the second shot is the signal. I'm going up on this rock pile here and see if I can get a shot at these varmints."

East Wind nodded and galloped back toward the herd.

Mase went to his horse, got his spyglass, and used it to scan the tops of the stone ridges and the columns. He saw no one there. He figured the rustlers were in the rock piles on the other side of the pass. He suspected Fletcher was lying about having a lot of men with him. He put the spyglass in his pocket and looked up at the big mound of rocks. The rough-edged red rocks were mostly bushel size, with a scattering of some half the size of a stagecoach. He started climbing.

He stuck to the smaller rocks, working his way up with one hand and the butt of the rifle, trying not to make any noise, wincing when his boot loosed a little gravel. He was about forty feet up when Fletcher called out, "Durst! If you don't quit stalling, we're going to dynamite this pass! It's no good to us! We got nothing to lose!"

Mase figured the dynamite was a bluff, too. He didn't want to reply and let Fletcher know he'd changed positions. He just kept going, climbing a few feet more, then started moving horizontally, creeping over ledges of fallen rock to a big boulder shaped like a haystack. There were smaller rocks running up one side of the boulder. Sweating now, his hand burning from the sharp rock edges, he started up the smaller rocks, praying they wouldn't come loose and take him down with them.

"Durst! Are you listening to me? I'll give you five minutes! I've got a good railroad watch right here!"

Mase reached the top of the smaller rocks and from there crawled on his belly across the top of the boulder. He inched forward—and saw three men on the east side of the pass about a hundred fifty feet from him. They were positioned in the rocks, staring toward the herd. Fletcher was there—judging by the hat—a little to the east of the others, mostly hidden behind a big rock. But Mase had a good shot at the other two.

Mase worked the rifle from his left to his right hand, tucked it against his shoulder, and aimed at the rocks just behind the men. He fired a warning shot, the bullet ricocheting as the rustlers looked around for the source of the gunfire.

"Fletcher!" Mase shouted. "Get out of those rocks and run! You can still leave here alive!"

Fletcher and the other men snapped their heads around to look up at him—and the two nearest opened fire with their revolvers. Bullets slashed over Mase's head. He picked a target and fired, and the man arched his back and then twisted away, scrambling behind a rock. Mase was sure he'd hit him.

Then came shots and shouts from the drovers, and the drumming of thousands of hooves. The herd thundered forward, driven by gunshots fired over their heads. The bullets cracked into the walls of the pass, ricocheting, kicking out rock dust.

Mase cocked and fired again, but the second of the two closest men was already clambering back.

Then the herd was stampeding through the pass, raising a cloud of red dust like powdered blood blotting out Mase's view of the pass.

The herd was stampeding out of the canyon, and he knew there'd be the devil to pay getting them all back in line. Still, the rustlers had one man down, they might not even be able to get to their horses in the chaos of the stampede, and Mase figured they'd get few if any of his cattle. The drovers were still sporadically firing over the herd.

Carrying his rifle, Mase quickly climbed down the rocks. He was glad to see his horse hadn't run off, though its eyes rolled in fear at the stampede and the gunfire. Mase mounted up, holstered his rifle, and waved his hat at the men to get their attention, his left hand signaling with a slashing motion as he shouted, "Cease fire! Cease fire!"

Pug understood him and took up the call. The gunfire shortly broke off. Coughing in the rising dust, Mase tugged his bandanna up over his mouth, drew his sidearm, and rode with the rear of the herd, squinting against the dust and sometimes shifting his horse to chase one of the beeves back to the herd.

It took time to get through to the open ground beyond the pillars, and it was a nervous passage for Mase and the cowboys, as they half expected to be fired on from the rocks to either side. But the stampede and gunfire had done its work—the rustlers were nowhere to be seen as the drovers emerged into the open range. . . .

KATIE AND JIM waited anxiously on the wooden walkway in front of the Butterfield stage office. It was a windy morning in May, and Jim had to keep a hand on his hat to prevent it from blowing off.

"Is it late, Ma?" he asked.

"Perhaps a little." It was a long way back to the ranch, and Katie hoped he was on this stage, as his letter said he would be. But she would come every day if necessary till he arrived.

Two ranch hands clopped by on their mules with the pleased looks of men heading to the cantina. Then Jim burst out, “There it is!”

The stagecoach was coming in from the west, streaming dust behind it, not in any real hurry, but its four horses rattling it along at a fair pace, and before long the stage had arrived. The driver called “Whoa!” and pulled the reins with one hand and the brake lever with the other. As the stagecoach squealed to a stop, its dust cloud caught up with it.

“Is he there?” Jim asked breathlessly, waving dust away from his face.

Forrest Malley stepped off the stage then, frowning down at himself, slapping dust from his coat. He was a middle-aged man in a three-piece dun sack suit and a homburg, a man with a small mustache just starting to go gray and a belly beginning to strain at his belt. Pince-nez hung from his lapel on a ribbon, the lenses catching the light.

“Uncle Forrest!” Katie called, stepping off the walk.

He looked up, his thick eyebrows bobbing, blue eyes widening, and a broad smile wiped his frown away. “Katherine!” he boomed in his deep voice.

He stepped over and clasped her outstretched hand in both of his. “Still the lovely young lady!” He looked down at Jim. “Who’s this young fellow with you? A cowhand?”

“I am that, too,” said Jim, raising his chin proudly.

Forrest laughed and stuck out a hand. “I guessed it was you! You’ve grown so! Why, you were no bigger than a jackrabbit last time I saw you!”

Jim took Forrest’s hand, and they had a solemn, manly shake.

"Have you had your breakfast?" Forrest asked, turning to Katie. "I have had none. The food at those stations is execrable."

"What's execrable mean?" Jim asked.

"It means very bad to the point of being nigh unholy, Jim!" Forrest said, taking his bag from the driver.

"There's a good café across the street," Katie said. "The food is not unholy. Right this way . . ."

They found a table by the café's window where Forrest ate a hearty breakfast of ham, eggs, and flapjacks. Jim had a second breakfast of flapjacks, and Katie drank tea. At last Forrest put down his fork, wiped his lips with the checkered napkin, and said, "Katie, we're going to have to go to Fort Worth to make our plea."

"Forth Worth! That's a long way, Forrest!"

"Your judge here, from what I can ascertain, isn't going to be any help to us. Now, there's Judge Holloway in Forth Worth. I was before him once, and he's got jurisdiction over the whole county—way down at this end, too. He's a hard man, but he's fair. Just now I've got to go over to the bank, introduce myself as your lawyer, and have a word with the manager. But I doubt I'll get him to budge if he's already started proceedings."

"He has." Katie took the paper out of her purse and handed it over. "It's right there."

He nodded, perched his pince-nez on the bridge of his nose, and peered at the document as Jim noisily applied himself to his flapjacks.

"Jim," she said, "I wonder if you could be persuaded to eat like a civilized person."

"I'm eatin' with a fork, ain't I?"

"*Aren't* I, Jim."

"Aren't you what?" he asked innocently.

Forrest looked up from the document. "It does seem they're within their rights to call in the loan. But if I can establish precedent locally . . . and take that to Judge Holloway, *maybe* we can get a delay till Mason returns with the money from the sale of his herd. But, Katherine—I can offer no guarantees."

DUSK. FIFTY-SEVEN DAYS into the drive to Wichita. Mase, Denver Jimson, and Lorenzo Vasquez came upon the appointed lawmen of Leadton waiting for them at the water hole. It was a muddy spot where the creek had widened into a kind of pond.

The sheriff and three other men, all with tin badges, were standing around near their horses, waiting, as Mase and the drovers rode up to them. Wearing a black suit and a derby, the sheriff was a man with a wide face, a cigar clamped in his big yellow teeth. He had a shotgun held in the crook of an arm and a Smith & Wesson revolver on his hip. The others wore six-guns—and the short, stout man with the bushy beard had his drawn. A man in a dirty yellow Stetson was standing with his arms crossed and a smug sneer on his face. He had long blond hair, his big ears sticking wildly out of it.

Mase recognized one of the other men; he had been with the rustlers—the man with knee-high riding boots, slicked-back hair, and pitted skin. He had one hand on the butt of his holstered gun, and he was giving Mase a look of undiluted hate.

"He's their boss," said the rustler, waving a hand at Mase.

"That a sheriff's badge I see?" Mase asked, looking at the man with the cigar.

"I'm Sheriff Greer," the man said, nodding. He glanced at Denver nervously, seeming to recognize him. "I'm the law in Leadton. And this here is part of Leadton."

"I don't see a town," Mase pointed out.

"Oh, we staked out the town bigger than the buildings and streets, mister. I heard your name was Durst?"

"Mase Durst. I'm bringing my herd through. Coming up from Texas." He pointed at the man with the high boots. "You know you've deputized a rustler?"

Greer shrugged. "I deputized Rod Kelso, is what I know. He told me him and his brother found those cows of yours. Said they were driven off from your herd by Indians."

"There were no Indians. Kelso and his friends are crooked as a dog's hind leg. Yesterday they tried to take half the herd by force, at Devil's Head. I warned them to get out of our way, and they opened fire on me."

"You shot my brother!" Kelso spat. "Doc says he ain't going to walk again. He's crippled up!"

"His own fault," Mase said. "He fired at me. Every drover on the drive will testify to it."

Lorenzo nodded. "We all see it. Mase, he fired a warning shot. Then Kelso, Fletcher, and those others, they try to kill him."

"That's right, Mike," said Denver. "That's how it was."

"You know this sheriff, Denver?" Lorenzo asked.

"Mike Greer? He was watching in Fort Griffin when Chester Kass and Fat Jack tried to kill me. He was a deputy there. Just stood around watching."

"You took care of them," Greer said. "I figured you would." He squinted at Mase. "You look like someone I know. You related to a Hiram Durst?"

Mase tensed at the name. He wanted to know what had become of Hiram, but he was afraid to find out, too. "I am. You know him?"

"He's done a little work for me. He's around."

Mase was going to ask for particulars—then he noticed Rod Kelso whispering to the squat, bearded "deputy." The man nodded and swung his pistol toward Mase—

Denver's gun was suddenly in his hand and pointed at the man with the bushy beard. "I dislike having a stranger pull a gun when I ride up. Makes me jumpy."

The man licked his lips and looked questioningly at Greer.

"Put the gun away, Cox," Greer said, sighing. "I never told you to pull no iron."

Cox holstered his pistol. Denver pointed his revolver upward—but didn't holster it.

"I'd kill you right now, mister," said Rod Kelso, staring at Mase. "But you got your gunman and your vaquero. You give me a chance, I'll gun you."

"Doesn't seem wise to give you the chance, then, does it?" Mase said dryly. "I'll try not to turn my back on you."

Denver laughed softly at that. Lorenzo grinned.

Mase looked at the sheriff. "You going to try an arrest?"

Greer rubbed his chin. "Thought about it. Figured I ought to hear your side. Not figuring on it now. But there's something else."

"What's that?"

"We charge a usage toll for the water and grass here for any farmer or rancher brings a herd through."

"How much would that 'toll' be?"

"That'd be four hundred dollars—in your case."

Mase snorted. "That's all the money I have—half of it's at the chuck wagon. I need that for supplies. And I'm not giving you any of my beeves. But I'll meet you in the middle. I'll give you two hundred dollars. Crane Williams told me something about this, and I brought that much along."

He reached into his coat, pulled out a roll of bills tied with string, and tossed it to Greer.

The sheriff caught it, untied the string, and flipped through the money. Then he nodded and stuck the money in his pants pocket with the air of a man planning to keep it. "Good enough this time. You've got twenty-four hours in town at that rate. Water and graze your beeves, get your supplies, and move on."

Kelso was staring at the sheriff in fury. "Mike, he needs to go down! Right here!"

"You going to do it?" Greer asked archly.

Kelso looked at the drovers—as Mase and Lorenzo pulled their guns. Mase just smiled at him.

"Don't make me shoot you," Mase said. "Be a shame to cripple up both brothers."

Kelso spun on his heel, stalked to his horse, mounted, and stabbed a finger at Mase. "Twenty-four hours is just long enough, mister."

Then he spurred his horse and galloped off toward Leadton.

Mase looked at the other two men with Greer. "These two aren't your full-time deputies, are they?"

Greer chuckled. "No. Just deputize 'em when I need to collect some money. Donkey there—" He nodded at the blond man. "He's half deef despite the ears. And old Cox—not much use. I do need to find me some good men." He gazed speculatively at Denver. "You ever want a job, Denver—come and see me. I'll pay you good." The sheriff turned away and mounted his horse. "Come on, boys."

"What you mean, I ain't much good?" Cox complained, pouting, as he climbed on his swaybacked horse.

Greer ignored him and rode off. Donkey looked confused, gaping first at the departing sheriff, then at Mase. Finally, he mounted his horse and rode off after the others.

"I probably should have killed Kelso," Denver said. "He'll be a problem."

Mase shook his head. "Then we'd have to pay the sheriff a whole lot more. Come on, let's move the herd up."

"I TOLD YOU," said Fletcher. "You can't roll over that man, Rod. Durst has got to be taken care of sly-like."

"I'll take care of him, one way or t'other," Kelso muttered.

They were drinking Old Overholt rye at the bar of the Jack of Hearts, about an hour past sunset. The place was starting to fill up, and the new piano player, a pretty lady with a stack of butter yellow hair atop her head, was playing a Stephen Foster song.

"Greer should've let us cut down on them when they come riding up," Kelso growled.

"Way I heard it," Fletcher said, leaning close to be heard over the piano without raising his voice, "is the sheriff doesn't want to cross Hiram Durst unless he has to. And he figured out that this Mase Durst and Hiram were kin."

Fletcher glanced over at Hiram Durst, who was in his usual seat, cuddling that damn ten-gauge. Hiram was talking to that tart he liked, Queenie. She was standing close in front of him, frowning, her hands on her hips. She seemed to be trying to convince him of something, and he was shaking his head. She probably wanted him to come and work at her place.

"The right moment comes," Fletcher said, "we can get Hiram, too, Rod. I've been interfered with twice by Mase Durst." He winked at Kelso. "That'll cost two Dursts. Anyway, we can still get hold of that herd. The whole thing next time."

"The whole herd? How you figure?"

"The trail will take him through Chuckwalla Wash. I know a spot—"

"He's got all those men."

"They'll run if we get Greer on our side."

"He wasn't no help today."

"I told you he wouldn't be. I said you were wasting your time going with him. He wants the sure money. But with the right enticement . . ."

"I don't want to wait. I want to kill that trail boss. You been to see my brother?"

"I saw him."

"All he does is swill that laudanum. When he runs out of it, he's crying like a woman. He's not going to walk without a crutch and probably won't be able to ride. What good is he? He's a ruined man, is what he is. And it's Mase Durst that done it."

"You think you're going to face Durst down?"

Kelso gave Fletcher a dark look. "You figure I can't?"

"I figure you oughtn't try. He's got too much backup. You just be patient. And stick with me. You'll see. Third time's the charm. . . ."

CHAPTER FOURTEEN

HALFWAY THROUGH THE afternoon and fifty-eight days into the drive to Wichita.

Dollager was driving the chuck wagon, Mase sitting beside him, as they bumped along into Leadton. Denver, Karl Dorge, Duff, and Lorenzo were riding along behind them. The wagon bounced over the rutted dried mud of the main street. It was a sunny day, but a cold wind sliced between the wooden buildings.

"There's the general store, coosie," Mase said.

They pulled up in front of the white-painted building; LEADTON GENERAL STORE was painted on its false front in ornate dark green lettering. Mase glanced around, noticing a dance hall and two sizable saloons on the street. The dance hall had a big sign with a painting of a poker jack and the words THE JACK OF HEARTS. Even from here he could hear the sound of a piano tinkling faintly from it. Farther down were the livery; a stock pen; a closed, boarded-over shop with a sign reading FANCIES; and a disused-looking building marked MINING ASSAY & EQUIPAGE. Across the street from the general store were a blacksmith, a feed store, and a large redbrick building with the sign WINGER'S SLAUGHTERHOUSE AND BUTCHER SHOP.

"Look at that—a slaughterhouse and butcher shop both in one building!" said Denver, smirking.

"Can't imagine my old ma shopping at a place like that," Dorge said.

"At least the meat in that place will be fresh," Dollager said, climbing down from the wagon. "I wonder if they have lamb."

"We can afford nothing so pricey," Mase told him, stepping down beside him. "Gave half my money to the town sheriff. We're going to be eating mostly whatever game we can shoot." He handed Dollager a small leather poke of money. "But you can get a side of ham if it's not too costly, and what supplies you can't do without: flour, kerosene, lard, and the like. Cornmeal, dried beans, and dried peas if they have them. I'll be at the blacksmith."

Mase turned to Dorge and Lorenzo. Mase had announced two men would be able to have a look at the town and a drink or two, and they'd drawn the winning lots. "Go ahead and get a drink if you can afford one. If you've got any money, keep a hand on it. This burg'll be alive with pickpockets."

"Come on, Lorenzo," said Dorge, beaming at the thought of beer. "Let's try the Jack of Hearts!" They rode off toward the dance hall, chuckling over their good fortune.

Mase took a bag of cracked horseshoes out from under the seat of the wagon and carried it over to the blacksmith. The rocky ground of the Red Trail had ruined many a horseshoe. Denver dismounted, tied his horse to a wagon wheel, and followed along behind Mase, a self-appointed bodyguard. He and Pug had insisted, and Mase had given in.

Mase glanced at him, saw the way he had the holster of his Smith & Wesson revolver tied low on his thigh. He remembered what had come out when they were talking to the sheriff about Fort Griffin. And what Pug had said about his time around Denver Jimson. "Denver," Mase said, "seems like every time I learn something new about you, I'm a little more surprised you came along on this drive. Sounds to me like you've got other skills that'll bring you more gold than punching cattle could."

"Those skills are just as likely to get me back shot as paid," said Denver. "I've had enough of that kind of living. I'm trying to learn some other trade. And I was broke when I heard you were hiring."

"There's always lawing."

"Did that for a couple years. Deputy in Virginia City. There is no more melancholy work, boss."

Mase nodded. "I can believe that."

They found the blacksmith just taking off his gloves beside his glowing forge. He wore leather overalls with no shirt; he was a big man who looked to be half Indian and half black. Mase introduced himself and Denver, and they both shook the blacksmith's hand.

"Name's Brightwater," the blacksmith rumbled.

"Got a bag of horseshoes here," Mase said, passing them over. "Hoping you can fix some, replace what you can't. We can fit 'em to the right horses at the drive camp."

Brightwater nodded. "What outfit you with?"

"I run the Durst Ranch. Herding to Wichita."

"Durst! You related to Hiram?"

Mase was startled to hear his brother's name again. "If he looks a little older than me but not so different—that's my brother."

"That's the man. Good fella. Always pays me right off. Treats me square. Him and Queenie don't put on airs."

"Queenie?"

"She's running the Stew Pot for Murch Sanborne. He ain't much, but I like Queenie, anyhow."

"What's Hiram doing around here?"

"Works over at the Jack of Hearts. He's the guard. They kept having trouble. He cut a man down not long ago in there. Outlaw name of . . . Cleland, I think."

Mase nodded. "Sounds like Hiram." Always skimming along on the edge of the law, looking for a meal ticket to the high life. And if it was a risky job, all the better.

"I can have these for you in the morning," Brightwater said, looking in the gunnysack.

"That'll do. We're moving on tomorrow afternoon."

"Say boss?" Denver said, giving Mase an inquiring look.

"Yeah?" Mase knew what he was going to ask.

"We going into the Jack of Hearts, or ain't we?"

"I didn't want to leave those two cowboys in there long, anyhow."

"That mean I can buy you a drink?"

"One beer if you've got the money. I'm not paying advances."

"I've got a dollar or two."

They waved goodbye to Brightwater and went down the street, passing a barbershop and a bakery before crossing to the Jack of Hearts. Mase was nervous about seeing Hiram but stirred with curiosity, too.

The double doors were nicely paneled, with red glass inlays shaped like hearts. Mase took a deep breath and opened the doors.

BINDER DOESN'T LIKE me sitting here with you, Hiram," Queenie said as she sat down beside him at the little table near the stage. The dancers were taking a break and the piano player, Milly, was playing a slow sad song that seemed to be making an old, bearded miner weep as he sat close beside her, whiskey bottle in hand.

Hiram put his coffee cup down and said, "Well, Binder figures you're spying or some kinda saboteur for Sanborne. He can go and pound sand for all I care." He had his shotgun propped on his left leg, pointing at the ceiling. It was getting heavy, so he moved it to the right.

"I *am* trying to do him a dirty," she said, chuckling. "I'm trying to hire you away! Sanborne is giving me hell for keeping time with Binder's man. He wants you at the Stew Pot."

"Sure, so he can start sending the gun-flashy saddle bums in here again. Any which way, I'm doing fine right here. I'm saving up, and when I've got enough, you and me are going to New Orleans. You want some champagne? Binder got some in. I figure we—"

He broke off, staring. His brother, Mase, was standing at the bar.

Mase was looking trail worn, with a day's beard on him and some sunburn. But he looked like a man who rode tall in the saddle, upright and strong. There were lines at the corners of his eyes that somehow bespoke the man he was.

Mase was looking around—and then their gazes met.

Hiram's mouth went dry. He felt his heart sinking, and he wondered, *What's wrong with me? I've got nothing to be ashamed of.*

He took a deep breath, stood up, and walked across the room.

"Aren't you going to drink your beer, little brother?" Hiram asked, gesturing at the untouched glass on the bar. "It's not bad here. For Leadton, anyhow."

Mase smiled. Those lines at the corners of his eyes deepened. He put out his hand, and the two men shook. It was a handshake that suited acquaintances more than brothers meeting after five years.

Hiram laid the shotgun on the bar. "Stanley, hold on to that for me, will you?"

The bartender nodded and stowed the street howitzer under the bar.

"What brings you to this run-down old mining camp, Mase?" Hiram asked.

"Running a herd through. All the other trails were shut down. Floods and Indian trouble. This one's not much better." He hesitated, then said, "Have a drink with me, Hiram?"

Hiram was relieved to hear the invitation. It was a shade friendlier than a handshake. He hadn't been sure where they stood. They'd quarreled when last they'd seen each other. Mase had told Hiram he didn't like the company his brother was keeping—men with bad reputations. Hiram was the older brother—but Mase often acted as if he were the older one.

"Sure, I'll have a beer. I need a champagne, too, Stanley," he added to the bartender, seeing Queenie bustling up to them.

She was looking narrowly between the two men, her brows knit, probably wondering why Hiram had walked off from her without a word.

"Queenie, this is my brother, Mason. Mase—this is the light of my life, Miss Queenie Jones."

"Well, listen to him!" she laughed. "That's the first time I've heard I'm the light of his life! But I have heard of you." She shook Mase's hand. "Hiram says you own most of Texas!"

Mase grinned. "Oh, I've got my piece of it, anyhow. Pleasure to meet you, ma'am. Folks, this is Denver Jimson. He's a drover for me."

"And almost figured out the job," Jimson said, shaking Hiram's hand.

Hiram looked at the clean-shaven man with the gun tied down and the lynx-eyed gleam, and thought he seemed more like a town lawman than a range hand.

Queenie accepted her flute of champagne and drank half of it off. "Why, it's *almost* cold," she said, setting it down. "Thanks for the drink, hon." She kissed Hiram on the cheek. "I've got to get back to work. I expect you two need to talk."

Hiram, Mase, and Jimson watched her walk off, and Jimson shook his head. "Fine figure of a woman," he said. He glanced quickly at Hiram. "If you don't mind my sayin'."

"Don't mind at all. Only it's look but don't touch, friend."

Jimson grinned. "Fair enough. Say, Mase"—he pointed at a smoke-wreathed table in the corner—"there's Lorenzo and Dorge. Took them no time at all to get in a card game. I believe I'll go keep an eye on them."

"Tell 'em it's going to be a short game," Mase said.

Jimson picked up his glass of beer and strolled to the table. Mase turned to the bar, drank some beer, and said, "Been a long time, big brother. You seem like you're doin' fine. Last time I saw you, you were riding with Goose Peterson and Cal Fogerty."

Hiram winced. "You can go ahead and gloat. You were right. I split up with them about two days after you went back to Dallas. Peterson was hung about a year after that, and last I knew, Fogerty was in the state prison."

Mase nodded as if he'd been expecting it. "I'm just glad you took a different trail. I hear you're working in this very establishment, keeping an eye on things."

"That's right. Sitting around in here about wears me out. Mase—how's Katie? And the boy?"

"Last I saw 'em, they were prime! Jim's already helping with the herd. He can ride, too. Not much more than a pony, but he rides it like a cowpuncher."

"I'll be damned! That little fella's chasing cows already?" Hiram shook his head in wonder, suddenly feeling that his own life had passed him by. What did he have to show for the last five years? A bullet scar on one leg and eighty dollars saved up. "Well—I'll tell you true. I've done little but bump from one job to another." He didn't want to mention his time in the south Montana range war. "Haven't put much by. But Queenie and I are talking about starting our own dance hall, down to New Orleans. Say—how many head are you running?"

"Around twenty-three hundred. Lost almost a dozen in a flood, and we've had two run-ins with a gang of rustlers. Fellow by the name of Joe Fletcher runs it. You know him?"

"I do. Never had the time for him. Might be in town if you want to find him." Hiram realized now that the cattle outfit Joe Fletcher had been talking about going after was Mase's. Hiram had heard before that Fletcher had twice tried to get a piece of some Texan's herd, and twice had failed. He hadn't known he'd been after Durst Ranch cattle.

Mase shook his head. "I've had enough trouble. We don't have time for him either. Got a herd to move."

"I don't know if he'd be fool enough to come after you now, if you've paid the sheriff off for free passage. But . . . best watch your back trail. And scout up ahead with your eyes peeled."

"You can count on that. Hiram, tell me about your plans with Queenie—and New Orleans."

Hiram smiled. It was a subject he liked better.

KATIE WAS JUST beginning to make supper when Jim ran into the kitchen. "Mama—it's that Tom Harning!"

She looked up from the kitchen sink. "Whereabouts?"

"Coming down our road right to the house!"

"Who's with him?"

"Nobody."

That surprised her. It was a relief, too. Unless he

had a gun in hand, she wouldn't likely need to get the shotgun or her pistol.

"Is your pony still saddled?"

"Yep, you said you were going to help me—"

"Never mind that. You take the pony, go on, and get Curly, just in case. Hurry up now. He's out checking on the new calves."

"Shouldn't I stay here and keep an eye on him?"

"If he's alone, it's all right. Go on."

He ran out the door. Katie took off her apron and changed her mind about the gun. Best to keep it handy.

She went to the bedroom, opened a dresser drawer, reached behind the pantaloons that she'd only worn once, and drew out the pistol.

Then she went out on the porch to wait for Harning.

He was about fifty yards out, cantering in on his high-stepper, wearing his best church clothes, and a friendly smile. There were two wooden chairs on the porch. Katie sat on one chair and put the gun underneath it, where it was hidden by her long skirt. She waited.

Harning rode up, dismounted, looped the reins over the hitching post, and said, "Mind if I sit down, Katie?"

She did mind. But she wanted to find out what he was up to with the minimum of trouble.

Let him talk at his ease for a time, she thought.

"Go on ahead," Katie said in a calm voice.

She saw no weapon on him. But it wouldn't surprise her if he had a small hideaway gun.

He stepped up on the porch and sat on the chair to her left. He took off his hat and fanned himself with it. "Surprisingly warm for May."

She said nothing.

He cleared his throat. "You and I have gotten off on the wrong foot. Things could be completely different between us, you know. Just the opposite." He leaned a little toward her and gave her a reptilian smile. "You're going to need my help—not my enmity, Katie."

"I have no need whatever of your help, Tom Harning," she said firmly, leaning away from him.

"Your husband, sad to say, bit off more than he could chew. I know all about that route he's taking. It's a fool's errand. A suicide trail." He softened his voice so it held a fair imitation of sympathy. "Renegades. Outlaws. Floods and disease. Rockslides. It's all to be found on that trail. I'm afraid we cannot expect him to return to you."

Her hands balled into fists on the arms of the chair. It took an effort to control her voice as she said, "Harning, I don't know what you paid the sheriff to lie to Curly Chavez. But I do know it was a lie."

Harning adopted a look of surprised innocence. "I paid the man nothing! He heard a rumor—I've heard it, too! Now, maybe that rumor was wrong. What I'm sure of is your husband left you here when things were unsettled. When there were legal questions and things were going wrong for you. He just left you! Who knows when he'll be back, Katie? Now, I can take care of you."

She looked at him, wondering if she'd heard him right. "What are you saying?"

"You won't have to work your fingers to the bone on this hardscrabble ranch! You can get yourself a servant! I'll pay for it all. I'll set you up—someplace comfortable. Maybe off in Fort Worth. I get up there regular. We can have an understanding. You'll be a woman of leisure and—" His eyes got big and his mouth clapped shut when he found himself staring into the muzzle of her pistol.

She had to take a long breath before she could speak. Her left hand was gripping the arm of the chair, and the trigger finger of her right hand was twitching. "Tom Harning. You have sent men to pull down my fences. You've sent hired guns to try to frighten me. You've sent men to target shoot at my property. You've fixed the judge and the sheriff against me. And I stood it. But I'm not going to stand this insult."

She cocked the gun.

He swallowed and raised his hands. "Now, Katie—"

"Stand up."

He stood up. His hat fell from his lap onto the porch boards, and she kicked it into the dirt.

"Pick up your hat," she grated, standing.

He stepped off the porch and picked it up as she tracked him with the gun. There was anger tightening his face now.

"Get on your horse. Don't say a word. Just get on it and ride off Durst land. When my husband comes home, you'd better hope he doesn't see you anywheres around here. Because he'll *cut you down*!"

Hand shaking, Harning crushed his hat onto his head, mounted his horse, and rode off. She watched him till he'd ridden through the gate. Then, feeling drained, she thumbed the pistol off cock and sank onto the chair.

"Mase," she murmured, "you'd better come home. You'd better get yourself home fast."

CHAPTER FIFTEEN

"YOU SURE YOU won't come out to camp for supper, Hiram?" Mase asked. Hiram and Mase and the drovers—who were only a little tipsy after an hour and a half in the Jack of Hearts—were standing out front of the dance hall. "We've got a cook John Chisum would envy."

"Can't do it, Mase," Hiram said, smiling. "Much as I'd like to. I've got business here. Me and Queenie have a plan, and I have to see to it. You coming in tomorrow?"

"Someone's got to pick up some horseshoes for the remuda tomorrow morning. I could do it myself."

"Well, I'm staying right here—they got rooms for rent up over the saloon."

"Supposing I come and get you for breakfast? I reckon you don't often get up that early, but . . ."

"I'll somehow live through it, Mase! You come and bang on my door, wake me up—and I'll drink a pot of coffee with you before you hit the trail."

"I'll do it. Hiram, I heard there wasn't much mail service to Leadton? Is that right?"

"It's true. We're damnably isolated. We don't have a post office or a stagecoach office—no Wells Fargo or Butterfield. Sometimes mail comes in—every couple months if we're lucky—with goods shipped down from Morrisville. The mayor collects it in his butcher shop."

Mase nodded. He'd told Katie she could try to write to him here, but the letter was unlikely to have arrived.

"Listen, Hiram—don't you kinda figure five years was too long?"

Hiram nodded. "It was, Mase. I'm sorry for it."

"You know where Durst Ranch is. You and Queenie could come down to the ranch for a spell. Katie and Jim will be happy to see you. I'm sure Katie would like Queenie."

"You think so? Queenie's a . . . well, a free-spirited sort of woman. If you know what I mean."

"Katie's free-spirited herself, just in a different way. She respects strong women, and Queenie seems like she'd fill the bill."

"She's a strong one, all right. Figures out what she wants and goes for it. And no shrinking violet. Fella tried to rob the bar once, and she shot him with a derringer. Didn't kill him, but it put an end to his capers."

"Now I know Katie'd like her! You know, if you wanted, big brother, there's something else you could think on, too—" He hesitated, then gave a small shrug and said, "Well, we can talk about that tomorrow."

Mase clapped Hiram on the shoulder and turned away, leading the three drovers back down the street.

Hiram watched them stride away. His mind was on what Mase had told him about his run-ins with Joe

Fletcher. The rustler boss just might not be willing to let loose of Mase's herd. Might not care what Greer thought about it. Come to think of it, who knew how deep Greer was in Fletcher's doings? Joe Fletcher had powerful connections around town. It came to Hiram then that his brother might be in far more danger in Leadton than he realized.

He'd already warned Mase. But there was someone else he could warn. . . .

Hiram set off the other direction, toward the Miner's Delight Saloon, where Joe Fletcher liked to play cards.

Fletcher wasn't hard to find. He was in the back room of the Miner's Delight, the high-stakes game. When Hiram came in, he found the place choked with cigar smoke. Sheriff Greer was there, peering at the cards in the pool of yellow light from a lantern hanging over the green felt table. Fletcher sat across from him. One of the players was Chas Winger, the slaughterhouse owner and the town's mayor. He was a burly man in shirtsleeves, counting up his money as he considered calling a bet. Next to him was Rod Kelso, who scowled at Hiram but looked fixedly back at his cards.

"Open a window while you're standing there, won't you, Durst?" said the sheriff, glancing up.

Hiram went to the window, struggled with it, then got it halfway open. Cold air blew in, and cigar smoke blew out.

"You plan to sit in on the game, Durst?" asked Fletcher, folding his cards.

"Hoping to have a word with you, Joe," Hiram said. "Outside."

Fletcher sniffed and said, "Boys, hold my spot for me." He got up and led Hiram out the back door.

They stood in the alley, where a couple of horses were tied up, the animals shifting impatiently as they waited for someone to take them to a barn where there was feed and shelter from the cold wind.

"Colder'n I thought it'd be out here," Fletcher said, hugging himself. He scrutinized Hiram curiously. "You have the air of a man on business, Hiram. Last time we spoke, you had your nose in the air. Something change?"

"Yes and no." He took a moment to think about it; then he said his piece slowly and in a low, flat voice. "Last time we talked, you asked me to help you steal a man's cattle. That was none of my business, so I didn't say anything about it to anyone. Only now it seems it was my brother you tried to rob. I've gotten to know you some, Joe. You're not a man to let a chance go. You know Mase and his outfit are still around, and I calculate you got something planned for him." He put a hand on the butt of his pistol and went on. "I'm here to say—don't try it. I'll warn him, Joe, and I'm going to find him and back his play. I'll ride with him all the way to the Kansas border and maybe farther. I don't care how many men you bring. I'll hunt you down and kill you if you make a move against my brother. I'll splash you all over like I did that fool Cleland."

Fletcher's cheeks were burning, and so were his eyes. But he managed a sour smile. "You've got me all wrong. I've got nothing planned. Your brother has too many guns with him. I won't risk it." He put a hand on his own gun. "But, Hiram—don't ever threaten me again. You won't live to make good on it."

With that, Joe Fletcher went back into the saloon.

Hiram shivered, maybe from the cold wind, and then walked out of the alley, thinking that if Joe Fletcher's lips were moving, it was a good bet he was lying, which meant he was lying about not going after Mase again.

Hiram walked out to the dirt road behind the buildings along the main street. There wasn't much back here, mostly storage sheds and privies. He walked thoughtfully up the road toward the Stew Pot, deciding he wanted to see Queenie. He thought as he went that he would tell Mase in the morning, early though that might be, that Fletcher planned something—probably an ambush. He'd let his brother know he was going to ride with him at least to the Kansas border.

Right now Hiram figured to get Queenie to go to the café with him, have some supper. He needed a woman's company to ease his mind.

He reached the back door of the Stew Pot—and then heard the sound of a gun cocking. He turned, his hand going to his gun, but the man standing in the shadows was already firing, and everything went red . . . and then deep, velvety black.

IT WAS ANOTHER cloudless day on the Red Trail as Mase rode back into camp the next morning, but that cold wind from the north was still nipping at the drovers.

"Everything okay?" Pug asked as Mase dismounted.

Mase wondered how Pug had figured out something was bothering him. He prided himself on being tolerably stony faced. But Pug, a quiet man, was always watching, looking close. He knew.

"Not sure," said Mase, untying the bag of horseshoes on the saddle horn. He handed the clinking bag to Pug. "Went to get my brother, Hiram, for breakfast. He didn't answer the door. It was unlocked—looked like nobody'd slept there."

"You sure you had the right room?"

"I checked. They said he hadn't come back last night. That bartender said it was surprising. Hiram was supposed to be on watch at the dance hall after suppertime, and not showing up isn't like him."

"From what you told me, he's always been a wild one. Maybe got into an all-night poker game. Hard to quit if you're winning—or for some people if you're losing."

"Maybe. Well, he can find me if he wants to."

"Did you ask in town about mail?"

"I asked at the butcher's shop and the sheriff's. Nothing for us. Let's get the herd moving. We're heading for Wichita."

Pug nodded and stalked off, calling at the top of his lungs to the drovers, "Move 'em on! Let's go! Head 'em north!"

Mase tied his horse to a wagon wheel and went to the big coffeepot for a cup of Arbuckles'.

Dollager looked up from cleaning tin plates. "You have your breakfast in town, sir?"

"Nope."

"Full out of porridge, but I've got biscuits and bacon."

"That'll do. You finish up there quick as you can, coosie. Get East Wind to help you harness up the oxen. We're back on the trail."

As Mase ate, he thought about the trail ahead. The

upper part of Crane's map was sparse. It named a place called Chuckwalla Wash about four days north with a mark for a spring and a scrawl that might say "Shepherd's Crook, high rocks, narrow." Beyond that, the map was unmarked except for the line of the trail, trending northwest, but if his memory of what Crane had told him was good, it was a clear trail, with good grass, up to Morrisville, where it rejoined the Texas Road in Kansas, which would take them to Wichita.

Mase finished his coffee, washing down a bite of bacon and biscuits. Then he remounted, setting out with Pug riding beside him to the drag of the herd so they could help get it moving.

It was more than an hour before they got the entire herd up and grudgingly traveling north.

Their route that day took them over a series of low, rolling hills for about five miles, then down into a shallow, flat-bottomed valley between two spiky granite ridges. The wind bit at them, stinging their noses and earlobes, but it was nothing compared to some real winter cold Mase had experienced on cattle drives. One drive that had started too late in the year ran into a series of blizzards and ice storms; the weaker cattle died, water barrels burst, and one of Mase's good friends lost part of his nose to frostbite.

On they went into the bitter wind, Mase pushing the herd harder than usual till the cattle bawled complaints. They were more than two-thirds of the way through the drive now, and Mase was feeling a renewed sense of urgency. Some instinct whispered to him that he was needed at home—needed badly. Mase was a little more worried about Katie and Jim every day. Now his mind chewed over concerns about Hiram as well. Maybe he should have hunted up Queenie, seen if Hiram was with her.

There was no use thinking about it now. Like as not, Hiram was doing just fine.

A BLAZE OF pain woke Hiram up. Everything was dark and fuzzy—except the pain. It was like a buzz saw in his chest. "Lord and hellfire, what is that . . . ?"

"Lie still," growled the doc. "That's a bullet coming out of you."

"Clamp your teeth on this, honey," said Queenie.

He felt a strip of leather pressed between his jaws. He bit down and writhed as Dr. Teague dug roughly into him. He could smell brandy and coffee on the doctor's breath; he could hear the man's raspy breathing. The pain became shriller. . . .

Then he felt an inner *pop*, and the worst of the pain ebbed away.

"There it comes," muttered Teague. "One inch higher you'd had it plumb through your heart."

"Where am I?" Hiram asked. It hurt to talk—every word hurt separately.

"My room," said Queenie. "Sally found you this morning out back, just lying in the dirt. You got a crease in the head—cut right along the side of your thick skull there, Hiram. Me and the girls bandaged you up. The doc was . . . Well, we couldn't find him till about an hour ago. Who shot you?"

"Couldn't see his face," Hiram said. "Shape of him—thought it was Greer, maybe."

"What! The sheriff?"

"Maybe . . ." He ground his teeth at the pain. ". . . has a . . . deal with Fletcher."

"And he left you for dead!" Queenie burst out. "He was pretending he was all surprised, hearing about it this morning!"

"Not sure . . . it was him."

"I don't want him talking now," said the doctor. "And I don't want to hear any more about this nohow. Don't ask me to repeat any of it anywhere. I don't want to be found shot in any alley. Now—you drink this down, Hiram. . . ."

Hiram felt a bottle thrust between his lips, and syrupy liquid, sickly sweet with a nasty aftertaste, gurgled down this throat. He coughed, spat some of it out. Knew it was laudanum. "No more of that . . . I got to—"

"Just lie still and heal up, Hiram," Queenie said, kissing his forehead. "I'll keep watch over you."

"Have to . . . Mase needs . . ."

But the laudanum was doing its work. He sank away into a muffled, cottony world of shadow-veiled dreams. . . .

CHAPTER SIXTEEN

It was sixty-five days into the drive as Mase rode back to the herd. He had been scouting north, and it was his guess they'd be out into the open range south of Morrisville in a day, two at the most. It was the cusp of evening; twilight was upon them, drawn over them by the long fingers of shadows stretching from the spiky gray ridges to the west. According to Dollager, as he'd spooned out the noon meal, the ridges looked like "the broken battlements of a bombarded castle."

Now Dollager was at work on the evening meal. East Wind and Harry Duff had gone out when camp was called and caught three grouse and two jackrabbits. The cowboys were sitting on the ground nearby, plucking and skinning.

Jacob and the other drovers were out making sure the cattle were settling in. All except Vinder, Mase saw, as he rode in behind the cowboy. Ike Vinder was drinking coffee and talking at Duff, who was just finishing cleaning a bird. Duff seemed to be trying to ignore him.

"I just think we all should've had a spell in town, not just two men," Vinder was saying. "Hell, we've been on the drive for a long damn time, and it seems to me—"

"Seems to me like your big mouth's about to get you in trouble once more," said Duff, winking at Mase.

Vinder turned and blanched, seeing Mase looking sharp at him.

"You enjoying your coffee, Ike?" Mase asked dryly.

"Boss! I was just— I was going to ask the coosie if he needed more wood for the fire. There's a dead tree over yonder." He put the coffee cup on the ground by the pot. "I'll just head over—" He started to walk away.

"Hold it right there."

Vinder reluctantly turned back to Mase. "Boss . . ."

"If you've got complaints to make, Vinder, why don't you make 'em to me?"

Vinder looked away—Mase saw his fists clench and knew the aging cowboy wanted to answer back. "Just say it to me right out, Vinder. Or do you prefer to grouse behind my back?"

Vinder cut him a cold look. "A man's got a right to let out a growl now and then! It's a long drive and for scant pay!"

Mase raised his eyebrows at that. "You didn't say anything about the pay when you signed on."

"It was hire on or give up eating. I was broke!"

"Go get that wood. Then you find a horse and get out on the herd. You're taking two watches tonight, back to back! Now *get*!"

Vinder's jaw muscles worked; then he stalked away from the camp into the thickening darkness.

There was silence as Mase drank some water, ladling it from an open barrel. Then Dollager said, "East Wind, save out the hearts and livers of those unfortunate creatures. I can use them in my cooking!"

"Well, if you put 'em in my stew, don't tell me 'bout it," said Duff.

Mase got back on his horse and rode out to find Pug and have a look at the herd. As he went, and as the sun sank below the ridge, it struck him that there was a strange feeling in the air tonight. He felt like something or someone was watching him as he rode along.

The rustlers? Or something else?

"YOU'RE A DAMN fool if you do this, Hiram!" Queenie snapped as—grimacing with pain—he stepped into the saddle. "Hell's bells, it's getting dark! You'll get lost out there!"

"There's a moon. That herd's tracks can't be missed."

"Get down off that horse this minute, Hiram Durst!"

"Can't do it. Wasn't for that damned laudanum, I'd have gone days ago."

They were outside the livery, Hiram sitting on his restless horse now, buttoning up his overcoat against the chill of the coming night. He could feel the wound in him, piercing and angry, just under his rib cage on the left side. His head throbbed under its bandage.

Queenie stood close to the horse, one hand on the cantle. "Send someone else, Hiram!"

"There's no one else I can trust. Move on out of the way, my sweet Amaryllis Jones. I'll see you soon's I can get back."

"Why, riding that horse on the trail the way you are now, you'll die before you get back!"

Hiram reached down, gently pushed her out of the way, and spurred his horse into the street. "See you soon, Queenie!" he called.

He cut into an alley to take the back road and avoid passing in front of the sheriff's office. He wasn't sure it had been Greer who'd shot him. He hadn't seen the gunman's face, nor a badge. The sheriff hadn't come to finish the job as he lay sick either. But then, Queenie had made sure she or one of the Stew Pot girls had been with him the whole time.

Every clop of the horse's hooves sent a streak of pain up through him. He'd healed some. But not enough. And he knew it. But when he'd woken up this afternoon, he'd taken the laudanum bottle and tossed it out a window. Kind of wished now he'd brought it along.

Somehow, he'd get to Mase. He figured he could catch up with the slow-moving herd in a couple days if he rode fast enough. He had to warn Mase . . . and stand by him.

Or die trying.

MASE WOKE SOMETIME after midnight, feeling that something was wrong. As he sat up, it came to him that the cattle were fidgety, and at the back of his mind, he thought he'd heard a wild cry in the night as he slept, something chillingly feral. Had it been a dream?

He pulled his boots on and was in the saddle within a minute, riding to the herd, looking for the night watches. He could see East Wind in the moonlight on the western side of the herd, drifting along on the mule. Something about his posture spoke of wariness.

Mase heard that call again from the darkness, off to the east. A yowl, a scream—a panther's hunting scream.

Mountain lions roamed western Oklahoma, and there could well be one come down from the ridge. It would have scented the herd and already be hunting down a manageable steer.

Coming to the eastern side of the herd, Mase looked around in puzzlement. Where was Ike Vinder? He should have still been out here since Mase had given him back-to-back watches.

Mase rode around the southern end of the herd, moving east—noticing cattle getting nervously to their feet now—and spotted Vinder. He was drooping in the saddle, looked to be sound asleep, about a hundred yards from the cattle.

"Damn cotton-brained son of a—" Mase muttered, riding hard over to the cowboy. "Vinder!"

He had to call out three times before Vinder straightened up in the saddle, looking around.

"What the devil you doing, Vinder!" Mase demanded, riding up to him. "There's a panther out there!"

"A what?"

"A cougar, a mountain lion! What do you think you're about, sleeping in the saddle?"

"I . . . two watches out here . . . just closed my eyes for a second . . ."

"Why, your horse carried you off! Look where you are! Hell—just come on!"

Mase galloped back to the herd, Vinder close behind him. They circled around to the eastern side, and Mase slowed, looking at the ground and peering off into the night. He noticed that the herd was squeezed in on this side as if they'd moved away from something to the east.

Then, looking out that way, Mase saw something on the ground catching the light about fifty yards out. A red glimmer. He rode toward it and soon found a small pool of blood. They halted the horses, staring at it. Blood was smeared across flattened grass around it

"Lordy," Vinder muttered. "Cougar got one of the beeves."

"Maybe if you'd been awake, you'd have been able to shoot that cat." Mase dismounted and bent to try to make out the marks on the ground in the thin bluish moonlight.

He could see signs of a scuffle, with both hoofprints and a big cat's paw prints. The hooves were small—it was a yearling. Dead by now certainly, for near the pool of blood were drag marks. The panther had dragged it off to some den out east.

"Can't have it stalking the herd," Mase said. "Might follow the drag marks, see if we can catch him. Put a bullet in him."

He heard Vinder dismount, then came an intake of breath and the rush of boots. Mase spun and saw Vinder coming at him with a big hunting knife, teeth bared, eyes wild in the moonlight like some feral creature himself.

Mase stepped to the left, barely avoiding the knife blade. It slashed so close, it cut through the fabric of his shirt just above his belt.

He punched Vinder hard in the side of the head, and the cowboy groaned and stumbled a couple steps away. Mase reached for his pistol—then realized he'd left it at his bedroll. And his rifle was out of reach.

He stepped in close to Vinder and caught the wrist of his knife hand with his own left, swinging an uppercut at the man's chin. He struck solidly so that Vinder grunted and shook his head to clear it. They struggled for footing, Mase using his right to force Vinder back, trying to get him off balance. Vinder was trying to hit him and only punching Mase's shoulder.

"Let go of the knife, Vinder, and you can ride out of here!" Mase shouted.

"No! I only got one chance to . . ." Suddenly Vinder hunkered down and lunged, trying to ram his head into Mase's belly. Mase twisted Vinder's knife hand to block him—and Vinder shrieked.

Vinder twisted loose and stumbled away, dropping the knife and clutching at his neck. Blood spouted from a gaping slash wound in his throat; it fell to mingle with the yearling's.

Vinder went down on his knees; then, trying to rise, he fell over on his side.

Mase turned, hearing Pug and East Wind riding up.

"I heard a cougar—" Pug began. Then he broke off, cursing under his breath, seeing the dying man.

Mase went over to kneel beside Vinder. The cowboy

was shaking, weeping softly, as his lifeblood ran out past his clutching hand.

Pug and East Wind dismounted and came to stand beside them. "He tried to stab me in the back," Mase said hoarsely.

"Mase . . ." Vinder choked, spitting blood. "Harning . . . hired me. Two thousand dollars. Getting old and tired . . . Sorry . . . my saddlebags . . . Mase, I'm . . ."

Then he went into a fit of coughing, began to wheeze . . . and fell silent. Staring in death.

The three living men looked down at the dead one for a while.

"Harning put him up to it," Mase said at last. He was stunned, his pulse still banging away. "Must've been Vinder who shot at me. And pushed that rock down my way . . ."

"Surprised he didn't just shoot you in the back tonight," Pug said.

"Wanted to make it seem like the cougar did it," East Wind said, looking down at the tracks.

Mase nodded. "Most like." He waved a hand vaguely at the drag trail in the grass. "Cougar's out there somewhere. I don't think we'll go after it. Let's just put extra men on the herd. Tomorrow we'll leave at first light."

"I'll get some hands to bury him," Pug said.

Mase shook his head. "I killed him," he said. "I'll bury him myself." It simply felt like his responsibility. "Just get me a shovel from the chuck wagon."

"He talked about saddlebags," East Wind remarked.

Mase was thinking about that, too. He went to Vinder's horse and opened his saddlebags. Nothing special in the first one: a box of shells, string, scrap leather, a rock-hard old piece of chewing tobacco, and a bunched-up shirt. In the second bag, he found a package in oilcloth. He unwrapped it, revealing four sticks of dynamite.

"What the hell was he going to do with that?" Pug asked, scratching his head.

"Scatter the herd probably," Mase said. "Harning's idea, I reckon." He shook his head, wrapped up the dynamite, and put it in his own saddlebags.

HOW LONG WILL we have before the bank forecloses?" Katie asked as they waited for the stagecoach to set out. "He spoke a great deal, and I wasn't clear on that." She stood with Jim and Uncle Forrest in a thin rain just after breakfast, their baggage on the wooden sidewalk in front of the Butterfield stagecoach office in Fort Worth. The stagecoach and its horses stood off to her left, awaiting the driver's return from breakfast.

"Three months," Forrest said, smiling. "Plenty of time for Mason to return with the money to pay off the bank."

Jim was watching a troop of Cavalry with their blue uniforms, yellow belts and bandannas, riding past in two lines of horses. The clean-shaven officers wore sabers and had gold braid and shiny brass buttons on their coats.

"Aren't they a sight!" Jim said breathlessly.

"You were right about Judge Holloway," Katie said. "He never smiled once, didn't seem to approve of me—I think he figured we were trying to squirm out of a debt. But he was fair–he gave us the time to pay off the loan."

"He's a decent sort, down deep," said Forrest. "Ruled against me once and for me once. I couldn't fault either ruling."

The Cavalry passed on, and now Katie could see the two men across the street. They were standing there in front of Forth Worth Fine Libations. Andy Pike and Clement Adams. Pike was leaning against a porch post. Adams had his arms crossed. Both men were staring right at Katie,

"It's those men, Ma!" Jim whispered, taking her hand.

"I see them," she said in a low voice. She felt as if her stomach had suddenly constricted to a tiny ball inside her, like an armadillo rolling itself up.

"What's all this?" Forrest asked, frowning.

"Those two men across the street, Uncle Forrest–they work for Tom Harning. They've threatened us in the past. Adams there, the man with his arms crossed–he's a hired gun."

"Can it be coincidence that they're here?"

"Could be. But I suspect it isn't. I think they got word we were headed up here. I saw that man Wurreck in town when we were paying for the stagecoach. He must've told them."

"Well, by God, I'll have none of this!" Forrest growled. "I'll go to the constables! I'll find the sheriff!"

"They're not doing anything but watching," Katie said.

"Clearly they're trying to intimidate you, Katherine."

She nodded. "Well, I'm not intimidated."

"I shall seek an injunction! I shall—"

Then the stagecoach driver came out of the café and called to them, "Let's load up and hit the road, folks! Bring your bags over, and I'll stow them up top!"

"I'd rather just go, Uncle Forrest," Katie said. "I don't want to give them any excuses to . . ."

"To what, Ma?" Jim asked, looking up at her.

"I'm not sure. I don't want to find out. But I do want to be on my way home."

Forrest nodded. "You're in the right of it." He picked up their bags, carried them over to the driver, and handed them up. "Perhaps I should come with you after all, Katie."

"You have law business here," Katie said, shaking her head. "But we'll need you soon as Mase comes home."

"I'll come to Fuente Verde sooner than that—in a week or two, maybe three. Goodbye, my dear." He took hold of her shoulders and kissed her on the cheek. Then he shook Jim's hand. "Don't worry about anything, Jim. Those men are just trying to scare us. And we're not going to let them, are we?"

"No, sir!"

"Good!" Forrest opened the stage door for them, and they got in. They were the only passengers, so they both sat at the back, each by a window.

Forrest closed the stagecoach door and Katie wished she'd asked him to come along, after all. But he was stepping back now, waving, and the driver called out to the horses, snapped his whip. Then they were on their way, clattering down the road to the southwest.

They rolled and bounced along for about ten miles, leaving Fort Worth behind, before Katie was ready to look. She lifted up the leather cover over the little window beside her and leaned over, craning to look down the road behind. A considerable distance back were two silhouettes against the thin gray rain. Two riders steadily following along behind the stagecoach.

CHAPTER SEVENTEEN

An hour past dawn, Hiram began to feel feverish. He had been riding all night, and both he and his horse were shaking with fatigue. Hiram's pain was a steady dull ache that sometimes became a sharp stab of agony, and he longed to get down off the horse and ease the hurt for a spell.

He had been trying to find water on the trail for the horse, but he'd come across none. At last he reined in near a patch of scrub brush. He dismounted, grinding his teeth at the pain, and went to his knees in the soft, thick grass. After the pain ebbed a bit, he realized he was grievously thirsty. He grabbed a stirrup and pulled himself to his feet. He had two canteens of water and suspected he should have brought two more.

He unhooked a canteen, had a long drink, then poured some into his hat for his horse. It drank all that was there and licked the inside of his hat.

Hiram splashed some water on his face to cool the

fever, closed the canteen, and holding the reins, lay down where the scrub protected him from the wind. The horse lowered its head and cropped a little grass, then seemed to doze standing up.

The pain surged up in Hiram all on its own, and he groaned, thinking that maybe he would die out here. Coyotes or wolves would take his body, and nobody would know what had become of him. Not Mase, not Queenie. The only two people who gave a damn . . .

Queenie had probably been right about this. But he wasn't going to quit. He just needed a little rest. He closed his eyes and lay very still. Before long, sleep took him into feverish dreams of shadowy gunmen and skeletons lying forgotten on the prairie. . . .

A cold rain woke him. Hiram sat up, blinked around. The sun wasn't very much higher in the sky. A few hours had passed. Long enough.

He pulled his wet hat onto his head, got to his feet, slung the canteen over the saddle horn, and dug in a pocket for some jerked beef. He opened his mouth to the rain, got a little down him, and then bit off a piece of the dried beef. He started chewing very slowly. *Breakfast,* he thought ruefully.

Then—gasping with pain in his chest, head throbbing—Hiram stepped into the saddle and started off again in the tracks of the herd.

"BOSS, LAST NIGHT some riders passed us in the dark," Karl Dorge said as Mase drank his morning coffee. Most of the drovers were in camp, waiting for breakfast. "I heard them clear as a bell."

"Didn't get a look at them?" Mase asked, glancing

around at the valley stretching out, yellow and green, to the rocky slopes lifting the granite ridges. Nothing out there but a couple of hawks circling and the shadows of clouds chasing sun over the crags.

"Nope. Clouds were heavy. Couldn't see much. I heard their tackle and the hooves. Sounded like shod horses."

"Maybe you were wrong."

Dorge shook his head. "Don't think so."

"Perhaps," said Dollager, stirring the Dutch oven nearby, "they were riders from Leadton going up to Morrisville. I believe it does happen."

"Funny time to travel," said Dorge.

Mase nodded. He called out to the other drovers. "Anybody else hear riders pass us last night?"

They all shook their heads. Except East Wind. "Woke up. Thought I heard something. Too many to be our people."

"Might be Cavalry, might be anyone, but y'all keep your eyes peeled!" Mase called to them.

The cold wind had abated, and it was a hot noon when Mase was satisfied that the herd was well under way. He rode north, scouting the trail and watching for signs of trouble. He cut the tracks of the riders Dorge had heard, guessed their numbers at seven or eight. The horses were shod. Could have been US Cavalry. Could have been riders from some outfit. But it could have been an outlaw gang, too. He was glad when the tracks angled off to the northwest, away from his route.

Mase watched the ridgetops, peered into the dusty distance, saw no glint of metal, no smoke rising, no sign of people at all. It was a wild place, growing lusher as he went north. Everywhere about him were stretches of wildflowers, yellow and purple, as if the plain had been splashed with bright paint. The copses of honey mesquite were blooming, too. Small pines and junipers were growing on the slopes under the granite crags now. The air carried the perfumes of flowers and blossoming trees.

Mase was alone in a world that might not have changed much for hundreds of thousands of years; the valley floor stretched flat all around him, but far from lifeless. He came across a prairie dog colony where small tawny heads bobbed up, regarding him gravely for a moment as he steered his horse well clear of their holes. A gray fox was easing through the grass, stalking toward the prairie dogs.

A little farther on, Mase spotted tracks he thought were buffalo—there were still some small herds around—and the prints of pronghorn antelope.

A couple more miles and the flowers gave way to knee-high grass. In the distance to the northeast, he made out a rock formation where the eastern granite ridge hooked to the west, like the sharp curve of a shepherd's crook. It followed the rough shape Crane had sketched on his map. Somewhere in that crook was the spring, feeding a small pond where the cattle could be watered.

Mase rode hard for it, and in another half hour, his stallion lifted his nose, nostrils dilating, in a way he did when there was water nigh. He eased the reins and let the stallion follow its nose, and in half an hour more, he reached a pool of green water in the shadow of the southerly curving ridgeline. The spring was a silvery line running down the black rocks to the pool. There was plenty of grass around it, too. An ideal place to camp. They'd be stopping a little earlier than usual, but he wanted to fill the herd's bellies with water and grass before heading into the unknown between here and Morrisville.

Mase let his horse drink and rest in the shade while he peered up at the ridges, looking for signs of trouble. Nothing moved except a vulture shifting on a high rocky nest.

Satisfied it was safe here, he remounted and rode south to give Pug the good news.

"YOU JUST GOING to let him ride off like that?" Kelso asked.

"Yep. For now."

Joe Fletcher and Rod Kelso were stationed in the boulders above and to the west of the spring, in a hollow formed by a rockfall. It was dark in there, and Fletcher didn't allow Kelso to raise his rifle or gun. Mase Durst hadn't been able to see them back there. But they could see him.

"I need to kill all those men, not just Durst," Fletcher said. "I need him to bring them down here under our guns. We'll get the other boys into position once dark sets in. And we'll catch 'em all down there because there's no doubt in my mind he'll camp near that spring. They'll all be out there at the same time for dinner. Except a couple on the herd. Greer will get them in place for us."

"You really think you can get that whole herd?"

"Sure, and sell it, too. You, me, and Greer taking most of the money. We'll represent ourselves as men from the Durst Ranch. Been asking around—this is the first Durst Ranch herd up this way. No one knows a damn thing about him."

"Suppose they find our tracks?"

"That's why I led us the ten miles out of our way you complained about so we could loop back from the north. They won't live long enough to see our tracks, Rod."

"Greer take care of the other Durst?" Rod asked, rolling a smoke.

"He did. Left him for dead. I saw him still lying there. Nobody'd even found his body the morning we left. Rod—don't light that till Mase Durst down there is long gone. We're going to have a cold camp and a long wait on that game trail up there. But it'll be worth it. Hell, once we drag their bodies out of the way, we can take over their camp."

"First one to make sure of is that Denver Jimson hombre," said Rod. "He's a real pistolero, what I heard. And that vaquero, too. Most of them Mex cowboys can shoot."

"I'll take down Jimson myself. That'll be the signal to start the general shooting. We got to make it rain lead and use every round smart so no one gets out of that camp alive."

Rod nodded, watching Mase Durst ride off to the south. "I'm going to aim my Winchester for Mase Durst. Me, Rod Kelso—I'm going to be the one who makes sure he dies."

IT WAS ALMOST suppertime when the stagecoach arrived in Fuente Verde. Katie and Jim were tired from the long, dusty trip. There'd been only one brief stop on the way, and they were aching from hours of jostling.

Jim jumped out of the stagecoach, and Katie climbed gratefully out behind him. It was cool, but the sky was clear of overcast, already tinted a vivid orange-red to the west. She looked down the road, half expecting to spot Clement Adams and Andy Pike. But they weren't anywhere to be seen. They'd probably slipped off the road when she got to town.

The driver handed down her bag, and they started toward the livery where Katie's mare and Jim's cow pony, Sam Houston, were waiting.

But seeing Tomas at the door of his store, Katie hurried over to him. He had his keys in his hand, seemed ready to lock up as Mrs. Tilliver came out. The widow Tilliver was a stout woman in a long black dress; she had iron gray hair and far too much white makeup. Katie thought she looked like a flour bag had exploded on her. "Tomas!" Katie called out. "Before you close!"

He turned and appeared oddly dismayed to see her. That certainly wasn't like him.

Mrs. Tilliver snorted and shook her head, seeing Kate hurry up to them. "You're a brazen one, Katherine Durst!"

"Brazen?" Katie asked, not sure she'd heard right.

"Everyone knows what you done—what you tried to do. Poor Mrs. Harning!" The widow shook her head and stumped off down the wooden sidewalk.

Katie stared after her. "Tomas—what is she talking about?"

"I— It is not something I believe, Senora Durst."

"What isn't?"

He looked at Jim. "I wonder if your son would like

to choose a piece of candy. Make it two pieces. My gift!"

"Thank you, Tomas!" Jim said, hurrying into the store.

Tomas cleared his throat and said, "Senora—Tom Harning, he is telling people you are the seductress."

"The seductress? Of who?"

"Why—of him! Or—you try. This is what he says."

She felt her cheeks go hot, and an equally hot outrage rose up in her. "That lying son of a . . . goat!"

"Yes, ma'am. But . . ." Tomas said. "But"—he shrugged—"there are some who believe."

"Then they've learned nothing about that man! You know what he's doing? He's been trying to scare me out with threats. Now he's trying to shame me out of town with lies, Tomas!"

"Yes, ma'am." He sighed. "I am to say—that the padre wishes to talk to you."

"Does he, now? I'll give him an earful, too!"

Tomas winced. "Was there something you need in the store?"

"I was just wondering—have there been any letters for me?"

"No, senora. I am sorry."

"Never mind. . . . There are a few things I'll get if you've got time. And if you're not ashamed to sell to me!"

He smiled ruefully. "It would be my honor, senora."

THE DROVERS WERE just setting up camp in the faded scarlet light of sunset when East Wind spotted the rider coming from the south.

The camp was about two hundred yards short of the water, partly to give the cattle room and partly because Mase was nervous about camping close under the hook-shaped outcropping of granite rocks. The curving rock formation Crane had named the Shepherd's Crook was a little over two hundred feet high. Mase had scouted it a second time, looking up at the rocks, seeing no one there. A thick brake of pine trees and underbrush grew along the farther side, and he couldn't see past it. But now, as he sat on his horse near the chuck wagon and watched the cattle trotting eagerly up to the water hole, he found the woods troubling his mind.

Too much trouble on this trip has made you jump at shadows, he told himself. Maybe, though, he'd take a few men and do a wider search on the other side of the rocks. . . .

That's when East Wind shouted, "Rider coming!" He pointed south.

Mase turned to look and saw a man slumped over a cantering horse about two hundred yards off. The rider seemed to be holding on to the horse's neck to keep from falling off.

He had a shivery feeling inside him, seeing that slumped figure. It couldn't be. . . .

Mase galloped toward the rider and soon saw that it was indeed his brother, Hiram, holding desperately on to his horse. His hat was missing. Mase could see a bandage on his brother's head.

East Wind got there first, taking hold of the horse's reins to slow it down.

"Hiram!" Mase called as he rode up.

Hiram lifted his head, blinking muzzily. "Mase?" came the croaking reply.

"We got you, Hiram! Hold hard now!"

They soon had him laid out on a bedroll beside the chuck wagon. Mase gave him a cup of water. Grimacing, Hiram got up on an elbow and drank it. Denver, Duff, Dollager, and Ray were looking on with concern.

"How bad were you hit, Hiram?" Mase asked.

Hiram put the cup aside. His face was pale and drawn. "A graze and a pretty bad wound just under the rib cage there. They tried to make sure I wouldn't warn you, Mase. Fletcher and his men—they're up here after you. Right before I rode out, Queenie asked around for me. They rode out a couple days ago. He's hired more men. . . ."

"Which one shot you?"

"I'm not sure. It was dark. Might've been Greer."

"Say now!" said Dollager, coming over with a tin cup of soup. "You must lie down there, cowboy!"

"Mick, this is my brother, Hiram."

"Mick Dollager, Hiram," said the cook. "You must lie down—you're running a fever, sure!"

"Can't lie down," Hiram said. "We can't stay here, Mase. Most likely they're waiting for you right close. Shepherd's Crook's the best spot for an ambush. They'll try to wait till you're bunched up. . . ." He took the soup and drank some off and made a face. "Thought you said this man could cook!"

Dollager grinned. "I've put willow bark in it for the fever. It won't taste right, but it'll help."

Hiram grunted and drank a little more. "Get your men under cover or move 'em back, Mase."

"There were those riders in the night," East Wind reminded them.

"Must've been Fletcher's men," Mase muttered, nodding. He was furious at himself. He'd been careless.

He went to the back of the chuck wagon, keeping part of it between him and the rocks, and stared up at Shepherd's Crook. "East Wind!" he called.

"Yes, boss?"

"Ride out and tell Pug what's happened. Tell him not to bring anyone in closer till he hears from me."

East Wind ran to his horse, vaulted on, and galloped to the south.

"WAS THAT HIRAM Durst?" asked Fletcher, looking down at the chuck wagon. It was blocking his view of the man they'd brought in.

"Couldn't have been," said Mike Greer. "He's dead."

"Too far away to tell," said Rod Kelso.

Fletcher, Kelso, Greer, and Donkey were standing on the deer path at the top of the ridge. A jagged line of boulders stood ranged atop the rocky granite slope overlooking the spring and the flat ground beyond. They could see through a gap in the stones that most of the drovers in the camp were on the other side of the chuck wagon. The wagon was farther away than Fletcher had supposed. Four of the drovers were amongst the herd, far back from the ridge.

"They didn't camp as close as you figured, Joe," growled Rod Kelso.

"Won't matter," Fletcher insisted. But he wasn't sure. His ideal ambush hadn't panned out yet. The Indian drover had ridden out of range, and the others were too far off to be good targets. "We'll get the other men to move off east where they have a shootin' angle on those cowboys. They'll have to get down in the rocks and open fire from there." The other men—three of them, including Cox—were down the deer trail, waiting for the signal to jump up and open fire between the boulders.

"They'd be seen climbing down there," Kelso said.

"There's another way," Greer said. "Norton and Jimenez and me . . ." It was Greer who'd brought those two into the gang. They were partners in a robbery, but he'd let them go, pretending he didn't have the evidence to hold them, when they agreed to give him the stolen money—which hadn't amounted to more than a hundred dollars. They expected to get paid two hundred dollars each for this job. "Now, suppose I was to take them with me to the camp. I ride in showing my badge. Those boys with me will have their shotguns. I'll say I'm there to arrest Mason Durst. Saying he actually stole those cattle. Now, maybe those cowboys will surrender. If they do, we'll disarm them—and then shoot them. But if they don't, I'll tell Norton and Jimenez to open fire. They're mean as snakes and they like killin'. That'll cut down some of the cowboys and draw out the others."

"Pretty nervy of you," said Rod admiringly.

"I'm no fool. I'll keep back some and ride to cover the instant the shooting starts. You boys'll be off to the east. You can move out while I've got those cowboys busy, and get into position—start shooting soon's you've got your targets in sight."

"What about the others with the herd?" Fletcher asked.

"If they come running into range, we'll shoot 'em. If they try to ride off, why, we'll hunt them down."

"Liable to lose Norton and Jimenez before it's done," said Fletcher

"Ain't no loss. Won't have to pay 'em then."

"It's not a bad plan," said Kelso. "But there's gonna be one change. I'm going with you and those other two because I want to be the one who kills Mase Durst."

MAYBE," MASE SAID, turning to Denver, Ray, and Duff, "we can send some men around the Shepherd's Crook. They can keep out of gunshot range and see what's on the other side. Could be they're not up there on the Crook at all."

"Say the word, and I'll ride, boss," said Denver.

"Me, too, Mase," Ray said.

Duff nodded. "Let's go!"

"Okay, mount up. . . ."

But Dorge rode into camp then, calling out, "Boss—men coming to the camp from the north!"

Mase stood up and said, "Denver, Duff, you get on the other side of the wagon, pull your guns and keep 'em on these men. Karl"—he glanced at Dorge, saw he was carrying a rifle—"lie down flat and have that rifle ready. Mick—get under cover but arm yourself."

Mase walked over to the front of the chuck wagon and saw four men riding up. Two he knew, Sheriff Greer and Rod Kelso. The other two looked little better than saddle bums.

Remembering that Greer might be the man who shot Hiram, Mase drew his gun and pointed it at the sheriff as the men reined in. He aimed it right at the tin star pinned to Greer's vest.

"What do you mean by drawing your gun on me?" Greer asked. He backed his horse up some, a little behind the others.

"You shoot my brother in Leadton, Greer?" Mase asked, his gun unwavering.

Greer looked past him, saw Hiram on the ground, and his eyes widened in surprise. Mase figured that most likely meant Greer had expected Hiram to be dead, which answered his question.

"Hell no, I didn't shoot him," Greer said. "But there's been a crime all right. It's been reported to me that you stole these cattle!"

"Stole them?" Mase laughed. "Every single one of those beeves has the Durst Ranch brand."

"Easy enough to steal a steer before it's branded and put yours on it."

"Which particular liar reported my cattle were stolen?" Mase asked.

"None of your concern—till you're ready for court! You men will surrender your weapons to me, and then we'll decide what to do with the herd."

Mase shook his head. "Not a whisper of a chance because I know you're lying to me, Greer. And I know that Kelso there rode with Joe Fletcher. And Joe Fletcher's a cattle rustler. I figure Fletcher and his men are up there in those rocks."

Again Greer registered surprise. Then he snorted dismissively and said, "I'll give you half a minute to think on it. Then we'll have to throw down on you."

Mase snorted. "Just remember who my gun's pointed

at, Sheriff. Now—I know Kelso there. Who are these other two jumped-up deputies trailing along with you?"

"That's Deputy Norton on my left, with the ten gauge he's likely to use on you if you don't stop pointing that Colt at me," Greer said. Norton was a hatchet-faced man with sunken dark eyes and a goatee. He was wearing a dusty low-crowned gray hat, a raggedy frock coat, striped trousers, and silver spurs. "Fella on my right with the twelve gauge, just as likely to cut loose on you, is Deputy Jimenez." A shorter, darker, thick-bodied man with up-curling mustaches on his jowly face, Jimenez wore a tall-crowned *diez galones* sombrero and a black Mexican jacket with silvery braids. Both men had shotguns in their hands. Kelso, Mase noticed, had his hand taut on his gun butt, like a man itching to pull it.

"Which jail you pull those two out of, Greer?" Mase asked.

Greer's eyebrows bobbed up at them and again Mase felt he'd hit the mark. "Rod, get a bead on Hiram over there—and if his brother don't lower his pistol, take your shot."

Rod Kelso started to pull his gun—and Mase made up his mind in a split second. He couldn't risk Kelso shooting Hiram.

He swung his Colt to center on Kelso and fired.

Kelso screamed as the bullet caught him in the breastbone, and he dropped his pistol, flailing as his horse reared, while Mase was swinging the gun over toward Norton, who was leveling the shotgun. Mase had a bad feeling he was going to be too slow.

But then Denver Jimson's Smith & Wesson cracked

out a shot, and Norton twisted in his saddle, grinding his teeth in pain as his horse sunfished, while a shot from Ray Jost hit Jimenez, the bullet catching him in the teeth. His horse galloped in panic through the camp, Jimenez slumping in the saddle. Hiram was sitting up, firing at Greer. But Greer was bent low in the saddle as he galloped north like the devil was biting his tail, bullets from Denver and Duff whining over his head.

Norton was still alive, yelling incoherently with pain and fury as he swung his shotgun back to Mase. He fired—a hair after Mase had thrown himself flat. The blast went over Mase, and then Denver and Hiram both fired again, their two shots knocking Norton out of his saddle. One of the outlaw's feet was caught in the stirrup, and he was dragged away by the panicky mount.

Gunshots cracked from up above now, coming from betwixt the upper boulders along the ridge of the Shepherd's Crook. Mase got up and ran to his horse, pulled it to the shelter of the chuck wagon, and fished his spyglass from a saddlebag. A shot cracked into a water barrel on the ground by the wagon, and water spurted from the bullet hole. Two more bullets cut holes through the canvas cover of the chuck wagon. Gun in his right hand and spyglass in his left, Mase ran to the back of the wagon, crouched, half hidden by a wheel, and fixed the little telescope on the Shepherd's Crook. He slowly tracked the lens across the ridgetop, but couldn't see anyone. Then as a bullet cracked by, a puff of rifle smoke drifted up between two boulders. In a dark place under another boulder, a muzzle flash showed as another bullet thudded into the dirt to his right. Mase fired up at the gunmen but didn't have much hope of hitting them.

Heads ducked low, Denver and the others came to Mase's side and commenced firing at the rocks. Bullets smacked into boulders and ricocheted, and the already nervous herd began turning away from the water hole, beginning to run south.

"You can see the muzzle flash sometimes!" Mase called as the men joined him. "And their gun smoke!"

"The herd!" Ray said. "Mase—they'll stampede!"

"Pug'll know what to do," Mase said. As he spoke, he swung the spyglass to the south. After a few moments, he found Pug in the glass, waving at the other drovers on the herd, mouth open in a shout, calling the cowboys out of the way of the stampede.

The cattle were running full out now, bawling. And left behind was a dead steer hit by a stray round. "There's our meat for the next week," said Dollager, coming to crouch near Mase. He had a rifle in his hand.

Mase fired several shots at the gun smoke in the rocks, then drew back, seeing, from the corner of his eye, Hiram getting to his feet. "Hiram, stay down, damn you!"

But Hiram had a gun in his hand and a determined look on his face. "I can pull a trigger, by God!" He stepped over to the other end of the wagon and fired up at the rocks, then ducked back.

A bullet cut through the canvas top, right near Hiram's head. He ducked down, cursing to himself. Another bullet cut through, and the men huddled back, shifting closer to the wooden frame of the wagon.

Harry Duff suddenly called out, "Mr. Durst! There's two of them coming from the north over on the western side! They're on the ground! They're firing toward the oxen!"

The drovers hadn't completed making camp, and the big oxen were still harnessed to the chuck wagon. They stirred, thumping their heavy hooves, lifting their heads and bawling as the bullets cracked into the ground near them.

"They're trying to spook them into moving the wagon!" Hiram said. If the oxen ran off with the wagon, Mase and the others would be exposed to rifle fire from the Shepherd's Crook.

Hiram crept closer to the front of the wagon and fired toward the men on foot. But this spooked the oxen even more. Dollager ran up to the oxen—alarming Mase, fearful the cook would be shot down. Dollager, half crouched, took hold of the nearest ox's harness with one hand and with the other stroked the beast, talking to it, trying to gentle it down. The oxen were between him and the gunmen.

"We'll have to unhook the team!" Mase called as he ran to the tongue of the wagon, kneeling to tug at the bolts holding the harnesses to it.

But more bullets cracked, and the oxen began moving forward, pulling the creaking wagon. Mase had to jump back to keep from getting crushed by a wheel. Dollager set himself and tried to drag them back by the harness. Mase tried to move into a position that would give him a shooting angle on the men firing toward the oxen—but a hail of bullets drove him back under cover.

"They're not getting away with this, Mr. Durst!" Duff called in fury. He ran to one of the nervous horses staked nearby, loosed it from the stake, vaulted into the saddle, and six-gun in hand, rode toward the two men crouched on the ground by the rocks to the northeast.

"Harry!" Mase called, lifting his head enough to see past the oxen. "Harry Duff, get back here!"

"Oh, God, help that fool!" Ray muttered.

But Duff's fire had hit one of the men—it was Cox staggering into view, holding his blood-spurting neck, even as he fired back. So did Donkey beside him.

Duff was riding down on them, still firing. Then a round from Cox caught him, and he jerked in the saddle, cried out, and fell heavily to the ground as his horse ran in terror off to the north.

"Damn you!" Denver Jimson blurted as he stepped right out into view beside Mase, aimed carefully, and shot Donkey through the heart.

Bullets struck the wooden seat of the wagon beside Denver, spitting splinters that cut at his face. Denver threw himself flat as a round cracked where he'd been a moment before. Mase stepped back for a shooting angle on the Crook and fired at the gun smoke. A bullet sang by his left ear, and he ducked under cover again.

Shots rang out from the other drovers sitting on their horses west of the herd. They fired their rifles at the rocky slope, where puffs of smoke showed in two places close together. Mase figured that Greer had gone around the other side of the Crook and climbed back up to a high bushwhacker's position.

"Damned shame about Harry Duff," Ray said, shaking his head as he reloaded his pistol. "He was a good hand and devilishly young. . . ."

Dollager was still struggling to control the oxen as

Mase—fuming over the death of Harry Duff—made up his mind about what he was going to do. He ran back to his horse, calmed the nervous animal as best he could, and searched through his saddlebags. He came out with the oilcloth package, unwrapped the dynamite, and said, "Who's got a lucifer?"

Hiram, leaning against the wagon, handed Mase four wooden matches. "You really going to fool with that stuff?"

"I got to get far enough down under the spring—I'll need plenty of cover. Every last man of you needs to open fire soon's I start. If I do it right, we should be okay here."

"Not so sure of that," Hiram said.

"They're going to start firing toward the oxen from up there," Mase said, holstering his gun. "The team will start running. It's got to be done."

As if confirming the prophecy, gunfire cracked from high in the rocks, striking the ground behind the oxen.

Taking all four sticks of dynamite in his left hand, Mase said, "Start firing!"

Denver, Hiram, Dorge, and Ray started firing at the rocks from every safe angle they could find, concentrating fire where the gun smoke showed.

Mase sprinted toward the pool under the spring, running across open ground, every step taking him closer to the ridge where the men above would find it harder to hit him without coming out and exposing themselves.

Three bullets slashed by, and a fourth one gouged the skin of his upper right arm. He ran—and the world seemed to slow down; the air seemed thick with imminence, and the metal taste of fear was in his mouth. Another bullet slashed by his left thigh, cutting a pocket, and then he was in the shelter of a boulder. Breathing hard, his chest heaving, he knelt down, put the dynamite on the ground, and lit two of the fuses. Then he got a good grip on the sticks with each hand, stood up, and threw them, loopingly overhand, as far up as he could. The possibility of one of them bouncing back down to him haunted him as he lit the other two and quickly threw them, straining to get them even farther up the boulder-snagged slope.

The cowboys were still firing at the top of the ridge; rifle shots were being returned as Mase ran to the right, sloshing through the pond up to his knees. Two little geysers thrown up by bullets rose beside him. He reached the farther bank, slogged up the muddy sides, and ran on, staying close to the boulders for cover from gunshots—

Two booming explosions came close together. Pieces of rock crackled down, boulders rumbled; then two more booming blasts, and a great roar set up behind him as a section of the Shepherd's Crook collapsed, undermined by the explosions. There came the piercing shrieks of men from the rocks.

Mase swerved to the south to escape the boulders. He ran through low shrubs, expecting to be shot at. But there were no more gunshots, none at all.

He reached a copse of mesquite and dodged behind it, crouching, and turned to see the big boulders rumbling and cracking down the hill, splashing into the pond. A great cloud of dust and mist rose. Some of the boulders to the west had been knocked loose, and as he watched, one of them rolled raggedly down to crunch into the rear right wheel of the wagon.

The drovers were running back from the chuck wagon; Dollager, close behind them, was helping Hiram along.

The rumbling and crashing went on. . . .

Then it stopped. All but the rising dust and little patters of gravel.

CHAPTER EIGHTEEN

I LIKED HARRY Duff," Mase said as they all stood around Duff's grave that night, lit only by the moon and stars. Hiram was there, too, leaning on a crutch that Dollager had made for him. Every man there had removed his hat and bowed his head. Jacob had constructed a cross of wood for the grave and carved Duff's name on it, the year, and the words *A Top Hand*. It was the greatest compliment the men knew.

"He put his life on the line for us," Mase went on. "He was as good a hand as any man here. Could be that he saved my life. We lost a good man when we lost our friend Harry Duff." His throat contracted, so it was hard to talk, and he'd run out of words anyhow. So he looked over at Mick Dollager. "You wanted to say a few words, Mick?"

Dollager nodded. "I saw him ride out against men who were trying to kill us all—he rode straight at them! I thought of these lines from Shakespeare. 'Disdaining fortune, with his brandished steel, which smoked with bloody execution, like valor's minion carved out his passage . . . ' And that is simply how it was, gentlemen. All that's left to add is 'We therefore commit his body to the ground, earth to earth, ashes to ashes, dust to dust, in sure and certain hope of the resurrection to eternal life through our Lord Jesus Christ.'"

"Amen," the men murmured.

Somewhere, far across the prairie, coyotes yipped and howled.

Looking at the cross, Mase couldn't help but feel the weight of it. He was boss, and he was responsible for the lives of his men. Maybe he shouldn't have taken the Red Trail. If he had waited, like as not Harry Duff would still be alive. Then there was Hiram—who had gotten shot because he was going to warn Mase about the raid. He might yet die from his wounds if an infection set in. Mase had that on his shoulders, too.

He sighed. There was nothing for it but to try to make sure every man here got to Wichita safely.

Mase felt the sting of the deep graze he'd taken from a bullet. That pain reminded him of something. He cleared his throat and said, "Boys, those men were here to murder us—make no mistake about it. I'm grateful I had good men with me for that fight. Because we're not the kind of men they were, we'll bury their bodies. Not Greer and Fletcher—can't be done. East Wind and I found their bodies in the rocks. Not enough left of them to be buried. Once we've buried the rest of 'em, we'll start out after the herd."

"I've scouted it some," Pug said. "Most of them cattle are within a couple miles. They remembered the water, I expect. We'll have to search wider for the others."

"We'll get the burying done, eat some supper, then get the main herd back here tonight," Mase said. "Tomorrow, we'll find the gang's horses. I don't want them left tied up in the woods. With any luck, we'll head out for Wichita tomorrow around noon."

"We've got to replace that wagon wheel, Mr. Durst," Dollager said.

"Is the axle intact?"

"It is, sir."

"We've still got a spare wheel left," Mase said. "We'll get it on there in the morning. East Wind, you go on and help him with supper. The rest of you, let's get some shovels and start dragging bodies. There's five men to put in the ground." He turned to Hiram. "Come on, Hiram." His brother hobbled along beside him as they headed slowly toward the chuck wagon. Mase said, "Hiram—I haven't had a chance to thank you for riding up here busted up like that. Must've hurt like hellfire all that way with a wound."

"Wasn't much fun, but I couldn't have done different, Mase. What would Pa have said?"

"Right now he'd have said he was proud of what you did. I sure thank you for it. Now we're going to get you bedded down in the wagon, and we'll find you the best doc they have in Morrisville."

"I'm about ready to find a bedroll," Hiram admitted.

Mase asked in a low voice, "You think there'll be a to-do around Leadton if Greer simply . . . goes missing?"

"There'll be talk," Hiram answered, "and there'll be a search, too, I suppose. But no one's heart will be broken." He chuckled. "Hell, most of the town will be glad Greer is gone."

"I'm trying to figure how much I should tell the territorial police about all this or maybe the marshal up in Morrisville."

"You want my advice?"

"I do."

"Tell them we were attacked by some known rustlers. Way I heard it, Rod Kelso is wanted in Dallas and Dodge City, too. The US marshal will know that. We can identify Kelso as one of the rustlers. Good chance Fletcher's wanted somewhere. They'll take our word on the rest, with all the witnesses we've got. No reason to mention Greer. Eventually, word about Fletcher and Kelso being dead will get down to Leadton, and folks know the sheriff was tied in with those owlhoots. The smart money will figure out Greer died an outlaw. And no one will give a damn."

GERTRUDE HARNING WAS pacing slowly back and forth in front of the closed door to her husband's den. She badly wanted to talk to him, and she badly feared it, too.

At last Gertie took a deep breath and opened the door. She stepped inside and closed it behind her. Harning was at his desk writing a letter, probably yet another one to Judge Murray. He'd been sorely harassing the man of late.

Tom Harning scowled up at her. "Well?"

She swallowed hard and said, "Tom—I need a word with you."

"So I guessed, Gertie. Out with it! I'm busy!"

She clasped her hands against her middle and said, "I'm going to take Mary and Len to stay with my aunt Lavinia."

"What! For how long?"

"Why, until this matter between you and the Dursts is entirely resolved. At least that long."

"That may take months! And she's in Missouri! I will not have my children gone so long from me! I'm teaching Len how to be a man!"

"That's part of the reason—your notion of manhood. The things you've been telling him. And then I saw him with Clement Adams! The killer was teaching Len to shoot! Adams told me it was your notion. Tom, Len is far too young to learn to shoot—but if he must, then you should teach him, not that . . . that man!"

"Indeed? What's wrong with 'that man'?"

"He's a hired killer, Tom Harning, and you know it!"

Tom slammed a fist down on the desk, making her stiffen and take a step back. "Woman, you will listen to me! I have no time for your hand-wringing nonsense! Forget about Adams!" He leaned back in his chair, breathing hard, then opened a wooden box on the desk and took out a cigar. He fingered it, sniffed at it, but didn't light it. At last he said a little more calmly, "I'll be sending Adams on his way when the job's done. Likely he won't have to fire a shot. I've gotten Fuller at the bank to push for calling in the note on the Durst ranch. They have a delay, but it don't amount to much."

"Mr. Fuller did that? He does not seem to me the type to foreclose when someone's out selling a herd!"

"Oh, well, now . . . there's things you don't know about our Mr. Fuller!" Harning's voice carried a note of self-congratulation, even glee. "Fuller's got a gambling problem. Misused some money from the bank! I found out and . . . well, he'll do what I say if he wants me to stay quiet!"

"Oh, Tom—you blackmailed the man?"

He shrugged and chewed a moment on the unlit cigar. "What of it? It's all for the best. Now, this nonsense about the children—I'll hear no more of it. Leave me to finish my work."

She shook her head. "I heard you talk to that man about killing Mase Durst, Tom. And now I'm hearing you talk of blackmail! I will not have my children in this house any longer."

She turned to go, but in a few quick steps, he had her by the arm, spun her around, and slapped her across the face.

With a wail of pain and fear, she stumbled back and fell, striking the floor hard enough to knock the breath out of her.

"Get up!" Tom snarled. "I'll have no theatrics!" He came to her, grabbed her hand, and forced her to her feet. "You will forget about taking the children anywhere, Gertrude! Or I swear to heaven I'll have you put in an asylum for the mad!"

Sobbing, Gertie pulled away and ran from the room.

A SOFT AFTERNOON rain was falling, seventy-six days into the drive, when Mase caught sight of

Morrisville up ahead. He reined in his horse atop a rise and looked the town over. It was several times bigger than Leadton, with some sizable buildings along the street winding up a high hill. A redbrick building that was probably a city hall stood with a cluster of other new buildings alongside the palisades of Fort Morris.

On the flats down below the hill were stock pens, grain silos, warehouses, and false-fronted buildings that were probably saloons. He could see farms and a ranch between here and the town. He'd have to figure out what was the acceptable route for a herd going past the town. He didn't want to get in a tussle with some sodbuster over trampled sprouts. He'd known a drover to get a rump full of buckshot for less.

He heard hooves drumming behind him and turned to see Rufus Emmer riding up the trail. "Hey, boss! Pug sent me to ask if we should bed down the herd this side of town."

"I expect we'd better. I'll be taking Hiram in the chuck wagon up to town. We'll get some supplies, and I can ask about where to take the drive, maybe out west of town a ways. . . . What's that look on your face like an excited prairie dog?"

"Me? I just . . . wondered if . . . um . . ."

"Yes, yes, you can come along. You can help Dollager. Then maybe you can go with him to a saloon if you think you're old enough and he's willing to keep an eye on you."

"Hot damn!" The boy grinned.

"I don't want to hear about you getting drunk! Two glasses of beer, nothing else!"

"Yes, sir!"

"Go on and tell Pug what I said. And tell Dollager. I want him up here quick so we can get Hiram to a doctor."

Rufus rode away, and Mase sat on his horse, thinking. They'd made Hiram as comfortable as they could in the back of the chuck wagon, but he had been doing poorly the last couple days. His fever was worse. Might need his wound cleaned and cauterized, which would take a good surgeon. The garrison would have the best doctor in the region. The commander probably wouldn't let him treat civilians—not as a rule. But Mase calculated that if he spoke to the commander, he could trade a couple of beeves to get Hiram into the care of the Army surgeon.

He nodded to himself and spurred his horse toward town, deciding to ride up to the fort immediately and see if he could make the deal.

HIRAM OPENED HIS eyes and, looking out the garrison window, figured it was not long after noon. He was lying in bed, aching and tired, but the fever had receded. He sat up a little. It hurt some. He tried standing up—nope, that hurt too much. He sat back and glanced down at the stiches in his chest. The Army surgeon had done a nice, neat job. It didn't look infected. He was starting to feel hungry, too. That was a good sign, wasn't it? Maybe he'd have the last laugh on Mike Greer after all.

The door opened, and he heard his brother say, "Thank you, Sergeant."

Mase came in, his hat in hand, a brown paper package in the other, a canteen on a strap over his shoulder. He smiled to see his brother sitting up. "Hiram."

"Mase."

He brought the canteen over and laid it down on the ticking. "Good and fresh. Got it from a spring outside of town."

"Thanks." Hiram lifted up the canteen and drank. He felt stronger just from that one long, clean drink. "Now, that's better than what they give us here. I think they collect it in an old boot left out in the rain." Mase chuckled and Hiram went on. "Where's the herd, Mase?"

"Off west. We had to circle around the town."

"You lost some cattle over me, I heard."

"I guess you're almost worth two cows."

Hiram grinned. "I'd like to think so."

Mase tore open the packaging and handed Hiram a new hat, more of a Texas-style Stetson. Hiram admired it for a moment and then put it on. The two men had the same hat size and it fit fine.

"That's for when you get up and get ready to come down to Texas," Mase said.

Hiram took the hat off and put it on his lap. "Thank you. Man don't like to be without a hat. I've been thinking about what you said. About . . ."

"About going into business with me?"

"Yeah. I'll see what Queenie says. I'd like to keep her with me if I can. And I'd like to go into ranching with you. I like the peaceful sound of it."

"Hasn't been peaceful on the drive," Mase admitted. "Next time I'll take the well-worn trail. Or send Pug to be trail boss and stay home."

"Now you're thinking smart. One thing I know: I'll

never go back to Leadton again. My letter go out with that liquor wagon?"

"Yep. Should get to Queenie in a week or so. I got one myself from Katie. It was waiting here. But she sent it a tolerable long time ago. More than a month. Mostly just talk of Jim and stock and . . ." He frowned.

"Anything about that varmint Harning?" Hiram had heard all about Vinder.

"Yeah. He's been pushing her to get off the land! Can you figure that kind of gall? The bank's asking for its money from us—threatening to foreclose. She said her uncle was going to get a stay of some kind. But I'm right worried, Hiram."

"Maybe ranching's not as peaceful as I thought."

"Wasn't this time. Anyhow, Hiram, I've got to get back. I'm sorry for it. I'd like to linger here and look after you."

"I've asked Queenie to come up. I think she'll show. And Dr. Sudbury's a good hand. I'll be all right."

Mase nodded. Then he glanced at the door and reached into his pocket, pulling out a pint bottle of Old Overholt. "Here's something to hide under your pillow. Don't overdo it, now."

"Overdo it? You hardly gave me enough to get me drunk. But I'll try!" Hiram winked, uncorked the bottle, drank a little, and offered it to Mase.

"You hold on to it." Mase stuck out his hand, and they shook. "Write to me when you know what you reckon to do." He stood up. "If I push the herd, I can be in Wichita in ten days. I won't be spending the night there. I'm going back home soon as ever I can."

"I'll write, Mase. Or I'll just come and tell you myself."

Mase smiled, clapped his hat on his head, and headed out the door. Hiram sighed, took one more swallow of the whiskey, carefully hid it away, and lay back down again.

Would Queenie come all the way up here just because he'd asked her to? Maybe so. Maybe in two or three weeks, Miss Amaryllis Jones would walk right through that door. . . .

IT WAS A cool dusk, eighty-seven days into the drive, when Mase Durst finished paying off his drovers and his cook.

They were standing around the rear of the chuck wagon, near the cattle pens at the south end of town. The drive from Morrisville to Wichita had been delightfully uneventful, and every man was smiling as he received his pay. The smiles were all the wider because Mase had included a one-hundred-dollar bonus. He figured that getting into gunfights for the sake of the drive was more than the drovers had signed on for. And he could afford it—his timing had been right. He had gotten to the market ahead of the other drives and reaped the reward of top dollar. Mr. Osgood had been as good as his word.

Mase paid Dollager last. As the cook tucked the money into a coat pocket, Mase said, "Boys—you all did a fine job. It was a hard trail. But you were the best hands I could've hoped for."

"Damned right," said Ray Jost. "We even built a bridge for you!"

Mase grinned. "You did at that!" He turned to Dollager. "What will you be doing now, Mick?"

"Was it you who spoke about me to Mr. Bentley at the High Steaks restaurant, sir?" Dollager asked.

"It was," Mase admitted. "I saw his sign—that he was looking for a top cook. I asked him about it, and he said he'd turned away three already as just not up to his standards."

"Well, sir, apparently I am up to his standards. He has taken me into his employ, commencing the day after tomorrow. Won't you come by and have a meal with us? There'll be no cost—that goes for all of you gents!"

"Can't do it myself," Mase said. "Wish I could. Taking the train for points south today. Heading back home quick as I can get there." He shook his head. He didn't want to burden them with his problems. "I've got to see to some things."

"How about Harry Duff's family?" asked Karl Dorge. "They deserve to know. . . ."

Mase nodded. "I found an envelope in his bag. It gives their address, so I'll be writing them a letter. . . ." The saddest letter he would ever write, he thought. "I'll send them his pay."

There was a solemn silence after that. Then, to break it up, Mase asked, "How about you, East Wind? You want to work for me? You're a drover now if you want to be."

East Wind shook his head. "I am going home, too, boss. The reservation. I asked Indian police—I'm not a wanted man. Seems they don't mind I kill renegade Apaches. I want to see my sister. Help my people."

Mase nodded approvingly. "They couldn't ask for better help. How about you, Denver?"

Denver Jimson shrugged. "Doc Holliday's in town. Invited me to a card game."

"Holliday? You'd better be careful not to lose all your pay, Denver." Mase wasn't surprised at Denver's plans. A man like Denver Jimson wasn't the sort to change his stripes.

"What about you, Lorenzo?" Mase asked, smiling at the vaquero. "You want to come to work for me in Texas?"

"Someday, maybe so, Senor Durst. But—I wish to go see my father now. I wish to make peace. I think now is the time. When those bullets fly past us at Shepherd's Crook—" He blew out his cheeks. "It makes a man think!"

The others nodded gravely at that.

"You other boys," said Mase, "you can always find work with me. First thing I need is someone to drive this chuck wagon back to my ranch. I'll pay fifty dollars for the trip."

"Me and Lorenzo were talking about that," said Pug. "Happy to take it down for you. We was thinking eighty for two of us."

Mase nodded. "It's a deal."

"Mr. Durst?" said Rufus tentatively. "Could I find work with you right away? I've got a lot of saving to do."

"Surely. You can take the train with me if you want."

"A train at last! But what about our horses?"

"Our horses will go in the stock car." Mase turned to the others. "You boys staying in town—y'all be smart and keep your money close. You get too drunk, you'll wake up finding it's stolen or spent. That goes for you especially, Ray Jost."

"Me!"

"I never saw a cowboy run through his money so fast as you do, Ray. I remember Dodge City—"

"You got the wrong idea there, Mase! Now, what really happened in Dodge was—I decided to bet my horse could outrace a feller. Well, my horse run so fast, the wind tore my coat off, and all my money went flying 'cross the prairie. I swear it's true!"

CHAPTER NINETEEN

MR. HARNING?" UNCLE Forrest said.

Katie and her uncle were just coming out of the courtroom in town as Tom Harning walked up. He was on his way into the building, carrying some papers with him in a leather folder.

Harning stopped and frowned at Forrest. "Who the devil are you?" he asked.

"I am Forrest Malley, sir, attorney for the Durst Ranch. We are well met. It saves me riding to your spread. I have something for you." He opened his own leather folder, took out an envelope, and handed it smartly to Harning. "That is your copy, signed, of the deposition concerning yourself, which we just gave to Judge Murray."

"Saying what and signed by who?" Harning demanded.

"It says that you stated you blackmailed Mr. Ralph

Fuller into taking legal action against the Durst Ranch."

"What!"

"And it further states you were heard hiring a man to make an attempt on Mason Durst's life."

"And who made these . . . these scurrilous allegations!"

"Why," said Katie, smiling, "your wife did, Mr. Harning."

"I don't believe it!" he sputtered.

"It's true, sir," said Forrest equably.

"Where is that woman?" demanded Harning. "She left the ranch when I was out on the range, and she's taken the children!"

"As to that, sir," said Forrest, shrugging, "I cannot say."

"She felt unsafe in your company," Katie said. "You struck her. You knocked her down. You threatened her. And doing that, you made up her mind for her. She decided to testify."

"So!" Harning jabbed a finger at her. "You've talked to her! Then you know where she is!"

"I have a notion," said Katie. "But I will not reveal her whereabouts."

"I will get an order from the judge to force you to tell!"

Forrest shook his head in mock sympathy. "I don't suppose Judge Murray will think kindly of that proposal, sir. We confronted Ralph Fuller, with Mrs. Harning in company, and he confessed. He admitted before witnesses that you blackmailed him into taking action. He signed an affidavit to that effect. It has been presented to Judge Murray!"

"Fuller! That lying weasel! Where is he?"

"He has resigned and, I believe, fled town."

"Lies, all of it! Conspiracy!" bellowed Harning.

"You tried to have my husband killed," Katie said coldly. "He sent a letter three days ago from Wichita to the US marshal at Fort Worth. The marshal sent it on by stagecoach, and it arrived yesterday. My husband is alive! And he is very angry."

"I'll have you all in court for these lies!"

"Lies, sir?" Forrest said mildly, eyebrows raised. "You are the very Prince of Lies. You even aspersed this lady's character. Do you know the Bible, sir? The Book of Proverbs? It tells us of the things the Lord despises. 'A proud look, a lying tongue, and hands that shed innocent blood . . .' The first two are simply your nature, sir. The third you have attempted. And you are guilty of these as well: 'A heart that deviseth wicked imaginations, feet that be swift in running to mischief, a false witness that speaketh lies—and he that soweth discord . . . ' The Bible has described you right down to the ground, sir. Now, I bid you good day. You would do well to stay away from Mrs. Durst and the Durst Ranch hereafter."

So saying, he offered his arm to Katie. She took it, and they walked away with Harning staring after them, stunned and trembling with anger.

"I will not stand for this!" Harning shouted after them. *"I will not stand for it!"*

I THOUGHT THE new trains were *fast*," Mase growled, not for the first time, as they approached Dallas, Texas.

"Mr. Durst," Rufus declared, looking out the window, "I'll say it can go faster than any horse I ever rode!"

"Seems to take forever . . ." Still, Mase admitted to himself, riding a horse would have taken longer.

They were seated two cars behind the engine, but smoke and cinders found their way in so that Mase coughed from time to time and waved the smoke away from his face.

"I expect you're plenty worried about your folks, Mr. Durst?" Rufus asked.

"Rufus, just call me Mase. This Mr. Durst business is wearing on my ear." He wasn't in a good mood. He kept thinking about what Katie's letter had said. Harning busting down the fence. Men threatening her. The sheriff being useless. For all he knew, she might be dead.

The thought struck him like a chisel through the heart, and his hands clenched on his knees.

No. He refused to believe it. Katie was strong, and she was smart. She would never let Harning get the better of her.

"We taking the horses cross-country from Dallas, Mase?" Rufus asked as if he wanted to try out using Mase's first name.

"We'll get there any way that's quickest. Roads, trails. Jumping fences. I don't care."

Grimly, he was looking forward to confronting Harning. But he was just as angry at Sheriff Beslow. The one man he should be able to count on had let Harning hound his family.

The train chugged on, maddeningly slowing now as

it came into Dallas. “Come on, Rufus,” Mase said, standing and reaching for his duffel bag.

They got up and went to the doors to wait for the train to stop. Mase wasn’t going to waste a second. Now was the time to get on that stallion and ride.

But he knew the ride home, even at gut-busting speed and risking his horse, would take a couple of days. What would happen to Katie and Jim in the meantime?

HOEING THE WEEDS away from her potato and corn sprouts, Katie glanced at the cloudless sky and wondered when it would rain again. It was June and starting to get hot. She just might have to get Jim to help her bring buckets of water out to the vegetable garden every morning.

The garden was between the barn corral and the gate, so she was the first one to see the riders. Five of them, one getting down to cut the knotted leather ties she used as a lock. That kind of impatience told her something. It spoke of a man obsessed.

“Jim!” she called.

He came out of the barn. “Yes, Ma?”

“Is Sam Houston still saddled?”

“Yes, I didn’t get a chance to—”

“Never mind! Get on that pony and go find Curly! He’s not far—he’s over by the creek working on that watering pond! Send him here quick! And then go find Hector. He’s probably working in their field. Go with him to the Smoles! See if Marty and Gwendoline will come over here quick as they can! Tell them to come quick but careful!" The Smoles were the closest neighbors and the ones most likely to come. "I'll come for you at their place later!"

"What's going on, Ma?" Jim asked, a catch in his voice.

"I need help, is what's going on, boy! Don't waste time on questions, just *get*!"

He ran into the barn. Katie threw down her hoe and hurried across the barnyard and into the house.

By the time the men were riding up, Jim was well on his way, and she was standing in the doorway with the rifle butt tucked into the hollow of her right shoulder. She kept back in the shade of the house so she wasn't a good target.

The riders were just who she'd figured on: Tom Harning, Clement Adams, Red Sullivan, Andy Pike, and the man Wurreck. They were sitting on their horses, lined up about forty feet in front of her porch, all of them looking at her. But not with the same expressions. Harning had a look of frozen rage on his face. Adams seemed calm, almost bored, slightly amused. Pike was nervous, his eyes darting around. Red Sullivan seemed smug and eager. But Wurreck—he looked bone scared, like he didn't want to be there at all.

Katie sighted the rifle in on Harning. He had his pistol in his right hand—he'd ridden up with the Colt drawn.

"Who do you intend to shoot, Tom Harning?" she called out. "Me? My milk cow? My son?"

His scowl deepened. "I don't want to shoot anybody, but I'll do what I have to! You send my missus and my kids out to me!"

"They are not here, you damn fool!"

"You're a liar! They're nowhere else to be found! I had a man ride all the way to Missouri! She ain't at Lavinia's! She's nowhere in town neither! I figure they're with you!"

"Whoever told you that is talking out his rear! Now, get off my land!"

"I'm coming in there, Katie! Or you can send her out!"

She considered letting him search the place but didn't want him in her house—because he could get the drop on her. Then he'd take the place over.

"I don't think finding Gertrude is the only reason you're here, Tom Harning. But if you put your gun in your saddlebag and come in alone, I'll let you search. There's a root cellar—you can look there, too."

"She's armed," said Adams. "Foolish to let her get you under her gun in there, Tom, and you unarmed."

"You're nervous about that woman, are you, Clement?" Sullivan said, jeeringly.

"I have looked her over and find her to be capable of blowing your fool head off, Sullivan, at the very least."

"He's right about that!" Katie said. "Right now I've got a bead on Tom Harning's heart. I'll let him come in if he puts aside his gun! Only then!"

Harning shook his head. "Wurreck! Get that kerosene down, and take it over to the barn!"

Wurreck looked at Harning, then at Katie. He took a long, shaky breath. Then he nodded, got off his horse, and untied a large can of kerosene hanging from his saddlebags.

"You'd better leave that on your horse!" Katie said, glancing quickly between Wurreck and Harning.

Carrying the kerosene, Wurreck turned and walked toward the barn. The muzzle of Katie's rifle wavered. She didn't want to take it off Harning—

She had to. She swung the barrel over and fired at the ground between Wurreck and the barn.

Wurreck made a sort of *yip* sound of fear and dropped the can, stumbling back. She fired again, closer to him, and he turned and ran back to his horse as Katie swung the rifle back toward the other men.

Wurreck mounted and turned the horse toward the gate. "This ain't my job, Mr. Harning!" he said, riding off. "I'm quittin'!"

Harning snarled and turned in his saddle to point his gun at Wurreck. Adams surprised Katie by reaching over and pushing the barrel of Harning's gun up. "Don't do that, Tom. Let's save it for where it's needed. It'll look bad if you shoot a man in the back."

Harning gave Adams a burning look—then turned angrily back to Katie. "Katie, I can send Sullivan or Pike to ride around the other side of that barn. You can't get us all. One way or another, we'll burn it down. Whatever stock you have in there's going to die! Now, I don't want to do that. I plan to use it myself when I take this place! You just drop that rifle and send my family out here!"

She heard a horse's hooves approaching from the direction of the creek. *Curly.* She noticed Adams and Pike looking in that direction.

Glancing over, she saw Curly, rifle in hand, riding up to the water trough. He jumped down and crouched, rifle in hand, behind the water trough near the corner of the barn.

Adams glared at Curly. "I don't like that man over there pointing his gun at me."

"Curly—hold your fire! Just keep an eye on them!" Katie called out.

"Yes, senora!"

"Katie, are you going to send my family out to me, or am I going to fight my way in there?" Harning demanded.

"They're not here!" Katie shouted. "You put that gun down, and I'll let you look! Only you! None of the others!"

Harning bared his teeth at her. But then he turned and angrily jammed his gun into his saddlebag. He dismounted and stalked toward her.

Katie backed into the house, stepped out of view, and lowered the rifle. "Come on in, Harning. You'll be safe if you behave yourself!"

The rifle was cocked and ready, and she was standing out of his reach as Harning came striding in, his boots creaking heavily on the wooden floors. "Gertrude!" he called. "Len! Mary!"

He listened to the silence of the house and then rushed from room to room, looking for them. At last he returned to her, eyes narrowed. "Where's this root cellar of yours?"

"Back door out of the kitchen. There's a porch out there where I do my washing. On your left there's a trapdoor."

"How am I to go down there without you locking me in?"

"Take the lantern on the back porch and light it. Shine the lantern in and have a look. You can see what's there. Not much. A ladder and some shelves, a few gunnysacks."

He turned away, made his way through the kitchen as Katie followed behind. She glanced over her shoulder to see if the others were creeping in behind her. No one there so far.

She followed Harning to the back porch, saw him peering down into the root cellar, lantern in hand.

He shook his head and turned back to her. "They could be in the barn."

She sighed. "Your men might shoot me if I was to march you over there to look."

"They won't. Your man is there."

She shrugged. "All right. Put down the lantern, head on back, and we'll go over to the barn."

He hung up the lantern and walked over the dusty ground behind the house. Her pulse thudding, feeling the other men watching her from their horses, she came along after him around the back corner of the house toward the barn. She held the rifle down at hip height, pointed at Harning's back. They got to the barn, and she let Harning look through it on his own. She waited, watching Adams, Sullivan, and Pike.

Sullivan grinned at her. "Fine figure of a woman. Tough, too. You get tired of that husband running off to Wichita, you look me up, lady!"

"Shut up, you damned fool," Adams growled.

Harning came out of the barn. "For God's sake, Katie Durst—where is she?" he pleaded.

Katie decided that what little she knew wouldn't help him find Gertrude. "I got a letter from her. You can look at that. She went to Lavinia's, but when your man got there, they'd already left. Lavinia took them to another town, a big one, where she has a friend. She doesn't name the town. You won't find them."

Harning sniffed and wiped sweat from his forehead. Then he said, "I believe you. But you're still going to have to leave this house."

"The law isn't with you, Tom," she said, shaking her head sadly. His obsession had made him thickheaded. He just refused to see. "Just bunking your men on my land won't make it yours."

"I've got a friend in the governor's office. He's going to fix it up for me. My lawyer says—"

"Your lawyer's taking your money in exchange for bad advice!" she interrupted sharply. "Get off my land, Tom Harning!" A hot fury was rising up in her, bringing her rifle up with it—she tucked it against her shoulder and sighted it on Harning's face. He was just five feet away. "Go on! Back to your horse!"

"You wouldn't dare. Not with those men there."

She saw Marty and Gwendoline Smoles in a buckboard coming down the road from the gate now.

"Don't test me!" Katie shouted. "I've had enough, and I'm plenty mad!"

Harning's face reddened, but he looked into her rifle's unwavering muzzle and turned away, walking stiffly to his horse.

"You heard the lady!" Curly called out. "All of you, *go*!"

Then she saw that Harning wasn't getting on the horse. He was pulling his gun from his saddlebag. He was turning toward her—

Curly fired, and Harning shouted in pain. Adams drew his gun, swiveled in his saddle, aiming at Curly—as Katie swung her rifle over and squeezed the trigger.

Adams arched his back, his head snapping back, and his own shot went wild, smacking into the water trough. Harning was going to his knees, firing into the dirt as Curly fired at Andy Pike, who fired back, missing.

Pike turned his horse to ride off toward the gate as Red Sullivan fired at Katie, the bullet cracking by her head. Curly fired at Sullivan, and he twisted in his saddle and slipped heavily to the ground.

And Tom Harning fell flat on his face.

There were the sounds of Pike's galloping horse, Sullivan groaning, the horses neighing, and water spurting onto the ground from the bullet hole in the trough.

But the guns were silent now as Katie stared around at the dead and dying.

THE AFTERNOON WAS overcast, the clouds dark. Katie had some hope it might rain. It would be good for the garden.

She kept hoeing, just to keep her mind on something. She still felt shaky from the gunfight, though it had been two days ago. Uncle Forrest would be back soon with news from the court. She was fairly sure she knew what that news would be.

She kept slashing at the weeds, wondering when she was going to hear from Mase. He should have found some way to get word to her. She was feeling more alone than ever before. . . .

"Pa!" Jim shouted.

Katie looked up from the garden. Jim was running toward the gate where two riders were coming through.

She knew Mase instantly from his posture on the horse, the outline of him. The other man, skinny as a rail, didn't seem familiar.

All this was totting up at the back of her mind as she walked toward him, slowly at first and then faster. Realizing she still had the hoe in her hands, she tossed it aside and ran after Jim.

Mase galloped up to them, and she'd never seen anyone but a trick rider dismount so fast. He scooped Jim up in his arms, hugged him, and then held him with one arm as the other went around Katie.

He was big and warm and strong and unhurt. He was back.

After a time, she realized Mase was talking. Somehow, through a mist of tears and welling emotion, Katie understood that he and their new ranch hand, Rufus, were tired and hungry. He was asking if they could find something to eat in the house. And maybe a glass of brandy if they had any left. Taking his hand, she led him toward the house.

"Rufus," Mase said, "just take those horses to the barn, unsaddle them, and come on in the house." Rufus took the stallion by the reins and trotted to the barn.

Mase and Katie walked Jim on to the house on either side of him, not letting go of his hands.

The men ate a late lunch at the dinner table. Katie sat across from them, gazing at Mase with a mixture of longing and suffused joy, and Jim sat close beside him, listening wide-eyed to Rufus. Between bites of chicken stew, Rufus was telling them the story of the drive. How Mase had saved his life at the Red River, how they'd built a bridge over another torrent. He told them of Vinder's treachery, and how they'd had to face down the Fletcher bunch three times in all, and how the last time had ended. He spoke more softly of the sad fate of Harry Duff.

"You blowed up a ridge, Pa?" Jim asked in amazement.

Mase winced. "Seemed like a good idea at the time. Was some risk to it. I don't recommend you fool with dynamite, son. Mighty dangerous."

"Ma shot Clement Adams dead," Jim said matter-of-factly, taking a piece of bacon from his father's plate.

Mase stared at her. "She what?"

She'd told him that Curly had shot Tom Harning to save her. But she hadn't yet gotten to the part about Adams.

Katie took a deep breath and told him in detail about the confrontation. And the fight.

"So many times we escaped fighting with them," she said. "But this time he was just too . . ." She shook her head. "That man was obsessed, Mase."

He nodded. "I'm kind of wondering what some folks around here will say about Curly killing Harning. You know how some of them are."

"Oh, the Smoles gave their testimony. They both saw Harning pull his gun and point it at me. And they saw Adams about to shoot Curly. And Red Sullivan had his gun ready to go. So . . . along with my deposition, and Curly's, why . . ."

Katie remembered that when Jim had ridden up soon afterward, he stared at the bodies with his mouth open. For once, he'd had nothing to say. He'd seemed appalled. She wondered how the sight might affect him. She could talk that over with Mase in private.

"What did the sheriff have to say about all this shooting?" Mase asked.

"You know, he's changed his tune. Maybe it was him seeing the deposition from Gertrude and that affidavit from Fuller. We sent Curly for him, and he came out in a buggy with the coroner. He just looked at the bodies, said he'd arrange for them to be picked up. He talked to Marty and Gwendoline. Then he said he didn't think anyone would find fault with what we did. There was something about the way he said it—like he was admitting something without quite admitting it."

HIRAM COULD FEEL it in the way Queenie held his hand that morning. There was a stiffness in her touch as if they were strangers.

He was sitting up in bed, and she was sitting on a wooden chair beside it. She was gazing at the window, her eyes focused on some unknown place far beyond the garrison at Morrisville.

"You made up your mind, Amaryllis?" he asked.

"I did," Queenie said.

"I guess I know already because you're so slow to tell me."

She gave a sad nod. "I'm going to New Orleans. Start the business there. I just . . . cannot become a rancher's wife. Children and keeping house and working in a barn—it's not in me to do it, honey. I wish it were. It would break my heart to fail you, Hiram."

With that, she squeezed his hand and drew hers away from him.

She didn't want to break his heart? *Would be hard to do,* he reflected. His heart felt like a lump of lead within him. "I guess . . . I knew that. I was hoping . . ." He didn't say the rest: that he was hoping she loved him enough to put up with that kind of life, anyway. But that just wasn't Queenie. "Anyhow, I'm powerful glad you came up here to see me. You've been a tonic for me. Just the sight of you."

Queenie's eyes filled with tears; her lips trembled. She stood up, clutching her purse to her, her voice husky as she said, "I have to go now, honey. There's a stage. I'm taking it east and south." She cleared her throat. "You don't have to be a rancher, Hiram. You could meet me there. You could come into the business with me. . . ."

He took a deep breath. Could he? Would he fit in, working at her dance hall in New Orleans? They might well prosper.

But would he be happy there?

IT WAS MIDWAY through July when Gertrude Harning came back to the Circle H Ranch. She was there two days before she came to see Katie and Mase, prompted by a note that Mase had sent her.

She had taken over the Circle H, hired new hands, and gotten tutors for her children. Her late husband's herd had been merged with another herd going north, and sold for good money.

Mase had sent her a note offering to buy one fifth of her land, adjacent to his own. She felt comfortable selling to Mase, she said. Because—she looked at Katie when she said it—"I am grateful to my good friends, Mr. and Mrs. Durst."

Gertie seemed happier than Katie had ever seen her. For some women, Katie reflected, becoming a widow was a glorious liberation.

On a hot afternoon a week later, Mase was at work erecting the new fences around the property he'd bought from Gertrude. Jim was there doing small jobs. Hector was doing bigger ones while Mase, Rufus, and Curly worked together setting posts. It was hot, sweaty work, and after a time, Mase declared a break in the shade of a nearby oak for water and some of Katie's oatmeal cookies. He was about to suggest they get back to work when Jim pointed off toward the north.

"Now, who's that, you suppose, Pa?" he asked.

Mase looked and shook his head. "Don't know." Then he went to his horse, got the spyglass from the saddlebag, and had another look. "By God! What do you think, Jim! It's your uncle Hiram!"

Hiram galloped up to them, dismounted, and shook hands all around. "Who's this man here?" he asked, looking at Jim in a puzzled way as if he didn't know who he was.

"Why, I'm Jim, Uncle Hiram!"

Hiram grinned. "Can it be? As big as you are? Lordy!"

Mase chuckled. "Hiram—have you seen Katie?"

"Who do you think told me where to find you?"

"How you feeling? How's that wound?"

"Hardly remember I had it. I'm fit as a fiddle, Mase."

"Maybe we should go on back to the house. You can rest and have a drink, and . . ."

"What! You're in the middle of all this work here, and the day is young, little brother! Now, let me ask you this—am I your partner on this ranch, or am I not?"

"That's what we talked about, and that's how it is!"

Hiram pulled two leatherwork gloves from his back pocket. He tugged them on, smiling. Then he said, "Well, what are we standing around for? Let's get to work!"